Seven Voices

VOLUME TWO

Seven Voices

VOLUME TWO

STORIES & REFLECTIONS

NORTH FORK WRITERS GROUP
LONG ISLAND, NEW YORK

The New Atlantian Library

THE NEW ATLANTIAN LIBRARY

is an imprint of
ABSOLUTELY AMAZING eBOOKS

Published by Whiz Bang LLC, 926 Truman Avenue, Key West, Florida 33040, USA.

Seven Voices (Volume Two) copyright © 2015 by North Fork Writers Group. Electronic compilation/ paperback edition copyright © 2015 by Whiz Bang LLC. Cover design by Andrea Rhude

For information contact:
Publisher@AbsolutelyAmazingEbooks.com

ISBN-13: 978-1945772986 (The New Atlantian Library)
ISBN-10: 1945772980

Welcome...

   North Fork Writers Group was founded in 2010 on the East End of New York's Long Island. Since the publication of our *7 Voices, Volume One* in 2015, the group has evolved. Some original members are pursuing individual projects as new members bring us their distinct literary voices.

   Seven Voices, Volume Two gathers our diverse styles into a collection that spans an array of genres. Social satire, quiet heroics, ethereal mystery, stark drama, and dark humor fill the pages that follow. We invite you to engage with our *Voices*, savor the variety that inspires us as writers, and share our enthusiasm for these tales.

Andrea ~ Christopher ~ David ~ Gerard ~ Helene ~ Joyce ~ Susan ~ William

~~~~~~~~

√ = Joyce

Our Stories...

BAD BOUNCE

GERARD MEADE

The summer day is near perfect. Sunshine, blue skies and pleasant temperatures are an excellent backdrop for the rare weekday afternoon game. Randy sits in his lounger with a neat Scotch in hand; the blow torch on the end table easily within reach. It's the top of the eighth, the bottom of his fourth Scotch. He hears the approach before he sees the intruder; a soft scratch-like noise followed by a faint thump. Resting his drink on the table before him, he refills it before extending his opposite hand for the torch.

The small ranch's living room is above a shallow, bare earth crawl space. It's uninviting and infested. In the regions where they thrive they're known as wetas, spider crickets, sand treaders, camelback crickets, criders, and also the name Randy had adopted for them: sprickets. Regardless of the unwanted guests' moniker, they are real scary looking things that, if enhanced, could star in a Japanese horror flick. Six over-sized spindly legs propel them and, when startled, those creepy appendages can launch them with speed in haphazard directions. The damn bugs sometimes leap to unimaginable heights. The hard shelled body is

1

elongated and can grow to almost two inches. Add those crazy legs and they can span six inches overall. That tough protective shell will provide a satisfying, though somewhat revolting crunch if you're lucky enough to snag one under your sole. They're pretty much blind and rely on, well - of course, *oversized* antennae for navigation. On long jumps that GPS kinda fails occasionally, hence the minute thump.

The insects often prefer, and keep to, uninhabited lower regions, comfortable in the dark and damp, but sometimes a lone renegade invades the living space. Several prior attempts at extermination, by costly professionals and internet inspired DIY, have been unsuccessful. To date, Randy has thrown out his hip doing an exaggerated jig while attempting to stomp one, and dislocated a shoulder in a particularly violent smack with a rolled-up magazine. He inadvertently discovered the blowtorch technique when a lucky shot with a lit cigarette effectively clipped one. Now, a precisely directed short blast instantly produces a crispy critter. Hospital visits and painful rehab have been avoided ever since, although he did have to replace the drapes once. That incident led to the purchase of a fire extinguisher...but I digress.

With one on and one out he waits patiently for the invader to make its move. The brand new torch head for the small disposable propane canister has one touch trigger ignition on its pistol-like grip. Randy the torch slinger listens for movement while keeping an eye on the game. The little bugger doesn't move. He reaches for the Scotch without his finger leaving the trigger and is about to drink when the spricket springs, jumping high before him and vaulting his lap. Randy follows it with the torch. His right hand holds the weapon and traverses his torso as he aims slightly ahead in the target's path. Having become quite adept with abundant practice he's pretty sure of his aim. He hits the trigger. The Scotch in his left hand ignites. Reflexively, he throws the flaming liquid but misdirects it toward him instead of away and it splashes up his exposed forearm toward his bicep, not quite reaching the cuff of his short-sleeved team jersey. The flames extinguish almost instantly but the stench of burnt hair and barbequed skin lingers. A meandering scrawl of burnt microfiber on his chair's armrest smolders for only a second before dousing.

Whether a result of the whiskeys he's consumed or the onset of shock, he feels no pain at first. Randy simply stares, frozen with disbelief as his arm turns an alarming dark pink. He's standing but doesn't remember rising. He collapses back into the chair and reaches for his phone on the end table. The pain arrives as he enters the last digit of 911.

Blisters rise quickly, like time lapse photography quick. They continue multiplying and growing, the largest beginning to resemble an opaque baseball...growing *out of his fucking arm*! Although nauseated by watching, Randy's unable to turn away. Smaller bubbles continue to form and the skin abandons the pink, turning instead to deep angry red around the whitish-rose of the numerous protuberances.

An ambulance from the nearby firehouse, arrives within minutes. The responders gain access through the unlocked screen door that leads directly into the living room. One looks Randy over while the other checks the chair and surrounding carpet for lingering fire. They've brought a collapsible gurney and insist that he be transported upon it. Strapping him in for the short trip to the curb, they cover his burns with a thermal blanket. The EMT pushing is obviously new to the job, and looks to be about twelve years old, the veteran who leads the way pulls, out of sight behind his head. The young guy asks twice how he's doing but Randy doesn't answer. The kid's nervous and doesn't seem to notice the lack of response.

Randy is loaded onto the bus and the young EMT jumps in back with him, asking again if he's alright. Attempting a reply, Randy opens his mouth and takes a deep breath before trying to speak; the pain is excruciating. Something begins to tingle under the blanket. It's hard to feel anything other than agony but a prickly sensation seems to be traveling up his arm, navigating the trail of scorched skin. Before his response is voiced, the spricket leaps from the blanket's edge. Randy's eyes bulge with terror as it arcs directly into his open mouth. The insect lodges itself in his esophagus and Randy begins to choke. The kid is distracted by something outside, but snaps his head back toward his patient. He recognizes the distress sound but doesn't know what to make of Randy's panic. He screams for his partner, the paramedic. Fortunately she's just outside the doors and jumps into the cabin, quickly analyzes the symptoms and undoes the strap that holds the patient's chest to the gurney. She sits him up abruptly, pain exploding from his forearm, and begins the Heimlich maneuver. On her second attempt, the critter is launched from Randy's mouth.

The insect is stunned, wondering what the fuck it's gotten itself into. It bounces off the wall of the bus and ricochets to the floor. Both EMTs are shocked, and grossed out by the creature's ejection from the man's throat. The young EMT knows he's going to lose his lunch. He bounds from the bench and heads to the door. His abrupt movement stirs the stunned spricket, which makes two quick jumps and beats the kid out. It hits the street, zig-zags drunkenly to the curb and screws up an attempt to propel itself to the adjacent grass, bouncing straight up and down instead. Another attempt at a sideways vault gets it into the lawn. The growth provides some cover from unwanted light but not enough security. The spricket forces itself onward.

Stu Berringer sits in his living room, aware of, but not caring at all about the ambulance at the curb. The vehicle's flashing lights illuminate the tears running down his cheek. His head is at half-mast, his blurred vision focused on the 9mm Beretta in his hand. He'd bought the pistol originally to protect them, but now that he'd squandered their savings and each of the equities they held had tanked, he was wondering if such a small gun was appropriate for blowing one's brains out; a large canon would definitely be more fitting. His blunder was monumental; the punishment must fit the deed.

A strange sound distracts him from his morbid thoughts. He dismisses it initially, but not when he hears it repeated. Looking from the gun up toward the open window, glancing at the ambulance flashing just steps away, the noise comes again, lower...from the floor maybe, possibly near the front door. He doesn't hear the car as it pulls into his driveway, fixated as he is on the curious sound. Stu rises from the couch and immediately feels the stiffness in his legs. He can't clearly recall how long he's been sitting in silence, contemplating his own demise. He remembers cleaning the gun this morning after his wife left for work. He can recall the breakfast beer also, but not how many have followed.

Stu focuses on the doorway, full of late afternoon sun, but fractured by the pulsing strobe of the emergency beacons. The spricket bounds from the shadow of a coatrack, just left of where his eyes are fixed. He sees it briefly reflected in the refracted rays of the decorative sidelight. Stu raises his aim. He waits for his chance. When it comes, he doesn't hesitate. The creepy looking bug shoots up from the carpet again in an amazing leap that peaks at almost chest height. He fires.

"Honey, what's up with the ambula..."

Stu's wife drops, falling to a crumpled heap in the foyer. Startled and scared, the spricket leaps again. The second shot catches Danny Wright, the new EMT, at the base of his skull as he straightens from spewing the last of his stomach's content. The spricket bounces yet again, springing this time off his wife's lifeless form. Stu fires and Patty McKeogh—covered in blood splatter and bone matter already—is spun by the round's impact while trying to aid her young partner.

The petrified insect, reluctant as it is to remain in the unfriendly light, knows it has to escape. It bounces along the lawn, scampering low between jumps and searching blindly for a damp, dark space inhabited by others of its kind.

Randy, his heartrate accelerated to a dangerous level by having the bug evicted from his windpipe, now hears friggin' gunshots. The paramedic's gone—having left him, he hopes, to get them underway—leaving just as the firing began. A ping is followed by a hollow thud before a second thump precedes a spray of blood across the open doorway of the bus. He watches in horror as the medic falls into view, dead in its wake. Alarm expels his shock. He bolts upright on the stretcher, suddenly racked by sharp chest pains, and fumbles desperately with his good hand to release the strap that still binds his legs to the gurney. His burnt arm, unprotected by the lost thermal wrap, is aflame with unbearable pain. The good arm goes numb and the ratcheting in his chest spikes, alarmingly off-beat. The torch slinger drops limp to the stretcher, fumbling no more.

Stu fires more shots, wildly and without aim. A strange laugh accompanies the volley. Finally he stops, looking first along the floor to the entrance and then beyond to the curb. The grief-driven dementia that took him hostage releases as the devastation he's wrought begins to dawn. The laugh trickles off to a whimper as sirens approach from a distance. He stares in disbelief at his dead wife. *"With her gone, you won't have to explain where all the money went"*. That truth untethers revulsion beyond all which had prompted him to retrieve the gun in the first place, and pushes him the last few inches over the edge. He raises the pistol to his temple and pulls the trigger.

'Click'

~ ~ ~ ~ ~ ~ ~ ~

SLOW-MOVING CLOUDS, 1957

SUSAN ROSENSTREICH

As we know, life is not death, wrote Pastor Jeremiah Entwhistle. Dottie Wright, his young Sunday school assistant who was at that very moment turning up the walkway to the church, had heard him repeat this observation for as long as she could remember. But she had never heard her Pastor's afterthought on this early June morning as he sat at his desk in the church sanctuary, reading over his draft of Sunday's sermon, certain he had closed the door of the church against any intrusion. "And what we know is not all there is to know," he prepared to add. Then he died.

The fat layer of the unknown seemed spongier than usual to Dottie this morning. She paused at the church walkway to glance across the street at Mr. and Mrs. Armbrust's garden, detonating its early summer bomb of baby-blue and stars-'n-stripes red Alabama geraniums. This sensation of a fragile surface that had just prompted her to slow her pace was not new to Dottie. Some years ago, she had been warming her body in the sun after plunging briefly into the ice-cold deep of Big Sandy Creek, and suddenly had sensed a rippling heave beneath her. She had never heard of earthquakes in Alabama, but Dottie was certain that what she felt was quaking earth. She screamed and burst into tears. Thaddeus, the older of her two brothers, had raced out of the water toward her, but as he saw she was in no danger, he became angry at her weakness. "Good Lord, Dottie. You just cry at any old thing. You girls!" And he stomped back into the water.

But later, when Thaddeus and Jimmy and Dottie turned up the garden path of their home, their mother was standing in the doorway, wringing her hands in her apron, her face blank. "Daddy's died," she announced. The boys had broken down, this loss of their father too visceral a rupture to call death. But not Dottie. She had stood stock still. Life and death. Death and life. Something ends, something begins.

After the birth of his daughter – "I want Dorothy for her name, but you can call her Dottie so's folks don't think we're uppity" – Mr. Wright, actually Seaman Wright, was shipped off to Korea, and after a year of combat had returned to Holts-ville honorably discharged and profoundly handicapped. A man of poetry rather than of brusque words, as an invalid he turned to telling familiar tales of childhood adventures, but now transforming them into great myths of forest spirits at war with murderous forces that turn a boy from tenderness to vicious spite. How could you choose good over evil? He was eloquent with his Darlin' Dot, affectionate with Mrs. Wright and complicitly male with his sons. But his heart weakened, and with it, his voice faltered, his lungs labored until finally, on that afternoon, Mrs. Wright had sent the children to the river and called Dr. Coleman.

As Pastor had chanted Psalm 23 over Seaman Wright's casket, Dottie peered into the small grave awaiting her father. Seaman Wright, who had gone out into the wide world. Wide world, small grave. Is that how we find our way through life?

Dottie was soon of the age when girls could choose to help Pastor deliver his loving counsel to the sick and the dying in spirit, or to wander off to the creek after Sunday sermon. For sure, Dottie would help that poor Annie Daughtry at Sunday school, her mother had done as much when she was a girl, though at the time it was Annie's mother who had charge of the rowdy Holtsville youngsters. Annie was older than Dottie by almost a decade. Annie had never ventured outside Holtsville, and now she looked as if she were a church fixture, as if she had just emerged from its white walls to hold them up like the wooden pillars that stood on each side of the church door. At first, her stolid presence had comforted the younger girl. Dottie had imagined she could take Annie into her confidence and confess while weeping that she felt her daddy by her side all the livelong day. But Annie was ponderous in every way. You had to repeat and explain all your jokes, and old Pastor Entwhistle became clearly exasperated with the Daughtry girl when he tried to explain Scriptures to her for the Sunday school lessons. Though Annie wasn't fat, she was of solid build and pounding ambulation, so that when she walked, her whole foot came into contact with the earth and was slow to rotate into the next step. Still, after her father died and took away his stories of vanquishing the world's evil, Dottie loved the distraction of Thursday evenings, when Mrs. Daughtry and Annie would come over with a quart of home-churned vanilla ice cream to play Bible word games.

But Dottie felt the undercurrent of her difference with the older girl. On a January Thursday this past winter, Annie had bared a part of her character that confirmed Dottie's unvoiced opinion of the older girl as a mean person, mean in the sense of small. The two of them had been dishing out four portions of ice cream into Mrs. Wright's little pink glass dishes when Annie had asked Dottie to keep what she was going to say a complete secret. Dottie froze. This was what terrified her in the world. She would be told something and be forbidden to speak about it, forced to act as if everything in Holtsville was as it seemed, all the while an accomplice in deceit. What was Annie going to reveal? Had she actually kissed that disgusting Jack Gilroy, the delivery boy who followed her around town, who was ugly as sin and stuck in the same place forever?

Her premonition was not even close. "What I gotta say, Dottie, is I am downright ashamed working for Pastor. You listen to him, the way he drawls just like a no-account? Like he never saw the Lord at all? Way he talks, why, it sound like he's sellin' snake oil. Makes me think th'other people in town, you know, the ones what don't go to our church, will think he's backward and his message is plain silly, and all of us in the church are stupid."

What on earth did Annie mean? What exactly had she said? Dottie frowned. There was something menacing in Annie's characterization of Pastor as a hick. Okay, maybe he spoke common-like, but then, wasn't that what he was, what they all were? Though he had been around. He had preached in Biloxi and down in Mobile and, for heaven's sake, he had even gone to Germany, spent a year over there. The army shipped him overseas – this was before Pastor studied to preach – and he had set about learning German and riding a bike one of the young German soldiers had loaned him so he could visit the little towns near his base. Once, on leave, he took the train to Wittenberg with a German soldier friend who found a way to get the two of them into the forbidden east.

"Now let me tell y'all," he had told the congregation early in his service to Holtsville, "they got small towns like we got here, but Wittenberg? Well, I never did see anything like it before. That's where we started, folks, right there on the doors of that great cathedral." And he held up a minute photo of the cathedral that he had taken with his Brownie camera. No one in the congregation had ever heard of Martin Luther, or of Wittenberg. You couldn't make out a single thing in Pastor's photo. The blurry mass, supposedly the cathedral, seemed to be leaning dangerously to the right, ready to crumble at the mere click of the young man's camera. But still, the image mesmerized Dottie. To her, the fuzzy outlines were the effect of some kind of illumination from within the edifice, where those forest spirits of her father's stories were resting from their fight with viciousness. The blurring of the cathedral's image was evidence of the spirit visible to Pastor Entwhistle. Why vilify such a person?

Dottie pictured Pastor Entwhistle to herself as she tried to grasp what bothered her in Annie's words. She saw his fat buttocks as he turned toward the church door to lock it after Sunday worship. She would pause at the end of the church walkway, watching as Pastor strolled toward his home at the end of the block, his plump hips like two biscuits rolling down a table sideways. That he was pigeon-toed made Dottie yearn to hold out her hand to him and help him scuff along, to keep him from falling. "That's really mean, Annie Daughtry. Pastor talks natural like that. I feel like he's talking just to me when he does that. He's not trying to be uppity, like he was speaking to people at some lord-high-pants dinner party. He is a simple man, Annie, a man of God."

"Now don't you be going off that way at me, Miss Dottie Watkins. Being a man of God don't mean all what you think it does. You're too young, you need to get around some, you should know, people judge us, and they listen or they don't, 'pendin' on what they see and how you sound. They don't hear a word you're saying if you're just talking like you would when you talk about the price of eggs in China. And when Pastor always says over and over 'life is not death' and that, well, don't I know life ain't death? Know what he's sayin'? He's sayin' all us don't know what's life and what's death, and he does 'cuz he's Pastor. Well, durn it, I do know, and I ain't no pastor." Annie finished and was breathless. Dottie spent the night tossing and turning.

Today at breakfast, toying with her fork and jabbing at the Sunday bacon, Dottie had told her mother that, contrary to what the town assumed, she, Dottie, wouldn't leave town to work in Birmingham when she finished school at the end of the month. She would stay right here in Holtsville. "Now, honey," her mother had protested, "you thinkin' you need to take care of me?"

"Why no, that ain't the point at all, Ma. It's what I want for me."

"That isn't the point, dear," Widow Wright murmured, clearing her throat. "You know it's always been like this. You young women go off to big cities, you work a bit in houses and stores, see some new fashions, other kinds of people and things like that, then you come home and settle down and live like the rest of us right here in Holtsville. It's what your daddy and I planned for you to do, and now he's gone, it's on my shoulders to see that you do it." But Dottie could hear a catch in her mother's voice. She was speaking the words everyone in town spoke to their daughters, but she was clearly feeling something else. What was she feeling?

"I ain't fightin' you, Ma, but what am I gonna do with all I'll learn when I go away? What's wrong with learnin' right here in Holtsville?"

"I'm not fighting you', you mean. It's just that you'll see different ways to do the same things, that's all. Maybe better ways, maybe not, you can choose."

Then what was the point? Dottie wondered. In the first place, it wasn't clear to her that what lay beyond her town was so different. Weren't there courthouse

15

lawns in every city of the world? Saturday Curb Markets, where farmers came to sell local herbs and plucked chickens? According to her Ma, according to Mrs. Daughtry, the market had offered the same goods, from different farmers, of course, when they were girls. "Our town don't change none, that's for sure," the Widow Wright had said, smiling at the patronizing thought that the rest of the world could go on changing till it fell to pieces, but their town would keep on doing as it had done since time began. No need to change. But like her husband had told her when he got home from Korea, it was good to see the different ways people did the same things. In the end, what you learned was just that the way you had always done things was the right way all along.

And yet, as Dottie reached the church door on this blazing hot Sunday morning in June, she felt a definite give in the ground, a sort of malleability to the concrete walkway. "Now ain't that strange," she thought, noting that Pastor Entwhistle hadn't left the church door ajar as he usually would do. But, Dottie told herself, it was strange only because she had felt it strange a moment ago that the ground was unstable. Just then, she was distracted by glinting water roundlets trembling on the Armbrusts' rhododendron shrubs across the street. She crossed over to get a closer look at the tiny glossy leaves, holding their portion of water granted by last night's thunderstorm, and she gazed at the sky's reflection in water pooling around the bushes. Such a blue sky. How far away?

She had sat transfixed as her father told his children what he had learned from his chief petty officer, that the Russians wanted to send a space capsule around the earth "so's they would own the skies." Why, how could you do such a thing, she had asked him. How could you own the heavens? "Why, Darlin' Dot, them Russian people, they ain't people of the spirit like us. You can't do no such thing, you can't stop the message of the heavens long as people like us go lookin' for it. So don't worry none. You jes' go seek the message, and come back home, have no fear." His words did not comfort Dottie. Why would anyone leave home to seek the Lord's message? Suddenly, standing by the Armbrusts', she had her answer. The sky, its domination of the space above, and the knowledge of its absolute blue beyond the earth's vagaries of atmospheric disturbances – you know what that is? It's our great and unfailing shield. Sure, it shields a big world, but wasn't it the world where evil awaited its match, the world of the unknown into which Seaman Wright sent his children, then showed them how to come home again to their small town where the sky was always overhead, blue and protective? It would be never-ending, the battle her father knew about, but it was not to be feared. Fear, those are the moments when we freeze, when we think that what we love is what we lose. But don't you see, Dottie told herself, you love something so as not to lose it. That's how come you come home over and over and you do not fear birth and decay and life and death for love is the enemy of evil and evil can't be victorious if you love.

Dottie headed back toward the church. She glanced once again at the precious sky shielding Holtsville before turning the brass knob, then noted a chaplet of clouds wafting overhead. How gentle they were, those promises of rain, there was no menace to them as they ambled across the heavens, making their way to a mountain somewhere, later to dissolve and soak some thirsty field of grain. For surely there were fields in need of rain wherever you went on this earth. She felt the ground heaving as if to sigh, she turned the knob. The clouds moved slowly and above them, the sky was blue. Dottie entered the church and turned toward Pastor Entwhistle's sanctuary.

~~~~~~~~

LOST TRAVELERS

DAVID PORTEOUS

Mervyn Frankel's brilliant mind is less daunting than his array of Diplomas for Psychology and Psychiatry, the latter with requisite M.D., and ancillary Degrees in Neurosciences. This likeable fifty-year-old's good heart raises the renown the credentials brought him. He reminds people of TV comedy professors, with clipped speech as his thoughts outpace it, and occasional vagueness when trying to resolve if the people he sees are patients, clients, or lost travelers in need of a guide.

Today he is trying to define that about Padraig O'Shea, who will face a murder trial. Mervyn just read a dossier from O'Shea's lawyer, who wants him to assess why the man is still vowing his innocence despite overwhelming evidence. All he read intrigued Mervyn enough to accept, and to tell a bronze bust of Sigmund Freud on his desk: "This one could be fun, Siggie... He seems a truly unique sort of lost traveler."

He phones the lawyer to set a meeting with O'Shea for three o'clock, and learns that it will be in a guard-protected interview room. In his drive to the prison, Mervyn mentally lists questions for O'Shea, but also considers the lawyer's curt depiction of the man, dismissing him as 'way beyond bizarre'.

After presuming that Padraig O'Shea will have traces of Irish features or a brogue, Mervyn is unprepared for the man standing to meet him. Gauntly thin with a pallid face, O'Shea looks almost wraith-like, but his style of speech sounding like an eighteenth century English novel confounds Mervyn more.

"Do I have the honor, sir, of addressing Doctor Frankel, the eminent guide to recovery for wayward minds?"

Mervyn opts to respond informally. "Feel free to call me Mervyn. Do you know why I'm here, Mister O'Shea?"

"I was advised by the exquisite Miss Ruffio, Associate at Beauchamp, Hashim and Walton, as an envoy of my attorney, Grantly Walton, Esquire, that you are retained to evaluate my competence to stand trial. So... Was I aptly informed, sir?"

Mervyn says only. "Pretty much. But today's half hour is for me to gauge if you'll talk freely enough in these pre-trial weeks for me to be any help to your lawyers."

O'Shea's pale eyes flare, but his voice remains steady. "As this room offers a table and chairs, sir, sitting in an informal atmosphere could well foster such a rapport."

"Fine. Let's go," Mervyn says, and heads for a chair.

O'Shea pauses to say: "Also, I sense that I can answer any questions you pose with confidence in your steering them to the uninhibited discourse you require."

While O'Shea sits, Mervyn hides a smile about the man's eccentricities by setting up his laptop, but says: "Fine start. So let's cut to the chase... Is there anything you believe is vital to your defense, but your lawyers don't see it that way?"

"Oh, good sir, your famous perspicacity is understated," O'Shea says. "You rightly grasp this issue's nub, and its cause of my discontent with allegedly renowned attorneys. Yes, one fact does underpin this case and all understanding of it."

O'Shea falls silently pensive, his gaze seeming to follow specks of dust on an air current, and Mervyn feels obliged to prompt him. "And...that nub of the issue...is...?"

"Half an hour, you say? A third of that is gone, so I shall explain it next meeting. When is that? Not that I have other engagements to prevent my being at your beck and call."

"I asked for an hour daily at three o'clock. I hope that's confirmed before I leave today. Your lawyer's working on it."

O'Shea sneers. "Do not expect such from my lawyer, sir. Grantly will drop it upon little Miss Ruffio. Fortunately for us, that pretty charmer is also a treasure of efficiency. So, were I you, I would confidently diarize those chosen times in ink."

Mervyn shrugs and smiles. "So we'll leave your nub until three tomorrow. But in our time left... Anything else I should know to understand how you see your best defense?"

O'Shea muses: "A modern Doctor with ancient wisdom... sensing there is more to the so-called evidence against me, and...dare I say 'intuitively'...knowing that I can avail you of the truth of it. I am in awe of your acuity, and vow to expose all my insights and knowledge to assist your efforts."

Something Mervyn can't identify in O'Shea's flattery nags at him, but he says: "Well... In your best interests, and all."

"Quite. But my intent was to convey my trust. If only you were my attorney... No, to have studied Law would rob us all of your expertise in humanity. They who stage court cases want only to win arguments, not to assist people. That is not a digression, sir. I feel a trust in you that my attorneys do not engender. Aside from the splendid Miss Ruffio, of course."

Mervyn glances at his watch before he says: "As time is flying, I'll just say thanks for that, and return to the bit about there's more to the evidence. Want to explain that for me?"

O'Shea's face crinkles in self-rebuke. "Please forgive my inapt loquaciousness. I appreciate your grace in chiding me." He seems to get lost in thoughts too dismal to arise from being too chatty, oblivious to Mervyn's growing curiosity.

"So, the evidence... Can you hear me, Mister O'Shea?"

As if coming out of a coma, O'Shea looks around in a way Mervyn interprets as the man having no idea where he is. "Oh, do forgive... I was... What? Oh, yes...the missing evidence."

"Missing, Mister O'Shea? Are you saying your lawyers do not have all the facts they need to defend you?"

Before answering, O'Shea leans over the table to look at Mervyn's watch. "Alas, time has flown. Please just listen, and later research what I tell you. Will you do that for me?"

"Sure," Mervyn says, as he prepares to make notes in the laptop. "But I'll be thrown out soon, so go for it."

"My home is in a restored Georgian mansion. In what is now my third floor apartment in that building...and in what is now my bedroom...a naked woman was killed –"

"I know, but –" Mervyn accepts a hand wave for silence, and nods for O'Shea to continue.

"It was exactly two hundred years ago. November first of that year, in fact. A knife through her left bosom to her heart." His look deters comment as he muses: "Vivacious twenty-two year-old...extraordinarily pretty...and engaged in incestuous liaisons with her father. He was hanged for her murder."

"And you know these arcane details... How?"

"That is inessential due to time constraints. Now, I am guiding your research of that crime to understand this one with which I am charged. You cannot help my attorneys if you are unaware of all the facts... Historical, and contemporary."

Before Mervyn can respond, the door swings open for two burly prison guards to enter, one saying: "Time's up, Doc."

"But I –"

"Now, Doc. Mike'll take him back... I'll walk you out."

As the guard named Mike takes O'Shea, Mervyn nods to the first officer, but his eyes are on the laptop as he closes it. His notes seal O'Shea's news in his mind so well that it blocks an alarm ringing in his subconscious. It is not until the drive back that it rises to remind him that, as usual, he had skimmed over the dossier's grislier details of the crime. Yet, he is sure all he saw about the victim matches O'Shea's story of the two hundred years old murder. He has never been as impatient as now to read the details of a murder by stabbing.

His secretary, Yvonne, hands him a note as he comes in, asking: "Yvie, can you get me the rest of today free? And every day from two to four-thirty...without traumatizing anyone?"

"No worries, Merv. I'll sort it out."

"Um, Grant Walton... Oh, and his Associate, some woman named Ruffio...may call. I don't know her first name."

"Irene. It's on the note. She already did, to ask how you got on with 'that creepy O'Shea'. Her description."

Needing to begin his research, Mervyn waves the note and says: "Tell her I'll try to call in an hour. Probably later."

At his desk, the O'Shea dossier confirms the similarity in Leonora Starr's death to the old murder; two nude twenty-two year-old women died from a single stab to the heart, and both on November first. As he considers that amazing coincidence, an oddly hypnotic swirl of dust in light through a blind's slats holds his gaze as it seems to form a human shape. His laugh at imagining that snaps the trance, and he wryly says to the always-serious Freud on his desk: "It seems that I'm the lost traveler, Siggie, but needing paranormal maps for guidance."

Although uncomfortable with morbid issues, he needs the O'Shea case's facts so that nothing else can surprise him. With that in mind, he tells his silent mentor: "Sure, Siggie... It's just O'Shea's say-so that another woman got killed there, and he could be projecting his crime, if he did it, on that one, but he wants me to check, so I have to assume he believes it."

Yvonne opens the door to say: "I heard you yakking to Sigmund, so I figured you're finished. Need coffee, Merv?"

"Thanks, Yvie...a big pot. I'm far from finished, so let Miss Ruffio know it 'seems promising', and I'll call tomorrow."

Googling old murders in the city's once-titled 'Knob Hill' he finds reports of a victim named Leonie Stark; this year's is Leonora Starr. One records Leonie's birthday as August 17, and the O'Shea dossier confirms that was Leonora's birthday. He is battling disbelief as Yvonne brings in a tray with a mug, cookies and a coffee pot, which she puts on a credenza.

"It'll stay hot for two hours till it shuts off, Merv."

"Thanks. I'll need it all. You cleared the rest of the day, Yvie? No one had an anxiety attack? No problems?"

"You'll have some with my rescheduling of everyone to get around your afternoon trips to the prison."

He smiles. "A treasure of efficiency." Too preoccupied to clarify that was O'Shea's praise of Miss Ruffio, Mervyn says: "You've done enough for today, and I'll be buried. Switch the phone to answer machine. See you tomorrow."

"Don't work long, Merv. With Gaye off fussing over your new grandkid, you have to look after yourself."

He waves as she goes, but is already reading reports of the old killing, making notes of even the inferences he draws from them. When Googling 'Leonie Stark' brings few new facts, he researches her murderer's trial. A True Crime book excerpt of it records, as Mervyn expected, the killer was her step-father, not father. Patrick O'Shaughnessy, known as Paddy O'Shaugh or O'Shaw, chillingly like Padraig O'Shea, married Joan Stark nine years prior, and was molesting her teenaged daughter. 'Purple Press' labeled him 'a brooding brute of bony frame and face', which fits the man Mervyn met today. Now uneasy, he keeps searching for facts and memorizing them before going home to cold leftover pizza, two beers, and restless sleep.

Patients the next morning find him unusually remote, but still offering insights for their consideration. Mervyn is eager to confront O'Shea with all he found, but knows it could put at risk the progress he is making. His mood is also due to having a rescheduled patient at lunchtime, delaying his leaving until two o'clock when he has to be at the prison before three.

He is met there by yesterday's guard, Mike, who says as they walk: "That O'Shea's weird. No trouble. Talks nice. But somethin' about him freaks the shit out of us. It's why you and his lawyers get big guys like me and Pete. But I don't see him as trouble. A huff o' bad breath'd knock him over. Still…"

Mike says no more, but Mervyn now knows that O'Shea hadn't put on an act just for him. He also has the name of the other guard he sees ahead at the interview room door.

"Good afternoon, Pete. How's your prisoner today?"

"Still fancy smart, but fucken crazy. Have fun in there."

Mervyn grins and goes in to find O'Shea on his feet to say: "I judge by your mien that you are now acquainted with the parallel incident with Miss Leonie Stark, Doctor. Glad I am, for now I can explain its pertinence to my case."

"And I have a long list of questions for you."

"I did expect such, sir. But you need my commentary to precede them. You will, please, agree, sir? I am imploring."

As he has weeks for his questions, Mervyn says: "If need be, I can listen for our hour. But let's get comfortable."

"Comfortable?" O'Shea muses. "Naught I say will be any comfort. But say it, I must. And I must ask you to indulge my dramatic air to best convey sequential

27

events for your grasp of my situation...and the emotional oddities within them."

While assessing that, Mervyn points O'Shea to a chair and sits opposite at the table, already feeling the 'dramatic air' of tortuous speech that, to his professional mind, is camouflage. He casually says: "The floor's all yours, and I'm all ears."

"I thank you, sir, and ask only that you visualize all I say. It will be important as we proceed. Can you try for me?"

"Sure. To see it all... Like putting myself in your place."

"Oh, no, sir! I want no one to be in my place. Just close your eyes as I describe a series of tableaux to take your mind to a place of linked events, and attendant emotions. Can you do that, sir, to help me help you see my situation clearly?"

"Sure," Mervyn says, but is wary of closing his eyes with this man, so tilts his head to hide one eye being open a slit.

"Thank you. So picture this... Alone in a room, I sit on a sturdy old wooden chair, gazing at nothing in particular, but attracted to a view of dust-like specks, drifting in the air. My gaze turns to a stare at them starting to swirl as an inexplicable dimming of the daylight in the room occurs. I dismiss it as a cloud obscuring the sun, but must be diverted by that thought, because my refocused eyes see no dust, just a girl, aged about six, approaching with arms out to embrace me. I lift her to my lap, where she rests against me with seeming affection. When I respond with a hug, she reaches into my vest pocket, extracts a cookie, and slowly eats it. The girl then rises, walks off into the gloom, and I lose sight of her, but sunlight's re-entry to the room fails to show any sign of her presence. I am again alone."

"Interpreting dreams can take time," Mervyn says.

O'Shea hisses his exasperation. "Do not dismiss this as a dream. Proof is my having crumbs on my clothes after that... I do not I carry food in pockets, sir!" His tone softens. "That was but the first tableaux of a series, and additional proof will continue. So, with your approval, I shall now do so."

Mervyn nods and, now more secure, closes his eyes, but his mind is deciphering what he heard as he listens to more.

"Now see the room and me on the chair, two years on, and feel the fear of seeing swirling dust coagulate into a girl aged eight years old as the light dims. You know, as I did, that what is to come is beyond our conception as the child sits on my lap, exuding affection. I am mournfully aware of that exhilarating experience's contrast with my barren life, and my tears flow. She takes from her embroidered velvet sleeve, a lace kerchief to dry them... But, as before, rises and vanishes in the gloom, leaving me that memory, and a lacy keepsake to treasure."

Mervyn's eyes open to see O'Shea signal for quiet with a raised hand. "I could recount each time I felt pain in too-brief exquisite love at bi-annual meetings, but I will spare us her at ages ten, twelve and fourteen as variations on the prior theme. In the November she was sixteen years and eleven weeks it all changed. For the first time, she spoke, and kissed me. Those entry factors of swirling dust in a dimming room were as prior visits, but this mid-teenager came with surprising maturity. I was entranced by her undulating hips and bosoms, and admit to having qualms about her being on my lap, but she sat and hugged me sensuously...the only apt word...then quietly said: 'My name is Leonie Stark', after which she kissed my mouth. I knew not what to do, sir. Do you now see how this is?"

"Mm, but that's Leonora, not Leonie," Mervyn says. "Can we discuss your interesting names swap before going on?"

O'Shea's eyes flare. "No, it was Leonie. And if you are so 'interestingly' obtuse, is there any point in going on?"

Mervyn slowly says: "As you couldn't have been there two centuries ago...we're left with some sort of visitation. Dream or ghost would be the popular options, but the same bi-annual date makes dreams unlikely. An emotional event may prompt the mind to revive images on its anniversary, but I can't see it every two years for a decade. Most dreams come from a day's memories... Or those of recent times. So–"

"So you say I could not be with Leonie, so she must be a ghost. But you, a Doctor, are 'unlikely' to accept the existence of ghosts, so must resolve... Why does she visit me? Who am I to her? Why is she sensually affectionate if I am a stranger?"

Mervyn studies O'Shea, hoping to sense a con trick, or a maniacally held belief, but sees only sincerity. He interprets it as a need for compassionate help that anyone who believes he experienced those events could feel, and says: "We'll get to that later, Padraig. May I call you that? It's friendlier."

"And kind. So call me Paddy, as friends do. And, friend, do you indulge me more of Leonie's 'visitations'?"

"Sure. You're right to lay it all out so I understand, but all I understand now is... I'm a lost traveler, with you my guide."

"Whilst more poetic than I expected of you, sir, I value its symbolic trust in me. So, to continue... Leonie did not go after the kiss, which I tried to see as just a 'farewell', but I had felt a lover's kiss. With our faces still close, hot breaths mingling our rising passions, I saw the sexual curiosity of blossoming womanhood. It scared me. I had no right to be there, doing that, so... When added to my perplexity about the sequential visitations... Can you imagine my mental state?"

"Imagine? No, but the Shrink in me senses some sort of guilt trip. Blocked guilt can lead to...'visitations'. That's glib, but let's not bog down. You have more to tell... Go for it."

As Mervyn's eyes close, O'Shea stares blindly, saying: "I know not how long she sat on my lap, her pretty face by mine, her soft bosom to my chest. I was unaware of reality. You may say of all I say that 'reality' is an inapt word, but I was there. Yes, two hundred years ago. Yes, you say it is impossible, but I was there when she stood to go, then lowered her face to give me as sensually arousing a kiss as I could, then, imagine. And I was still there, in a glorious daze, as she walked away into the gloom and vanished just before the daylight returned."

Mervyn frowns, which he usually hides so people cannot draw inferences, but he is assessing a story he knows must be delusional, yet seems truly believed by O'Shea, so time drags before he can respond. "I'm thinking it'd be wrong to say a thing while you have more to tell. My comments can wait."

"Yes, let us leave the sixteen year-old temptress to later, but her image haunted me until her next visitation." O'Shea adopts the far-away look he has while describing those visits. "See the fateful meeting with me, the room dimming as I am transfixed by swirling dust that becomes beautiful eighteen years old Leonie. She is changed, not only by riper figure, but also by rouged cheeks and kohl-edged eyes. More startlingly, she is naked. A breathtaking sight, but I see lust personified, and it alarms me. More so when she does not sit on my lap, but instead straddles it to sit with her...you know, pressing on where my manhood lurks in my trousers. As she kisses me, I think 'what can I do?' But I have no control. I kiss as ardently as she, and we lie on the floor, now both naked. I will not talk of the depravity to which we descended. Suffice it to say that when she finally left into oblivion in the dimmed room, I lay like a sunken galleon on a seabed, a wrecked and rotting hulk. That last memory from the day still scars my mind."

An almost eerie silence chills the room. Mervyn knows he should say something, but his mind is flooded by images it has created. He tries: "If that sixteen year-old haunted your head for two years, this one must have blown your mind."

"Yes! You now see the nub. But see the torment I had for two years in a hell of self-loathing, fearing the sequence's next step, as each prior had advanced me to the hell I found."

Mervyn asks: "How do we do this? Options I see are to discuss how you reacted then to that hell, or you tell me your next encounters and we cover the lot at the end. Your call."

O'Shea looks relieved. "For that option, I thank you." He falls silent, his mind apparently far away.

Mervyn allows a pause before saying: "But time is slipping by, and I'd like to hear it all today."

O'Shea's vacant stare remains. "Talk about my mind then covers the next two years. My festering thoughts deepened, and self-loathing included disgust for her and all she made of me." He scowls, and turns to tell Mervyn: "More on that will be repetitive, but what I have said leads to what I was thinking just prior to Leonie's manifestation at twenty. I decided to kill the lass to stop her tempting me to wallow in hideous ecstasy. I do not see intimate congress that way... Physical love is life's gift, but our cavorting was despicable, and my sanity could be restored only by her death. More precisely, by my killing her."

"So she died at only twenty? Not twenty-two?"

"Alas, she looked too ravishing... I was incapable of all but joining in her sordid games. At day's end, I felt potent, but shame and revulsion soon regained my mind's control. See me spend the next two years planning her death, as you read of it, but see this... In that November, I sat with a knife at my side. As before, she came naked, but this time doing an erotic, twirling

33

dance to me. I stood, as if to greet her, thinking she would teasingly dance about me, and I knew Leonie well, for she did so. I awaited a twirl that let me grab her from behind, reach around and stab into her bosom. Then, lost in thoughts and emotions, I slumped on my chair, staring at what I had done, and only slowly aware that sunlight had returned to the room, and her dead body was still there. Did you see it all?"

"Not sure what I see. Top-of-the-head textbook stuff is you studied the old crime to tell an insane tale to be found not guilty of a murder you did commit. Police reports list no proof you knew the girl, so a random killing. If I testify you told me that story, an insanity plea could get you a few easy years in a psych cell... But I don't believe that's what you want, Paddy... And I can't figure out why I don't believe it."

O'Shea sits pensively until he says: "I will tell you that, as Leonie Stark died two hundred years before Leonora Starr, I also stabbed Lena Stahk two hundred years prior to that." He waves-away a response. "Before her, Leah Schtahk. Records of those two must exist back in England, and any relating to William Shakespeare's later life may mention Lena. I recall that she knew him... In her childhood, so not intimately."

Mervyn's patience expires. "Enough! My best advice is to not add that embellishment in court. The jurors will hear it as over-the-top lies to convince them you're insane, so know you aren't. Stick to the Leonie dreams driving you to kill Leonora."

"But I am always executed. It is my fate, as is killing a girl fated to die. If you do not see that, what do you see?"

Mervyn stares sternly at the pale man across the table and signals for quiet, but knows that he should provoke a reaction from O'Shea. "What I see... First, you're right. I find no logic in the idea of ghosts, so can't accept them. I accept that people believe in them... Even believe they are one, reincarnated... however that's said to work." He sees O'Shea wants to speak and again raises a hand. "If it were possible to live again with a repeating 'fate', we'd all know about it. But what we know is that any who claim it are found to be charlatans, or delusional. I don't see you as delusional, Paddy. But a charlatan? Maybe. Though I'm yet to figure out what you could be after."

O'Shea sighs sadly. "So you have no idea what I'm telling you. What a shame... I need you to. What a waste."

Mervyn's ire shows. "What's wasted is my time. It's you who doesn't get this. So see it from the other side. Okay?" He doesn't pause. "Say your story's true...dead girls, Shakespeare and all, going back every two hundred years, and each time you're executed. It's your fate to die, because you did back when many crimes got you hanged, but that has all changed... Here, and in every civilized country...even those with a death penalty...take forever to do it. Appeals stretch as long as you can afford lawyers. Really, Paddy... You have more chance of dying in prison by being killed by an inmate you've pissed off while waiting to be executed.

And that's if your jury happens, against the odds I see, to convict you. Don't you get that?"

O'Shea looks genuinely troubled. "But I always am, so I must be. What will become of me if I do not die?"

Mike and Pete entering, signaling the hour is up saves Mervyn from answering, so his smile at them includes thanks for the intervention. Noting that O'Shea has stood to go with Mike, he is surprised to see that the man's obvious concern of moments earlier is replaced by contentment. Mervyn is more surprised when O'Shea addresses the guards.

"You are in the presence of an astounding man. Doctor Frankel can see all sides of an issue, and also its core element." Turning from the guards, he tells Mervyn: "Please know that I greatly appreciate your advice, and will follow its guidance." He then turns and leaves the room with Mike.

Pete says: "Seems you're a big hit with him Doc."

Finding that as surprising as the contrast he just observed in O'Shea, Mervyn smiles. "His lawyer sent me, but it can't hurt to offer some advice that he values, eh Pete?"

"Can I ask what it was, Doc?"

Mervyn chuckles. "I wish I knew." He then recalls saying that O'Shea's tale of earlier murders would alienate jurors in court. "Seems he's found advice in something I said critically. We Shrinks are a misunderstood lot."

On the drive back, Mervyn hears from Yvonne that his last patient cancelled, so he tells her to go home, and gladly heads to his home after a demanding day. A stop for a pizza delays his arrival, and all the way he ponders O'Shea, sensing that a subconscious insight is eluding him as his mind reviews the man's unique characteristics. His top priority once at home, though, is to call Gaye for news of their new granddaughter.

Despite his fatigue, Mervyn sleeps poorly after playing his O'Shea session recording to allocate key points to categories in notes. When awoken, his mind is slow to register the time is 6:40, five minutes before the alarm is set, and it is the phone ringing. Believing that only Gaye would call so early about an emergency in their daughter's family, he tries to sound calm in answering: "Mornin', honey. What's up?"

After muffled men's voices in the background, a woman says: "It's Irene Ruffio, Doctor Frankel. I'm –"

"I know who you are, Miss Ruffio...but I don't know why you'd be calling me at this hour. What's going on?"

"My boss, Grant, sent me out to the prison to get O'Shea's personal stuff before it...disappears. And I –"

"Wait! What?" Mervyn interrupts, his mind struggling to function. "The prison? What for? Why call me? Now?"

In reply, a long and seemingly anxious sigh ends with: "Oh... You didn't see last night's news? Sorry... He's dead."

"No, early night. How? What happened, Miss... May I call you Irene? I'm Mervyn, okay? Tell me all you know. "

"He got an improvised knife...shiv, in the heart during an argument. Grant saw the ten o'clock T-V news, and called me to be here before the six A-M shift change to collect O'Shea's belongings, and to find out all I can."

Mervyn offers: "Poor kid, you must be exhausted. But, I mean... I wasn't due out there until three o'clock, so what's the rush in calling to tell me now at...not yet seven?"

"There was a note in his cell for you, and –"

"O'Shea wrote me a note? What's in it?"

Irene's breathing is all he hears until: "It...looks to be very old paper, folded in half. Your name outside... Inside has the words 'thank you'... And it's all in faded ink. But –"

"Paddy thanked me? For what? Any idea, Irene?"

"That's one odd bit. The writing's a woman's, delicate and ornate. So some woman thanked you, and I'm calling, because Detectives here hope you can explain...who she is, for a start."

"No clue. But that's all you can tell me about the note?"

"Well, no," she says warily. "It's in a plastic bag to go for forensic tests, because they can't find fingerprints on it. What I see looks old, but it can't be with your name on it. So that's odd, too. And the letters... Oh, sorry, I didn't tell you... Under 'thank you' are initials... Though the Detectives say they could be part of some coded message to you. Are they?"

"No," Mervyn scoffs. "Initials? In the same hand?"

"Yes. That's the oddest part. She wrote 'L' and 'S', which would be Leonora Starr, except she was dead before you knew O'Shea, so how could she write your name on the front?"

Mervyn says: "Tell the Detectives I don't know who wrote it, and that the only logical 'L-S' is who you thought of... The late Leonora Starr. Now, I must rearrange my day, so I'll call about this later. Thanks for letting me know. Bye for now." He hangs up and, seeing dust floating on the early sunlight pouring through the window, he laughs as he says: "So...L-S? Maybe Leonora, given Paddy's story. But the Cops could try to pin it on Leonie Stark, or Lena Stahk, or even Leah Schtahk. Right? Um... Are any of you ladies hearing me?"

~~~~~~~~

THE INHERITANCE

ANDREA RHUDE

Grandma used to get very nervous come October...about her garden. The house could be shedding its peeling paint, the driveway could be all broken-up by grass and weeds until it resembled a jigsaw, but the garden had to be harvested, and tilled, and replanted by October thirty-first. After that she would never set foot in, or remove anything - not even snow - from the garden. If any child in the neighborhood tried to enter the carefully tended marvel, she would fly into a rage, become a whirl of shawls and walking sticks, and scare them off. She was that crazy old woman the neighborhood kids alternately torment and avoid.

To me, she was the eccentric woman who told strange wonderful stories. She was the adult who would laugh at my mother when she became inexplicably angry with something I said, and smile at the stories I'd tell about my tiny imaginary friends...and who you had to watch, because you never knew what would send her into a nervous panic. One day when I was young, I moved one of the stones that surrounded her garden. She flew into a frenzy, ripped the rock out of my hand and placed it back along with a slice of bread and some butter. Then she took me inside, had me strip and then put all my clothes on again, back to front. I thought she'd lost her mind. She scared me so badly I cried and cried until my mother forbade me ever going there again. I had to beg and plead for months before she relented and I could see my Gran again.

She did lose her mind a bit, a few years back, and began calling me by a name I didn't know. The only reason I even know it was a name is because of context, like a little puppy responding to the same repeated, meaningless, sounds that somehow corresponded to me. There is no way to spell that 'name'; there is no correlation to any alphabet I've heard.

I have spoken the name to numerous linguists, scientists, folklorists, even alchemists. No one seems to hear it. They kind of blink at me as their minds erase history back to the last thing I said before I mentioned the name. It happened so much that I started to use it as a party trick, one only I could appreciate. It got old and started to make me feel very alone. I tried a new tack; I'd hand the scientist some samples of earth and plants from my Grandma's garden, and ask for them to be tested because something is 'wrong' with them.

The scientists all apologized, mumbled something about the samples being contaminated, because the test results were negative; including a carbon test they ran 'just to make sure'. I never came up with an alternate plan for the linguists. I cared back then, had hope of understanding Grandma. Now I just want to know. What I mean is not 'to understand'. You see, to know you just have to listen and remember. But to understand you have to 'eat' all they tell you, you have to make room for it, make it a part of you.

I own Grandma's house now, much against my mother's advice, and it's not just the garden that needs looking after. There are 'odd corners' of the house that I can't put anything in. Things will break, or vanish, or... The wall, the freaking wall, will blow out if you don't place a saucer of milk in the corner at night. A neighborhood kid took a blueberry off our bush after October thirty-first and he got sick. He told everyone the berry had no taste. Now I shoo the kids from the garden as if I'm an old crone in a fairytale, like Grandma was.

I know not to do anything in the garden after Halloween. I understand that it doesn't belong to me between Halloween and Easter. I know I will never understand who owns it. But now that I live here, I hear voices at night. First, when I set my bed near one of the 'odd corners'. When they woke me for the third time, I think I mumbled something back. Now I hear *Them* whenever and wherever I sleep. *They* use that name my Gran used. Strangely, I feel closer to her now, and I've begun answering to that name.

Soon, I know, I will go with *Them*, and I worry; a stranger will buy my family home and they won't know anything about the garden, or the corners, or any of the other things I have learned since I've taken over the home. What will they think? How will they keep the kids safe? Will they figure out how to placate *Them*? I know that they will never understand. No, truthfully, I understand that they will never understand, but I hope they might know...

Remember the milk and don't eat from the garden after Halloween. *They* are calling. I do understand what *They* are saying, but I don't know it, and I must go.

~~~~~~~~

THE PAINTER

JOYCE deCORDOVA

It wasn't your cookie cutter kind of cruise ship. This was small and exclusive. It was touring the Yucatan in Mexico and held only 85 passengers, with about the same number of crew; an almost one to one ratio.

What made it so distinctly exclusive were certainly not its accommodations, they were clean and simple at best; it was its passengers. They were all Princeton, Harvard and Yale alumni and as they and their families were the only ones on board, it was very clubby.

However, it was not an exclusivity that was earned. They had not really accomplished much themselves, and were not self-made. They were basically free-loading on ancestors, their parents and grandparents. They were your quiet, rich family money types, and none of their names ended in a vowel.

David Gilbert, an archeologist and historian, was guest lecturer for the cruise, giving daily talks on the Mayan sites they would be visiting. Truth be told, the passengers really weren't interested in the Yucatan, but the lectures were part of the pattern of the day which also included the acceptable hour to have the acceptable drink: 10am for Bloody Marys... noon beers...5pm cocktails...7pm wines...9pm brandies, and so on. The passengers came to the lectures, started taking notes, and then dozed off with pen or pencil in hand. But every afternoon, David earned his keep.

The nights however, were his own. He was a painter...a very good portrait artist. He would ask the sailors to come to his cabin and pose for him. He loved men. You could tell by the way he painted them. His brush caressed their form. He was not interested in painting women, and never asked the ship's hairdressers or the laundresses to pose. Just the men. He primarily painted for the health of his soul, and he usually gave the finished portrait to the sailor. David's passion was in the art itself...the love of the line...the lights and shadows of the form...the palpable connection he made with the sailor. All this satisfied him.

Because it was a small ship, word spread that David was a painter. One night, when he had just completed a portrait of one of the cooks, a huge coal black man with an almost incredibly kind and open face, there was a knock on his door. It was one of the women passengers.

She was in her 30's...waspishly beautiful. Her slim body was expensively dressed in a quiet understated fashion. Her blond hair, cleverly streaked, was fashionably cut and framed her perfect oval face. She wore little jewelry--just diamond studs in her ears and an expensively cut gold bracelet. Her nails had no polish, but were buffed to a subtle sheen. Though she smelled fresh and young, she also smelled of money...old money, and walked into David's stateroom uninvited, as if she had every right to be there. And, in a way, she did, because the ship's golden rule was that passengers ruled. Whatever they wanted, was theirs, including the bodies of young sailors if that was what they fancied.

David remembered her because she was one of the few passengers who had been to every one of his lectures, and had managed to stay awake. More memorable was that she had actually seemed interested in what he was saying. Oh yes, she was interested, but not in the Yucatan ruins.

She was interested in him. She found his earnestness and dedication to his craft appealing and refreshing, unlike all the other passengers who bored her with their talk of money and mergers. Physically, she liked the leanness of his body and the tight curls about his head that looked carelessly combed. Yes, she reasoned, he fit the profile of an academician and an artist, because he gave no thought as to how he looked. It was his work that mattered, and he was consumed by it. And, because of that, she was consumed by him. He was a challenge. She would be the one to turn that beautiful head around.

She looked boldly at David, glanced at his paintings and told him she wanted her portrait painted. She knew she was beautiful, so there would be no possible reason that he could refuse her, she thought.

David's eyes took on a look of panic, but he was a gentle soul, and his feeble attempts to dissuade her were useless. So she sat. David sighed, arranged his palette and began to paint. He felt he had no choice.

If the definition of a good model is one who can assume a pose and hold it for a length of time, then she was it. Her pose, however, was provocative: her blouse casually slipping off a shoulder and her skirt just a bit too high, revealing her smooth thighs. But yet, the pose was as rigid and unbending as she. While she sat, her thoughts went to David and the romance they would have once her portrait was finished.

Interestingly, David hardly looked at her as he painted. His jaw was set and he was doing as he was told. After a time, he put down his brush. There was no mistaking that it was she, but now the minimal lines on her face were exaggerated. Her blue eyes were washed out as though she had cataracts beginning. Her blond hair held more gray and hung limply about her now sagging shoulders. One could imagine the rest of her figure, which would be flat and sterile, devoid of curves, sensuousness or feeling. He had placed her against a light background, and since she was fair, she blended into the canvas as if she was not important enough to have definition of her own -- and whatever definition he did give her, was not worth knowing.

David had painted her soul.

He then signed his name to the painting. She knew the significance of that. It meant that he liked what he did. He gave it to her, and her good manners could not refuse it. After all, she was well-bred.

~ ~ ~ ~ ~ ~ ~ ~

WINTER ROSES

KIT STORJOHANN

I sneezed into the dishtowel, hoping to catch the inevitable afterbirth of mucus that poured out of me almost unchecked since the winter roses had taken over our town. The tissues were gone and the penultimate roll of paper towels had grown thin. I hated using the towels this way, but knew that my husband, Will, would never complain, even if I used my wedding dress for a Kleenex. His reaction to my struggle with Surgensblight, a now unimpressive derivation from the Latin word for rose paired with "blight" to name this ghastly affliction that struck a select few of us as though we were plants, was a seemingly inexhaustible anger - but none of it was ever directed it at me. Instead, he hurled his fury at the world that had reduced me to a house-bound invalid. Every window in our two-story, 4,000 square-foot house stayed tightly shut most days, the gentle breeze of the late summer air sacrificed to keep one more barrier between my ravaged sinuses and the heady poison.

I was an outlier, statistically speaking. "It's just bad luck," the prevailing wisdom had informed me over and over. But, in spite of the many times my hopes had been dashed, I hoped the latest test results might prove a change in fortunes. Will, although unaffected by Surgensblight himself, had become a crusader for sufferers: those of us who had fallen prey to this new pollen that clung invisibly to every surface in our little corner of the world. He attended meetings, held up signs at rallies, circulated petitions, harangued lawmakers, and made sure that the now-thriving area would not forget our suffering.

The flowers were certainly pretty, and 'winter gardens' that survived the ice and snow painted monochromatic landscapes with their palette of vernal purples and reds. The yards of our neighbors - which had previously been abandoned to winter's drab, fallow tomb - now adorned family Christmas cards, where broad smiles dotted amidst knitted winter finery clustered about a fully blooming rosebush dusted with snow. "We are standing beside a miracle," they silently boasted.

The handcrafted phenomenon of rime-crusted flowers had caused the recent renewal of local prosperity. When we moved in, the area was in the process of shuffling off its rotted, post-industrial-bust past. The promised gentrification that lured us here had proceeded slowly. The old guard clung steadfastly to their extinct world, fighting fate and progress for every foreclosed house. Those who had stayed were now rewarded as they enjoyed the succor the winter roses offered to the local economy. Our little outposts of cafés, galleries, and bistros – once the spear point of our advance – celebrated the town's previous incarnation, and all now had rose-themed names. Regional television news stories and viral articles delivered goggle-eyed tourists in droves to where old winter carnivals and lighting displays had failed. Local nurseries were suddenly inundated with orders from all over the area, and cheerfully charged top dollar for their miraculous crop. People wanted to spar with death, to claim little oases of life in defiance of winter. The town and its spirit were revitalized, and I could almost forgive them for destroying my life.

There was no apparent rhyme or reason as to who was afflicted by Surgensblight. It was technically a severe allergy, but often left unscathed people who usually struggled against onslaughts of pollen, heat, or dust. A few families had several members reduced to coughing, aching invalids, but it was rare enough that most households had no sufferers. Schools saw only a handful of children missing for weeks or months due to Surgensblight, and not necessarily the same kids who needed peanut-free environments, or routinely sucked on inhalers between wheezes. Suffering seemed to be apportioned by nothing more rational than divine whim.

That morning, I waited for a call from my doctor. Most doctors refused to believe in Surgensblight, and I'd severed ties with a long string of them - including ones I'd trusted for years - when they'd repeatedly suggest that I see a psychiatrist instead. Many fellow sufferers got the same advice, some of them receiving it for their children as young as five. For most of the medical community, that approach was easier than shrugging and saying "We don't know what's happening, so we've chosen not to believe you." I'd finally found a physician willing to not write me off as a hypochondriac, but he had no solid answers. A handful of pills to hold the symptoms at bay for a while was the best he could do.

Will's continual scouring of the internet had unearthed a hypotheses of how Surgensblight was escaping detection and which tests might be more effective. Dr. Mallinas was open to them, and I'd been duly prodded and bled. When the phone rang, my idiotically high hopes allowed me to stride to it with an unaccustomed ease.

My cheery "Hello," was greeted by an angry, but familiar, exhalation; I was about to be scolded or threatened.

"I'm onto you," a male voice said in a throaty whisper, like a bad guy in a film trying to disguise his identity.

"I'm sorry," I said, as though I hadn't understood.

"I know what kind of scam you're pullin'," he said, his voice rising angrily at the end. The dropped "g" betrayed a hint of southern twang which indicated that he was not from the area. *Interesting,* I thought, *the hate calls are starting to filter in from farther away.*

"There is no scam."

"There is scientific evidence," he said, enunciating every syllable as though each was indisputably arbitrating a truth, "that this whole thing is a hoax. Alarmist bullshit."

These calls used to pour in constantly, and we'd already changed our home phone number twice; I had no cell phone anymore. Many of the initial calls were discernible as voices of our friends and neighbors. I grew to hate the people who asked Will with great concern about how I was when they saw him in the supermarket, and then called the house later to anonymously berate me for lying to get attention. Strangers were easier to dismiss. I tried not to take it personally, with mixed success. "I assure you," I said, "Surgensblight is real. I pray no one you love ever experiences it."

"They won't," he retorted, any attempt to hide his accent disappearing as he slid into a full-on drawl. "All my family works for a livin'. We aren't jumpin' on the gravy train to live off welfare and charity money."

The financial hardships Will and I had endured were severe. There was no math we could devise that would let us keep the house more than a few months. I couldn't work, of course. The office had readily accepted my resignation after repeatedly turning down my requests for medical leave. As no doctor had found anything 'definitive', I was not eligible for any sort of disability. Will was quietly dismissed from his own office when his activism became known. They claimed his 'partisan activities' had nothing whatsoever to do with it, but was due to all the 'sudden irregularities' in his schedule. Since then, he'd held down minimum wage jobs, carrying boxes of textbooks around a warehouse and stocking shelves overnight in a supermarket, all for the sake of preserving a few waking hours every day to carry on the fight. He cared for me as best he could, and made sure that we had at least a few minutes together every day, but aside from that, he was in meetings, at protests, making phone calls, or going door-to-door with petitions and pamphlets, braving endless abuse. Amateur fund-raising barely covered mailing costs, let alone the lavish lifestyle the caller imagined us living.

"Listen, I don't know where you get your information—"

"I get my information from reputable news sources. Not your leftist propaganda nonsense. You people want to make us all scared to go out of our houses. Just so you can cash in. You're what's wrong with America, dammit. Get a job!"

I tried to be patient. Obviously he'd suffered through a collection of unscrupulous con artists, deliberately making his life harder. There was a time when I might have felt similarly. I used to habitually roll my eyes when I heard about the plight of illegal immigrants, or the hardship of welfare queens and their dozens of children. But since I'd gotten sick, I'd found it harder to get angry at people whose stories I didn't know.

"I'm afraid you're mistaken." My voice had inadvertently hardened. "A lot of us are sick, and-"

"Oh yeah? Yer sick? What about us? We're sick of you on the news whinin' every night! Sick of seein' your crisis actors cough at the camera!"

I wondered what news program he could be watching. This was a local issue - regional at most. Will, probably the foremost advocate for Surgensblight's victims, had never been on television. His schedule allowed for no more than brief quotes in a local newspaper with few readers left. I wondered if the caller was delusional, or mistaking me for someone else he didn't like. Or perhaps the news had spread to become a national issue without our knowledge.

"We're sick of you livin' off our tax dollars for some fake disability."

"Fake!" I yelled. "How dare you. You..." I trailed off, and tried deep breathing which turned into a wheeze.

"Fuck you, cunt," he drawled. "Start prayin' I never find you and your commie husband, bitch! Yer sick? Well, I've got a second amendment cure for you! You think--"

I hung up, resisted answering the next ring, and let his vitriol pour directly into the machine. He roared accusations that I was a plant for powerful environmental lobbyists, or a government agent who wanted to whip up panic to grab more federal power. I was anti-Christian and anti-America, I was Hitler. I told myself that it had nothing to do with me, but for the first time in a long time, the abuse had me in tears. I did cry frequently due to Surgensblight, but had not been goaded to it by a stranger for quite some time. If I hadn't been waiting for the doctor's call, I would have shut off the phone.

Dragging myself around the house in a pathetic imitation of housekeeping, I half-heartedly slid a duster along the living room shelves, then sat down and wheezed. It wasn't much of a life. The woman I used to be had evaporated since the winter roses had taken root, replaced by a frail scarecrow who she would have dismissed with either pity or contempt. My hard-won Master's degree in accounting had gotten me into a firm nearby. From what I deemed pure hard work, that entry level position had burgeoned into one of making presentations to boards and acting as an ambassador to leading companies in sister industries. Vertical integration was the buzzword tossed around, but for me it was a wonderful exploration of how innovation and will fit seemingly unlike things together. I loved what I did, I worked hard, and I was damn good at it.

And I once had a similar attitude to the caller. I believed that laziness and self-pity were the roots of most of the world's problems. Besides, I'd known people who suffered far worse. So when my health began to wane and I found myself trying and failing to keep up with my job - remotely or in person - I assumed the fault was mine. That I was too weak-willed to conquer the pain. My efforts to fight through Surgensblight's symptoms by virtue of sheer will completely failed, bonding to anguish at my new-found helplessness. As I had adjusted over time, I found a deeper well of patience.

Back in the kitchen, I regarded the dishes in the sink, and resolved to finish at least that task. Rolling up the sleeves of my three sweaters, I began filling the sink to soak them. As I rarely had energy to scrub vigorously, any advantage I could give myself was worthwhile. I no longer looked like a thirty-four-year-old woman, but a worn-out crone. My prematurely withered hands turned off the tap and let the dishes sit in the soapy water like shipwrecks. The doorbell sounded a bleary chime. I let it whimper again before going to it, ignoring all the prickles of pain that shot through my limbs.

In the vestibule, I held my breath as I took the gas

mask off the coatrack like a doughboy in the trenches, and fitted it over my face. I'd asked Will to get me one with the rounded eyes and terrifying, birdlike beak of a medieval plague doctor. The panache tickled me as much as the irony did.

The figure on my stoop was swaddled like a Berber in the multiple layers of clothes that were now the unofficial uniform of our sad tribe. This person wore goggles and bandanas over its face instead of a mask. The bent and diminutive form was positively desiccated, so I was surprised when a robust male voice asked: "Is Will Segovian here?"

"No," I said. The Darth Vader-like distortion afforded by the plague mask tended to hide my gender and any trace of identity, so I added: "I'm his wife. He's at a meeting now."

"I need to talk to him."

"I don't know when he'll be back. Can I take your number and have him call you when he gets home?" That would be many hours later. Will would have just a few minutes with me between jobs after dropping off his clipboards and canvassing materials. By the time he got home from his shift it would be after midnight. I'd be tossing and turning in our bed, soaking our sheets with snot and sweat. He'd be at his desk, trying to respond to the endless correspondence amid a flood of threats and mocking before getting a few hours sleep on the couch, just so he could do it all again. He answered my entreaties for him to slow down and take care of himself by saying he was doing it for me, and for everyone with Surgensblight.

"I didn't know you were a sufferer," the man said.

"I try to stay out of the limelight. I'm not the story."

"You are the story," the man said. "So am I. And so is my granddaughter."

"Your granddaughter?"

"She's three months old," he said. "And won't grow at all. Has gained only a few ounces since she came home from the hospital. All she does is cough, and spit everything up. They had to feed her intravenously several times. My daughter and son-in-law don't believe Surgensblight exists. But their little one has it." He leaned in conspiratorially. "She must have gotten it from me." He evidently believed that he'd dropped something insidious, like hemophilia, in the gene pool, which would torment and obliterate the life of his granddaughter.

"It's not your fault," I said. "We didn't ask for this. It –"

"We pass it on," he said. "To the children. I know it."

"I think you're right," I said. "I'm sorry." As he staggered off, disappointed and shaking in the morning's burgeoning heat, I sat in my easy chair and cried. Tears were another effect of Surgensblight that I loathed. As a little girl, uniquely in our neighborhood children, I didn't cry at all. Knees were scraped, tree-climbing ended in falls, wind was knocked from lungs, and feelings got hurt. But through it all I shrugged and kept playing.

I'd stoically accepted my father's death when I was in high school, and the pain of ovarian cysts which made every breath and movement a study in agony, gritting my teeth resolutely. For some reason,

Surgensblight played hell with my emotions to a degree that trauma, chronic pain, or hormonal chaos had never achieved. Will had told me many times that he loved my strength. Yet he loved me no less now that my vaunted strength was gone. Part of me secretly hated him for being more understanding than I think I'd have been in his place.

When the phone rang again, I was less enthusiastic than I'd been before the venomous calls poured in, and heard the voice coming through the machine before I could get there. "It's Valerie calling from Doctor Mallinas's office. A message for Kate Segovian. Kate, we'd like you to-"

I scooped up the phone and croaked: "Hi. It's me. Sorry I didn't get to the phone in time. You got my test results?"

"We did," she responded, volunteering nothing further.

"And?"

"Could you come in for a consultation with the doctor?"

I sighed, and said: "It's difficult to leave the house. Can we discuss this over the phone?"

She also sighed. "One moment please," and left me in the care of a Muzak version of 'You're So Vain.' I sat in an easy chair, trying to take pressure off without relaxing so much that it would be hard to stand again, dragging a towel across my sweat and mucus-soaked face, over and over.

"Kate," the doctor's voice cut into an oddly cheery flute and synthesizer rendition of 'Cat's in the Cradle.' "It's Doctor Mallinas. How are you feeling today?"

"Hi, Doc. Pretty rotten. But I've had worse days, I guess."

"Well, I'm sorry to hear that," he said, his tone betraying the fact that he likely wouldn't lose any sleep over it. "I have your test results. Can we discuss them for a moment?"

"Yes. I'm just sitting here. It's all I can do right now."

After a palpably somber silence, he continued. "We ran every test you requested, but none shows any evidence of those antibodies." I sighed. Dr. Mallinas was open to the possibility of a heretofore undetectable affliction, but as his medical bag of tricks had been bested by Surgensblight, he'd begun to fall back to trusting his tests rather than his patient. More tears had mingled with the ubiquitous mixture of other secretions before I realized they were flowing again.

It's all over, came churning up out of the depths of my mind. "So what do I do?" I asked.

"I'm not sure there's much more we can do. I'd prescribe the meds you were on before to help alleviate the symptoms, but I can't prescribe them longterm."

"They didn't help," I said sharply. "All they did was put me to sleep all of the time."

"Well, there aren't really any options in that drug family," he said. "If you can come in, we might discuss -"

"What?" I said, practically yelling. "Discuss how it's all in my head?"

"Kate, you know I've been open to your hypothesis this whole time. No, I don't think it's all in your head, but I do think you'd benefit from counseling. I have some names that I've given to other patients who...experience similar-"

"Surgensblight," I said calmly. "Just say it. You might not know how to test for it, or treat it, but I've got it."

"I've done a lot of reading on the subject," he said. "And your symptoms are consistent with the ones attributed to this so-called Surgensblight. But there still isn't enough data to definitively talk about the disorder."

"I've done a lot of reading too," I said. "Believe me. It's Surgensblight. Just because you don't know how to find it doesn't mean it isn't there."

"Well, I'm in agreement with you on that," he said. "I'm just skeptical of giving it a name when I can't prove it. And I can't move to a course of treatment without knowing more. The best we can do, now, is to try to control the symptoms. I can call in a prescription for -"

"Call in whatever prescription you want," I said. "I'll take it. Thank you for calling." I tapped the End Call button gently, lamenting the loss of slammable phone cradles of my youth. Of course, I was so weak I probably couldn't have managed a good slam anyway. All I could think was: *It's all over.*

A few pity-soaked moments later, this was replaced by the thought that I still had to wash the dishes. As I trudged to the kitchen, I wondered if Will would be able to see that I'd gotten bad news when he got home. A glance at the clock told me it was time for a local talk radio show that I had grown to enjoy after finding myself housebound. The voice of Fay

Heltzberg, indiscriminately fascinated by every topic and guest, would be the perfect company for washing dishes and giving up.

Through a cruel coincidence I hadn't imagined could exist outside of a sitcom, the program's subject was Surgensblight. Fay's guest, an 'expert in natural healing,' had written a book on the juices which would 'properly attune' one's body to the world. She didn't advocate research and funding, but asserted repeatedly that Surgensblight did not exist, adding: "I think a lot of people bought into the medical-industrial complex's propaganda telling them that they are inherently 'sick.' You see," she continued in a voice simultaneously saccharine and didactic, giving me two reasons to want to strangle her. "The medical-industrial complex - crisis-based doctors, hospitals, Big Pharma and insurance companies - is interested in selling things to us. Like vaccines against diseases our grandparents got through unscathed. They sell us pills to 'treat' endless symptoms. And what causes these symptoms? Take a guess."

"Hmm," the host said, as though considering it. "The power of suggestion, perhaps?"

"Maybe," the guest said in two obnoxiously mellifluous syllables. "But the main culprits are chemicals and synthetics around us. They've *made* us sick. Think about what gets jammed into kids every day with needles, airborne chemicals and refined sugar. It's making us 'allergic,' for lack of a better word, to the natural world. But we've evolved to live *in* nature, not in spite of nature. You didn't hear of cavemen's seasonal allergies. Or migraines. Or autism, or peanut allergies. But as soon as there are pills to be sold, suddenly we're all sick."

"Are you saying that the people with Surgensblight are faking their symptoms?"

My hands in the sink looked safe beneath the layer of soap bubbles like some breed of aquatic plant. The outline of bones was visible, like on my grandmother's hands. My mom didn't live long enough to become an old woman. Nor would I, I now realized, but I would look very old before the end. *It's all over.*

"I think," the guest said airily, "that might be overstating it. I'm saying that we've made being sick into the norm. So what is natural suddenly *feels* sick."

I felt sick all right, but it was definitely a deviation from the 'norm,' and my illness arrived with the winter roses. I wiped fluid flowing from my mouth and nose on the shoulder of my outermost sweater, and stared into the water at my hands, which no longer seemed to want to move.

I had never been able to listen to daytime radio while I was working, but had grown to enjoy this show's discussions on the need for education or conservation, freshly discovered planets, and reviews of new books. Fay's forays into health news usually dealt with the benefits of meditation for cancer patients or the importance of working exercise into our daily routines. This episode was just reinforcing the nonsensical claims that sufferers of Surgensblight were attention-seekers, or whiny hypochondriacs.

"Activists claim," Fay said, drawing out the word to belie the certainty of the connection, "that Surgensblight is caused by the so-called 'winter roses,' a local strain of flower that was bred - some say 'bioengineered' - to survive cold and snow. Is that an argument against genetically modified crops?"

"Well, genetically modified crops themselves are the best argument against genetically modified crops. They can be quite harmful in, say, vegetables, where the benefits you find in organic produce are stripped out and replaced by possibly carcinogenic chemicals. That's self-evident, but I don't think it's what's going on here. There is no scientific evidence that the winter roses are causing any specific illness."

Fay didn't challenge her on this point. Will had a sheaf of scientific evidence sitting on his desk pointing not only to correlation, but definitive causation. He constantly updated the website, linking to every study he found that supported the cause. Yet no one wanted to read them. People got on the site to argue bitterly with each other, the threads devolving into name-calling and accusations of ignorance or hate. Part of me wanted to think that if I was hearing this show and had no idea what Surgensblight was, I'd Google it to learn. I would study the data, and read accounts of victims, like me, who'd posted testimonials of how miserable their lives had become. I knew, though, that I probably would have accepted what was said on the air as gospel truth, then forgotten about it before I tuned in the next day for a discussion about whether drones should be allowed in our national parks. When the calls started coming in, I was reminded that there's a wide variety of people ready to hate me without even knowing me - some, I was willing to concede, with good reason.

"I think one of the problems is a cost-benefit analysis," the first caller's gruff voice said. "My family's been crammed into a tiny apartment since we lost our house. I ran my own greenhouse and nursery for twenty years, and it was killed off by cheap plants from Walmart and Home Depot. They get cheap imports, so I got run out of business...can't pay the mortgage. We were..." He trailed off, apparently struggling to not let emotion bleed through into his voice.

"You were living without hope," Fay prompted.

"Exactly! We had no hope. Now I own a nursery again, getting bigger every month, and employing a few locals. A pal of mine was watching his restaurant go down the tubes, and now he's doing great. This town is packed with tourists, and everyone is doing well. All thanks to those roses."

"So what would you say to all those people suffering from Surgensblight?"

"They keep saying 'How would you feel if someone in your family had it?' I lost my business and house without a word from anyone. How's my being able to feed my family more selfish than them grumbling about having to take Benadryl?"

The guest described the evils of Benadryl, of course, but added sly insults about the 'illusory nature' of Surgensblight. She then extolled the benefits of Ayurvedic juicing as a path to health, much to the amusement of the host, who gleefully stumbled over the word in her attempts to pronounce it.

"I say," a caller droned in her painfully slow basso voice, "it's just another panic the government made up to get more power. It's what they do. Invent a problem that the government has to come in and 'fix.' They send our tax dollars to 'experts' who invent reasons why they need even more. Some people just want someone else to fix all their problems. My husband has hay fever, but he's not on welfare because of it."

"Thanks for the call," Fay said. "Interesting point about the role of government, which has to get involved to fight an epidemic-"

"When there *is* no epidemic," the guest ended that for her, unbidden. The host made a humming sound of agreement. While the next caller was being put through, I raised my hands out of the water, and slumped them on the counter. Before someone of the same mind as the anonymous caller who had harassed me that morning could begin her tirade, I lifted my hands and brushed the tightening fingers on a towel as best I could. When they were dried enough, I turned off the shrill woman who'd already launched into Surgensblight being "as big a lie as Al Gore's global warming."

Exhaling heavily, which started a coughing spasm, I had to slump into the kitchen chair, and heard the same refrain in my head: *It's all over.* Part of me wanted Will home right away. Another part hoped he would get in the car and drive away forever, to build a life somewhere where he didn't have to take care of me, or fight the world on my behalf.

Once more, at the phone's behest, I dragged myself to the far counter where I had left the handset. The call had already gone to the machine before I got there, but when I heard the voice of Will's friend - and my fellow sufferer - Rick, I doubled my strenuous efforts. He was crying, bleating out Will's name into the machine before I reached it.

"Rick, it's Kate," I said. "What's wrong? Are Jessica and Sloane okay?" Their two daughters, seven and nine years old, were both suffering horribly from Surgensblight, and the social isolation and teachers' chastisement that came with it.

"It's Susan," he said, referring to his wife. "I need some-one here, and I can't get Will on his cell."

"Is Susan okay?" I asked.

"I need to see Will."

"He won't be back for a while," I said. After listening to Rick weep through the phone, I said: "I'm on my way." I hung up before he could protest.

A short time later, I was bundled in additional layers of clothing with my mask on. It was unclear why more strata of cloth helped, but they did. Since their house was only a few blocks away, I walked, leaning on a stick and looking like some frightening stranger whose arrival in a picturesque village would start off some fairy tale. Taking the car was a dodgy proposition, and I'd been in danger of losing control due to being sick at the wheel too many times to risk trying it again.

Rick answered the door, his own face masked. I assumed Susan was at the real estate agency where she worked. It had gotten busy as people wondered if they'd like a second home in our rural-flavored corner of suburbia. With two sizable cities not far away, a quick drive or train ride could have them here on weekends. Our Chamber of Commerce was advertising us as 'the perfect home for holidays.' The revitalization we had dreamed of was briskly underway; I just hadn't counted on Surgensblight being its price.

Jessica and Sloane were evidently in their rooms. The upstairs hall looked down on the living room, and I saw that both bedroom doors were ajar, allowing at least one of the girls' soft snores to be heard. In their magnificently decorated living room, so impeccable that it looked to have been staged for a photograph - and probably had for Susan's brochures or website - Rick flopped miserably on a couch, his diminished, skeletal fame sinking into the sheer size of it. As I pulled off my mask and sat nearby, he didn't insist on any disinfecting measures, looking too exhausted to care.

"What happened?" I asked.

"Do you think...I've somehow given this to the girls?" he asked. I forewent honesty and just shook my head. "They are having a terrible time of it. We've seen seven pediatricians... not one could find a thing wrong with them."

"I've been to a lot of doctors, myself," I said.

"Me too. They just say we need a positive attitude, herbal supplements and exercise or whatever. Or that we're making it up." I sat silently as he sobbed. "Did they get this from me?"

I closed my eyes and took as deep of a breath as I could before answering: "I don't know. But I met a man today who thinks we're passing it to our children genetically."

"What do you think?" he asked.

"I think he could be right," I conceded. Both of our gazes drifted up to the doors of his daughters' rooms.

Aside from the thin strand of gentle snoring, there was no sign of any life.

"It's my fault they're suffering like this," he said.

"No, it's not," I told him. "It's just some genetic lottery."

"This is..." He sought a word to illustrate the injustice before giving up and settling on "...miserable."

"How is Susan?" I asked, regretting the question as soon as I posed it.

"She left."

"For work?"

"She left for work three days ago," he said, tears flowing freely again. "Hasn't come back. I've had nothing but a few texts saying that she's 'on assignment,' whatever that means. She's never been on assignment before, let alone disappeared for days. I... I don't think she's coming back."

"You don't know," I said. "She may...need time to herself. It's hard enough on Will. I can't imagine what it's like for..."

"For someone with three invalids to care for?" he asked.

"You're not an invalid," I said.

"I am. I can't tell you how often Susan has yelled at me to just 'pull myself together.' I can't. No one believes us."

I touched his bony shoulder. "I understand."

"She'd rather believe I'm just feeling sorry for myself than for all of this to be real. If she thought it was just me..." He wiped his face off and looked upstairs again. "She'd have taken the girls with her."

"She'll be back," I said, beginning to doubt it as

soon as I'd spoken. "No mother is going to just abandon her husband and two daughters. And certainly not Susan."

"I called the police," he said. "They said they called her, and she told them that she was 'on assignment' for the office, and that I knew it. They thought I was nuts. Her office told me that same thing."

"Well, there you go. Maybe she took the assignment even though she usually doesn't...for breathing space, you know?"

"What sort of 'assignments' do local real estate offices have that would keep her out of town for three days?"

"Scouting new areas, or something," I said, trying to sound confident, but I was almost positive that he was right. I hugged him while he cried, and promised to tell Will as soon as he got home. When I left I heard the same verdict echoing through my head again: *It's all over.*

Tottering down the street in my plague doctor's mask, I decided to treat myself to the long way home. Before the roses invaded, I'd driven through adjacent neighborhoods countless times, seeing nothing but nondescript backdrop. That day, however, I tried to imagine the people inside each house I passed, basing stories of their lives on the exterior of their houses, including the ubiquitous roses.

I turned a corner and came face-to-face with a hedge-wall formed by rosebushes which had thriven and grown through the winter and spring and the present summer heat without having to die off and start again. The softball-sized flowers had been carefully sculpted into a perfect wall of eternally blooming ice roses, the most expensive and prized strain of the new breed. The cyan-tinged ivory petals of these enemies wiggled in the afternoon breeze, taunting me. I recoiled at first, as if encountering a savage dog. After staring at them head-on for a moment, however, I allowed myself to begin to see the same beauty that everyone else did.

Like all living things, the plants had bested the eons-long attempt by everything else to destroy them. To have created a niche in the world was an admirable legacy for any species. Human exuberance and interference caused the niche to over-flow and swallow mine; it was an unwelcome and unpleasant reality, but perhaps not as unnatural as I had thought.

Removing one of my gloves and touching the bloom, I was surprised to find it strangely cold, as though it had preserved a pocket of winter frost through the ensuing thaw and heat. When I raised my mask to inhale its fragrance, I caught a whiff of autumnal chill, that crispness that would soon creep into the edges of day and remind us of dying. I couldn't tell as I replaced the mask, coughing and sputtering out my mélange of mucus and spittle and tears, if that chill was present in the air, or emitted by the rose itself.

The sun was already starting to slide down the other side of the sky. I cried until my vision blurred within my mask's cold, glass eyes. *It's all over*, I thought again. A sentiment I echoed aloud a short time later as I stood in our living room, already mentally packing its contents into boxes.

When Will got home, holding a clipboard and

tension he had accrued from having doors slammed in his face all day, I followed a greeting with "You don't have to do this anymore."

Unbeknownst to me, I'd married a warrior. When we first met through mutual friends, I had dismissed him as 'meek.' Hectored by his friends and family, dumped on at his office, and mercilessly henpecked by his then-girlfriend, he evinced none of the resolve he had shown since the Surgensblight scourge began. "There's a lot more to do," he said.

"Please relax for a while," I said, and saw him bristle about the strident phalanx of foes who wanted their roses, no matter what it cost us. It was as if even a slight pause by him would deepen their already considerable advantage. "I don't know how much more you can do. You barely sleep now."

"There's much more to do. We're not letting them win."

"You do more than anyone could be expected to," I said. "The fact that you haven't left me is all I could ever want."

"I would never abandon you," he said.

"I know," I replied, thinking that Susan had probably told herself many times that she would stick it out.

"I want to give you your life back," he said. "I want us to go hiking again...out to dinner...away for weekends. Not lock ourselves in a fortress of air filters and humidifiers."

"I want to move," I said simply.

"And let them win?" he asked. "Where can we go? What happens when this stuff gets everywhere?"

"We keep fighting," I assured him. "We go someplace where there are no roses, and warn the people about them. We can hold the line somewhere. But not here anymore."

He crumpled, slamming his head onto my shoulder and sobbing into my outermost sweater. "I'm sorry," he said. "I can't stop it. I can't stop them. They've taken everything."

"Not everything," I stroked his thinning hair and laid phlegm-laden kisses on his scalp. "We'll find somewhere else to live. I can work again. We both can. We can live again."

After a bout of crying, then going through the agonizingly slow and careful process of making love - during which I held in coughs and sneezes as best I could - we began making plans. I lay beside him, cocooned in layers of blankets and sweat, watching him excitedly chatter on about the prospect of our new life, his night job already forgotten. I'd mention Rick to him later, not wanting to deflate his rebirth of enthusiasm.

I didn't share my entire plan with Will as he padded naked through the bedroom we would soon desert, dreaming our revitalized life aloud. We could manage a move, maybe two, but tactical retreats would buy only a few years, at most. The roses were an implacable foe; we had no way to win this war. They would eventually rampage over every line we could draw in the sand. Time was, after all, on their side. Once we arrived at whatever distant piece of the world would be our new home, I would do my best to prevent Will from totally dissolving into 'the cause' again. Perhaps when my eternal anguish no longer confronted him, he might find that keeping up the website and attending a rally now and again was enough to assuage his fighting instinct. No matter what we did, ultimately the war would be lost. I'd resolved that when the final defeat came, I was ready to fall on my sword.

Given Will's veritable resurrection when I insisted that we surrender this position, I had no doubt that he would adapt and thrive once I was no longer around. He'd still be young enough to start over wherever he wanted. He would never admit it, and perhaps not even allow himself to imagine it, but I suspected that he'd be happier once I was only a memory. I'd give him as long as I could, and make it as painless for him as possible, but I no longer had delusions that the roses could be stopped. The same unwritten laws of nature that allowed humanity to thrive in the first place was now fostering the succession of a portion of our number by the winter roses. I chose not to dwell on the details of the end, focusing instead on how my husband's taut body strode through the dying light of the afternoon, his arms waving around passionately in the midst of his planning as though he'd been granted a stay of execution. In a way, perhaps he had, but my fate was less ambiguous. The only condition I would demand, in whatever instructions left behind when I finally laid my weapons down forever, was the perverse stipulation that winter roses be planted on my grave in lieu of any prayer or appeal to God, who was as helpless as the rest of us in this winter-proof Eden.

~~~~~~~~

THE ELUSIVE CONSUL

HELENE MUNSON

The oil portrait in a gilded frame was dated 1944 on its back. How had my great-grandparents managed to get out a painting done in Germany in the middle of World War II? I speculated: *'Maybe it was a pity purchase...they had given a commission to a painter who was down on his luck in those desperate days'*. It was of an old man with a white mustache, dressed formally, though a bit old-fashioned, even for those times, in a suit with a stiff collar and white shirt. The bright blue eyes expressed the great sadness of a man who had seen a lot in his life. He was my great-grandfather, but our family had always referred to him as *The Consul*.

The painting had been in the possession of his daughter, my paternal grandmother. Once she told me: "You know, I have sold off all my fine jewelry, the jade and the rubies, and even gave up the silverware I inherited, because I needed the money. And I moved so many times...but everywhere I went, I took this portrait."

It was of her beloved *Pappchen* – Little Papa. According to my grandmother, the Consul's family had fifteen servants living with them in a magnificent teak house in the British colony of Rangoon, Burma. Now, after subsequent political regimes, it is renamed Yangon, Myanmar. They had lived a privileged, expatriate life until the end of World War I, when political circumstances in the form of anti-German sentiment forced the family to return to Bremen, Germany.

I had heard my grandmother's stories over and over, but I had never seen any documents. Had the Consul really been a German diplomat? Or was it just a loving daughter passing on some glorified family legend, bestowing on him a title of respect? But an album full of sepia-colored family photos my grandmother had left me was proof enough that they had been there. I became determined to find evidence of his life in the historical records of the period.

My initial research yielded that my best resource would be the British Library in London, and reminded me that the last time I used the British Library was in the 1980s. At that time its venerable, awe-inspiring reading rooms were still in the British Museum, with green-shaded lamps that shed light on high-ceilinged rooms paneled with bookshelves. The new British Library, near Kings Cross Station, was as impressive, with its red exterior, reminiscent of a Chinese Palace, and its striking, white interiors.

After being photographed and issued a reader's card, I was sent to the Asia & Africa reading room on the third floor. A friendly librarian with a heavy Eastern European accent helped, but her computer search yielded nothing concerning my key words:

'German Consul, Rangoon, Schrader 1900- 1918'. Getting frustrated, she asked condescendingly:" If you are looking for a German consul, why are you searching the British colonial records and not the German ones in Berlin?" It seemed like she had a point.

I responded defensively: "I have contacted the German archives, but was told to refer to British colonial accounts, as they kept meticulous records of everything that went on in the glorious days of the Empire. Besides, many records were lost when Berlin went up in flames in the Second World War." Having found nothing helpful in the computerized database, she showed me how to locate the original paper annals of the British administration of colonial Burma.

Those thick, leather-bound books' pages were yellowed, brittle and covered in small print, so had to be turned gently to avoid ripping them. I started my search by looking up German Consuls, but none were named Schrader between 1900 and 1918. I learned only that Carl with a 'C' must have been a popular boys name in imperial Germany, nostalgically invoking the grand empire of *Charlemagne* 1000 years ago. In Germany this king is known as *'Carl the Great'*.

I persevered and checked other records. There had been a *'Deutscher Klub'*, a German club in Rangoon since 1867, attesting to a relatively large number of Germans there. The Consul might have been a member, but his name does not appear on any of the organization's lists. The Grand Lodge of Burma's Freemasons had its share of Germans: Friedlander, Lutter, Müller—but no Schrader. I checked the Rice Brokers' Association next, as family lore had it that the

Consul had also been an agent of a German rice trading commodities firm. In fact, a family photo shows him on top of a mountain of rice, surrounded by porters. Again nothing!

In looking through the yearly editions of *Thacker's India Directory*, subtitled *Embracing the whole of British India and the Native States,* published in Calcutta, old Rangoon came alive for me. In the 1912 edition, Thacker's also sold ad space to the businesses it listed: *Siemens Brothers* advertised their services as contractors to install electric lights; *Misquith Ltd.* was selling imported pianos and organs.

Many Rangoon businesses had addresses on Merchant Street, and the Chamber of Commerce was at number 68. An illustrated advertisement showed the posh dining room of *Romani's Restaurant* at 69 Merchant Street. I pictured my great-grandfather having a businessmen's luncheon there with Chamber of Commerce members. He would probably have been smoking a Burmese cigar from *M.E. Negda & Co*, who advertised their ability to ship their products in airtight tins to anywhere in the world. Romani's Restaurant offered *'Choicest Wines & Liquors, Le Carte and Afternoon Tea'.* It was a fascinating glimpse into a long-gone era, but there was no trace of the Consul.

In a failed attempt to find out more about this part of my family, I had gone to Burma just after the restrictive military government finally allowed individual tourists to visit the nation. What I saw was very different from how it must have looked in 1910. In Yangon's downtown business district, I ate in a restaurant like the other diners: with my fingers. In the last 100 years, plastic chairs had replaced the Mahogany ones in the circa 1900 photo of Romani's Restaurant. In modern Yangon, fine liquor was nowhere in sight, but each table had a little fixture to hold a roll of toilet paper to wipe one's fingers in lieu of napkins. No pianos or organs were for sale, only cheap household goods imported from China. In the British Raj era, Burma supplied the world with rice. Now, suffering abject poverty, it barely fed its own people.

I really disliked that many tourism facilities were run by government agencies. I had to go looking for privately owned accommodation, so my tourist dollars did not benefit a regime whose human rights record I could not support. My young daughter had come on the trip, and while looking at places to stay with me, she caught on quickly. If she did not like what she saw she would comment: "Mama I do not like this hotel. It must be a government place."

I would caution: "Shush darling, don't say those things aloud, or you will get us in trouble." She had been so excited to go to the place where her great-grandmother had ridden on an elephant as a child. Since she was little, my daughter had seen the old photograph of the whole family sitting up on one of Burma's about 4000 timber-logging elephants. What a disappointment it had been for us to find out that now the only elephants left in Yangon were in the zoo. In order for us to ride one, an angry elephant bull was tied up and subdued with an injection before the riding frame could be strapped to his back. We left feeling very sorry for the abused animal.

The British Library staff announced that reading rooms would close in half an hour. In a final frustrated attempt, I looked through the *Alphabetical List of Residents in India, Burma and Ceylon* of 1914. Interestingly, it contained only western names, but a far smaller, less detailed section in the back had '*List of Principal Indian Inhabitants*'.

'*Were there no Burmese in the country?*' I thought; the list's authors had felt no need to include any. It was consistent with what my grandmother had told me. Invited by the Brits, many Indians lived in Burma and held prominent positions, displacing local elites. She had taught me how to prepare a few Indian Curries, but could not recall a single Burmese dish. It had been payback time in 1962 when Myanmar's military regime forced those Indians' descendants to leave the country.

I leafed through the list with little hope. Finally, on page 353, I found an entry: '*Schrader, H. mangr. Mohr Bros. & Co. Ltd and Consul for Austria, Hungary.*' It did not occur to me to seek his records in Vienna. He had been a German Consul all right, but not a Prussian one. Today's Germany is almost synonymous with what was the Prussian Empire, but the K&K Austrian Hungarian Empire had been a second Germany in 1900, and its multi-cultural makeup would later play such a tragic role in the outbreak of WWI.

But a fact about my great-grandfather confused me. His first name had been Johannes. Why was he listed as H? In a town where the telephone exchange had just three digits, it was unlikely that there would be another man with the same surname. Now that I knew what I was looking for, I checked the list of Austrian consuls and there he was, listed as Hans. That made perfect sense! Hans was the shortened form of Johannes. The Consul probably felt that in Rangoon's multi-cultural society, 'Johannes' was too long and changed it to a more fashionable 'Hans'. His eldest daughter, my grandmother, had loved her father very much and named her oldest son, my father, Hans as well.

I went back to the company directory, where I found the Consul listed as the Managing Director of Mohr Company, and as a Member of the Board of the Rangoon Chamber of Commerce for 1914. But when I returned to the records from 1913, again there were no listings. What had the family done in the earlier years? Those thoughts were interrupted by the announcement of the room closing in fifteen minutes.

I told the librarian excitedly: "I found the record of my ancestor in the section of the Austrian consuls." She was delighted and shared with me: "I am actually Polish and few people today know that where I grew up was once part of the Austro-Hungarian Empire as well." As a courtesy to me, she ran another computer search.

"Ah, here is a document with the title: *The Government of India's objections to the Consul of Austria-Hungary M. Sevastopul,*" she said. From my research, I already knew that this man had been Consul Hans' predecessor. Maybe there was something there worth exploring that would shed more light on the elusive Consul. But would there ever be another

Saturday afternoon of working myself through the dusty papers at the British Library?

~~~~~~~~~

SOUND AVE

GERARD MEADE

Ott's running late. It's Thursday, not a particularly ominous day for most, but for her it's now precisely that. Out of fiscal necessity she'd become an instructor, attempting to teach creative writing to secondary school kids. The class was library-sponsored in a well-to-do district some distance from her east end home. Conceived as an informal, 'old school' extra-curricular activity for those who'd displayed aptitude and the desire to create, the program seemed promising.

The salary exceeded the minimal remuneration typically offered for such publicly funded courses by a wide margin, so the offer was hard to refuse. Privately she hoped the exercise might also inspire. Her writing had suffered of late, become cumbersome and difficult in ways it never had, a sophomore curse after the successful publication of her first novel. Sadly, the initial excitement was more fleeting than the unblemished fruit of just-sliced apples. Once besieged by crudely composed tales of vampire villains and reality star heroines in plots as unlikely as peace in the Middle East, Ott's enthusiasm had vanished by week two. The blues that followed thwarted her creativity and the profound disdain for 'T-day' was born.

By trial and error, Ott's found that a combination of diversions keeps her from sinking into depression before the dreaded evening event. She starts by reading some of the kids' stuff—a chore always avoided until then—takes a break to attend to personal business, and fantasizes about what else she could be doing before trying to focus on her current project, giving up on that, having lunch, reading some more and then formulating an agenda for the evening's class. The final step is to find something to look forward to, be it simple or elaborate—anything to salvage the day. Frequently, that seemingly easy task is as frustrating as trying to write. Most Thursdays lack heroes, so often it is the modest default of a leisurely drive west that assumes the role. On rare occasions she'd have dinner in the library's vicinity, someplace she'd not otherwise visit, but a scarcity of funds and having to forego wine before class often left her with only the drive.

Ott does love driving Sound Avenue, despite its failure to offer even a glimpse of the large body of water that lends it the name. A lovely two-lane country road that snakes its way through farmlands, nature preserves and vineyards—well, tasting rooms, anyway, as most of the vines grow farther east—is a pleasure to maneuver. Old churches, vintage barns and quaint farm stands border the route, and travel is slowed only by the few traffic signals or a crawling farm vehicle. It's a narrow stretch, just shy of eighteen miles overall, where passing is prohibited by bold, double yellow lines dividing the east-west flow. Sporadic backups are irritating, but for Ott the reward outweighs the risk.

Her favorite time to make the trip is just after sunrise when its shine wakes the landscape, lighting diamonds of dew in the vast sod fields and orchards. Driving west into the sunset is magnificent in its own right but not always fun for the driver. After dark the route is a different animal, bristling with hazards. Ott opts for Main Road then—usually.

This morning, Ottavia—elegantly, albeit inaptly named fourth and last child of hard-working immigrant parents who had provided her opportunities they could never imagine for themselves—knows today will be different as she reads the second submission. She'd assigned a rather broad theme that seemed innocent enough, but the story she reads scorns it, offering instead a dark, disparate essay of failure, self-loathing and loss. Its author ignored her guidelines, earning rejection on that alone, but rather than dismiss it, she's drawn back; her pulse quickens, a seed of wonderment sprouts: *'What is this? A plea for attention? Cry for help? Or finally what I'd hoped for when I desperately, but naïvely, agreed to this arrangement?'* Plodding through the others' mediocre efforts, she remains with the dark tale, missing nothing of consequence while absent-minded.

Her writers—now eight ironically and down from twelve originally—submit their work anonymously. Over time she's grown familiar with their handwriting and can identify their alleged 'style', so it isn't hard to guess who is who, but she is stumped, wondering who's thrown her a curve. The chicken scratch on the two lined pages, torn from a spiral notebook, isn't identifiable, but the prose is a sleek, welcome contrast to the haphazard appearance. If it's fiction, it's good, but if not, and is instead what she prays it isn't... Ott skips the dreary banking, decides randomness is the evening's agenda, and stares down a blank page, on which she eventually, edgily but purposely, begins nursing a new story to life. The deftly composed but disturbing pages serve as a springboard.

Now she's late. The words on her page are bizarre—that's being kind—and the time lost conjuring them distressing. It's nearing four o'clock and she'd vowed to be off by three for a leisurely jaunt west. An earlier check of the forecast, while desperately seeking distraction, was unsettling. Snow will arrive tonight and is expected to fall heaviest on the island's east end. Scoping the sky from the study's window, she frowns, finding sun-filtering Cirrus clouds already. She jogs to the bedroom to change. If she hurries she'll still make the drive in daylight when the lowering sky will make its own unique impression on the landscape.

Ott compares two blouses–thinking one too suggestive, although it is quite modest–still reflecting on the harrowing tale, the impending storm, the nonsense she'd scribbled, and the minimal reward of the drive, when a guilty but promising thought prompts abandonment of the wardrobe dilemma in favor her tablet. *'Perhaps they'll cancel evening activities due to the coming storm?'*

The school district's website shows no changes to the scheduled events, but Ott's only mildly disappointed in light of her discovery. She chose the sexier blouse after all, but its allure is now buried under a heavy, buttoned sweater and her warmest three-quarter coat. Leaving through the kitchen's door, she pauses to glance at the Merlot on the counter and smiles, knowing it will wait patiently for her return.

Driving Route 48, Ott challenges the speed limit, as she often tends to do, but then slows to the pace she intended. The clouds have thickened through Cirro and Alto to looming Stratus in just the short time since she left home. Darker storm clouds pepper the Southwestern sky, at times eclipsing the sinking sun. Turning on the radio, Ott's greeted by an urgent voice updating the storm. It's developed a real need for speed, approaching with mounting intensity and widening in mass as it hugs the coastline, traveling north. A tingle of anxious energy brings a shiver as she considers this, but her thoughts seamlessly migrate to the mystery author's possible identity. Recognizing the tingle as excitement, *'in this blouse possibly the dangerous variety'*, she recalls the novel promise of the class and misses the rest of the news. The opening strain of a favorite song brings her attention back to the road. She's at the last traffic signal before these four lanes funnel into the two of Sound Avenue.

At the first of many bends, deep dusk engulfs her as the road winds through a canopy of towering oaks. Emerging moments later, it's not much brighter, the leading edge of the dark clouds sending scout tendrils north. A few fat, random snowflakes appear and a pulse of flurry activity follows but ends quickly. Winds have increased out of the west, pulling cold air with them, and darkness descends as if managed by a slow moving dimmer switch. She turns on the headlights. Traffic's steady but not heavy after squeezing in to the single lane. The speed suits her leisurely intent, the cars moving atypically at ten to fifteen miles an hour below the posted limit. Ott glances about in the last of the light but deciphers little of the beauty she normally equates with the region. At this point, she's well beyond the boundary of her sprawling home town, and tapping the brakes more often. A quick check of the speedometer shows they're moving downright slowly, less than twenty miles per hour.

Dark is full-on, ahead of schedule, and the intermittent flurries have become squalls, still sporadic but impressively threatening at times. Traffic has come to a dead stop, with oncoming headlights less frequent. She's at least a mile from the nearest intersection and inching forward occasionally as cars ahead abandon the wait, maneuver a tricky turn, and go back the way they came. Ott weighs each of her students' profiles while waiting, still seeking a clue, and assumes an accident ahead prevents a detour. She checks her phone and fiddles with the radio, confident there's still time before the six o'clock class. Once the road clears, her destination is just twenty minutes ahead, weather permitting.

Of course, as if on cue, a strong gust rattles the old Volvo and she hears the sand-like sound of icy precipitation above the radio. The view of stalled traffic is replaced by a swirling fog of white before the gust dies off. In its wake, a heavy band of fine snow angles across the road, backlit in the red glow of taillights. The wipers become necessary, and reveal motion ahead, the long line of cars at a crawl, but promising nonetheless...thickening snow and more frequent gusts, not so much. The crossroad is visible as she crests a slight ridge, and her suspicion is confirmed. Emergency vehicles crowd the intersection with beacons flashing, and a policeman is directing traffic to a southbound lane that leads to Main Road. It's agonizingly slow with drivers stopping to ask directions, or looking for signs of carnage with morbid curiosity. car-lengths As she finally nears, just several back, the officer who was veering cars south breaks away from his duty and begins removing the cones that block the road ahead. Ott reviews her options.

The significant time lost has potentially become an issue. If she follows the other drivers, all choosing the alternate route even after the roadblock's been lifted, she'll have to return north to reach the library. If she continues the direct route on Sound, it'll be in the dark, without streetlights, in a strengthening storm. Having come this far, she's committed and no longer harbors guilty hopes of aborting. The return trip will most likely be worse. It'll be quite some time before she reunites with that Merlot.

The curious stimulation had been tainted while snarled in traffic, and her underlying concern grew more prominent, dampening the thrill of her potential discovery and sounding an alarm for whoever penned the disturbing tale. She's conflicted and unsure how to proceed or best approach the class to unearth the author. Ott's only a writer, not a trained psychologist, or even a teacher.

No longer flashing, the police cars leave and no evidence remains of what caused the delay when Ott reaches the intersection. Her fingers drift to the direction lever, intending to opt for the safer route, but it fades in flakes as she drives past that option. Within a hundred feet she's questioning her unrealized decision as the snow bears down and the image of a particularly treacherous hill that lies ahead comes to mind.

The road remains accumulation-free, residual warmth from the day's sun is grudgingly held by the blacktop, but within a few miles she sees patches of white. Ott checks the rearview and frowns, finding that no one else has chosen her path. She's confident of the Volvo's traction, steady at thirty miles an hour, but the eerie solitude of being the lone vehicle on the road mounts. Visibility continues to deteriorate as she drives and more icy patches dot the road. The forecast for better conditions west looks questionable, but if the surface remains mostly wet until she's conquered that hill she should be fine past that point.

Ott enters a curve that leads onto a particularly desolate stretch, devoid of commercial buildings and homes. A sod farm spreads over hectares to the south, and a stronghold of nature to the north. As the turn unwinds into straightaway, she's dismayed by the uniform glaze ahead.

The first loud thump comes from the front grill, two more reverberate below her foot and a grinding squeal soon follows. Before she can brake, the car slows on its own, the steering wheel pulling against her grip and aiming the wheels to an almost non-existent shoulder. Ott knows she hit an animal; she's had that unfortunate pleasure before. Both times, the small bumps from below rolled along the chassis until, once a squirrel, and the next time a chipmunk rolled out to scamper off, scared but seemingly unhurt, into the woods. This is different. She glides to a stop barely halfway off the road.

The snow is intensifying, whipped by now near-constant wind, bringing down the *real* cold and icing the road surface. Some asphalt is briefly revealed by random powerful gusts but the road has lost the battle. No traffic approaches from either direction. Ott finds and powers on her phone, then hesitates, undecided. If she calls for roadside assistance she will wait forever in the worsening conditions, and though not dressed for crawling about in the snow under her car, the damage may not be as bad as it sounded or felt; she could at least take a look. A check of the time shows she'll be late, so she searches out the library's program director's number and calls, but is forwarded to voice mail. The message she leaves is brief; she's having car trouble but isn't far away, so hopefully she'll be just a few minutes late. Ott bundles her coat, pulls on her gloves and steps out of the warmth.

As her toe hits the snow, headlights rake the road from south to north as a car comes from the turn she just passed, bearing down with reckless speed. She quickly moves to the front of the Volvo and turns back to find the car already upon her. It flies by in a cloud of snow, leaving a swirling vortex in its wake. She's shaken by the brazen pass, too close to her, despite her flashers, and wonders if the driver even saw her.

Ott slip-slides by the front bumper to the passenger side in dress boots not meant for snow. With the tenuous support of the ice-crusted hood, she kneels, immediately feeling the frozen ground through the light wool of her slacks. She looks under the bumper, sees nothing, so pulls her phone from her pocket to activate its flashlight, but has to remove her glove.

A ball of fur, a rather large ball of fur, is visible near the left side front wheel's axle; no identifiable features, just a grayish coat. Bending lower, she lights up the lowest region of the wheel well and can see part of it, but not much. The fur is twisted, scrunched upward, rust-red tainting the gray from somewhere out of sight. Ott knows that even if she could somehow reach it she couldn't possibly bring herself to touch, never mind dislodge, the poor creature.

Her knees and bare fingers are numb and she retreats for warmth, abandoning the wish for a simple fix. Reaching the spot where she'd stood when the car sped past, another pair of lights rounds the curve. These appear weaker, veiled by the swirling snow, yellowish and dim, perhaps an older car that travels much slower. Ott shakes accumulation from her hair, hopefully watching the approach of a truck—but it's impossible to tell. As the lights draw near, still dull even up close, the cabin is no more than a shadowy contrast in a wall of white. She prays for a kind farmer, a local unafraid to offer help on an isolated road in times when most wouldn't. She hears the engine slow to a rough growl before she sees the change in speed. Her flashers don't light the cab and she can't make out the driver, but it is an old truck, a vintage one. And as it accelerates away, she briefly spots the winch fitted in the rear bed before snow intervenes and blocks her view.

Ottavia sheds the heavy jacket and reenters the car, her emotions alternating between disappointment and a strange sense of relief with the motorist's decision to pass by. The engine's still running and the heater blasting, comfortable at first but soon she's flushed. She lowers the thermostat and fan before sending an update to the librarian and searching the accumulated clutter in the glove compartment, assuming her insurance card has a number for roadside assistance. She unbuttons the sweater and lowers the heat a few more degrees. With her head in the glovebox she's oblivious to the weak headlights cresting the rise in the west.

Ott finally finds the insurance card and straightens in the driver's seat. A familiar growl draws her attention as the old truck materializes, ghostlike, out of wind-driven flakes. It drifts across the buried center line as it slows, pulls to the shoulder behind her and stops, facing the opposite direction. Her pulse quickens. The relief returns, but hope's quickly compromised and blossoms to fear. Ottavia shivers, thinks she should step out to meet the stranger, but stays still, eyes flicking pointlessly to the rearview mirror, then the side, but the truck is only a shadow. Minutes pass in silence, the quiet intensifying her qualm.

The snow-muted thump of the truck's door startles her, even though she's anticipating it, and she alternates glances in both glazed side mirrors, to see which way he'll come. The sharp rap sounds from the passenger side while she's focused on the other, causing her to jump in the seat as she turns. A hooded figure looms outside the door, bent to the wind and apparently looking in but indistinguishable beyond a coating of frost that refuses to succumb to the blasting heat of the cabin. Ott fumbles for the window control, hitting the back one before lowering the passenger side to half-mast. A blast of snow rushes in, blocking the stranger's features from view. When it settles, Ottavia is looking at a broad, hunched figure turned away in the window's frame, its head buried deep in a parka's vast hood as a violent gust whips the loose material taught. Ott fights off a sudden impulse to raise the glass.

The wind eases and the fur trimmed hood creases at the shoulder as the stranger shifts to the open window. Ott locks in on cobalt blue eyes blazing from the scorched rouge of blistered, weathered skin; wisps of long blondish hair blow from the hood, snow renders the bushy eyebrows Santa-white. Ott studies the face, trying not to linger on the ghoulish blisters as the cracked, red lips snag her attention. The voice stuns her.

"Evenin' miss, saw ya stuck on my way out but had a bit of an emergency call first. What alls got you holed up to the side of the road?"

Ott can't respond; her mind is stuck in a gaping synapse crevice that prevents the connection of sight to sound. It's a young woman's voice, articulated by this rugged face of a man. Relief frees held breath and she finally refreshes with a deep draw in. Emerging from...wherever, she replies quickly and leans toward the stranger as she begins, softly at first, but after in what she jokingly refers to as her classroom voice.

"Sorry, yes well, I hit some kind of animal. I never saw what it was but I looked underneath and it seems twisted in the axle or wheel or something. Might be a possum?"

The hardened woman's eyes size Ott up and down before another gust turns her away again. She speaks as it recedes, still nearly shouting over the sustained wind that persists.

"Ok, roll 'er up, let me take a look."

With the window secured and the warmth returning, Ott assesses the situation. She was bordering on panic when the truck returned, but reassured by a brave woman's surprising presence. Any gal driving a pickup with a winch in back must know a thing or two about removing critters from cars, and this sure as heck is one tough looking girl. That stirs a thought but Ott pushes it aside and clings to her vision of rescue by the kind local she'd hoped for...of course substituting heroine for handsome hero. That's interrupted when the car rocks; the large girl rising from lying beneath leans on the hood. The wipers reveal her walking carefully around to the driver's side.

The car blocks much of the wind this time as Ott opens her window. Closer, the bulk of her rescuer is obvious even under heavy layers of sweatshirts and sweaters tucked under the thermal, bibbed, union suit that's topped by the parka. She leans into the car and delivers a verdict.

"Yup, damn varmint got itself tangled in your front shaft pretty good, but I think I can free it up. You'll have to shut the engine...can't take no chances. Hopefully I can get it without hooking you up to the truck for a lift but it might take me a bit. Come wait in my truck while I give 'er a shot. You'll be warm and not have to watch in case...well, ya know. Oh, and miss, dim the damn headlights will ya?"

Ott switches to parking lights and kills the ignition, but is leery of leaving the safety of the car. Clutching the phone, she looks at the girl, now backed from the window but still focused within, the intense eyes lingering as Ott snags the keys and reaches for the door release. A large gloved hand slaps the door's upholstery, the light dusting of snow billows.

"Think it best you button up miss, that pretty silk thing won't do much against the cold. Oh, and leave the keys."

Ott glances down to find her sweater undone and the blouse she'd thought suggestive tented open below the collar. She pulls the sweater tight and fumbles with the buttons. The big girl seems oddly relaxed in the midst of the storm, a half-smile on her lips and a glint, no doubt from the wind, in her sharp eyes. Ott keeps her in view, shuts the window, pockets the phone and takes her coat. Anxiety she'd felt at the truck's first approach, more at its ghostly reprise, revives. She bites her lip, pulls the handle and steps into the road.

Four inches have accumulated since she last ventured out. The boots slip as soon as her full weight is on them, and her savior steadies her. After helping Ott up to the high bench seat, the big gloved hand releases its grip but slides down the sweater along the contour of her back. Ott's afraid to look at those piercing blue eyes but has no choice. The worrisome look and questionable glint are gone; the local girl smiles.

"Alrighty, let's see if I get you back on the road. Make yourself at home miss, don't mind the...well, whatever. I'll be right back."

Reluctant as she'd be to admit it, Ott's seen some prison flicks and her subconscious pulls up some scenes, making her more wary of her predicament than when expecting, and fearing, a man. *'Whoa Ottie...chill out, think this through.'*

With the unknown lurking out of sight behind her, Ott doesn't care for the arrangement, but if this woman is true to her word she might soon be free. She stirs her phone to life but stares blankly at the screen. A flat-back window directly behind leaks cold air on her neck as Ott turns to look out; all that's visible is an indistinct glow near the Volvo's hood and the haloed red dots of her snow covered taillights. Ott's not streetwise, only lived on an actual street as an infant, so the need never arose. Her childhood's Lanes, Trails, and Ways were as peaceful and dull as one might imagine. Lack of that extra sense doesn't deter her; Ott's awareness was born in books and that cognizance has voiced a concern. A bounty of 'what if' scenarios spin as she waits.

The seemingly distant sound of her car's door snaps her back. Ott's surprised to see the phone in her hand, her finger over the touchpad, two of three digits already displayed. She wipes the glass behind her as the Volvo's engine and brake lights come to life. A new fear flickers but reason assures Ott as her eyes dart left, noting the stick shift. No, surely this girl wouldn't want a vehicle that's seen only a few less winters than she. From what Ott can see through near-opaque glass, the violent gusts have subsided and snow seems to be falling less intensely. The Volvo bumps forward and angles out onto the roadway, the brakes are applied and backup lights guide it to rest near its original location but fully off the shoulder. The door opens and the big girl's vague shape steps out, holding Ott's attention as she approaches the truck.

The dim overhead bulb brings a candlelight glow as the driver's door opens. The girl pulls off her parka and rolls it, sleeping bag style, then jumps up into the cab and tucks the coat carefully under the seat before removing her gloves to warm her hands over the sole center vent in the dash.

"Got lucky. I got the darned thing free and it don't seem it bothered nothing none. Looks like you're on your way."

The morbid episodes that Ott had imagined vanish and pure relief floods in. Gibberish pours out at her first attempt but she eventually manages a coherent expression of gratitude before segueing to nervous explanations about lateness and her need to go. The local eyes her carefully. Ottavia catches a glimpse of that half-lidded look that troubled her, before a slow, somewhat sad smile erases it and the girl returns to the warmth of the dashboard vent. Ott reaches for the latch.

"Not sure if you're from these parts or where it is you're headed but you might need to change your plan.

There's a bitch of a hill up ahead couple miles, and ain't no way you'll climb it if they ain't plowed yet. Best bet, hang a left the next intersection and head on down to Main Road, that one'll be cleared. I was you I'd forget that stuff you babbled about and get your sweetself home. Seems this storm surprised most everybody, and folks may not be handlin' it too good. "

"Thanks, no...sorry, thank you *so* much. That sounds like good advice, but...I'm closer to where I was going than where I'd much rather be. I do know that hill though."

"Suit yerself but it won't be easy out there, stuffs piled up pretty good. Just don't even think about goin' straight."

"No, I don't think I will."

Ott bolts from the truck, slides as she lands, but remains upright. Her heart pounds and she shuffles through the snow as if wearing a too-tight evening gown. Steadying a hand on the car, she hopes the old Volvo is up to the task; a coach to whisk her to safety. She's going home and doesn't care what it takes to reach there; her mysterious author isn't forgotten, but has been abandoned for the night. Ott's forced a belief; the story's no more than conceivable fiction, most likely by someone not in her group, slipped in to trip her up—just adolescents being adolescent. Ott's outta here and it's entirely possible that they're long gone as well. It'll be a tough drive, but she can already taste the wine and feel her warm 'jammies'. She reaches her car door just as the truck's flies open.

"Oh, hey miss!"

Ott freezes. She's so close, can jump in and go–the car's already running–but owed appreciation intrudes. The large local jumps from the truck and clumps behind the Volvo, pulling up at the bumper, up-lit in the tail lights' muted glow. From a distance, even with the resurging snow, Ott spots the big girl's eyes and is sorry she chose to drive Sound, sorrier to think that she may never choose it again—a close friend lost. She flexes her fingers on the door pull, ready to flee and wondering if she's quick enough to make it. With a hunter's intuition, the woman senses Ott's intention and moves, but starts too quickly and slips rounding the rear fender before regaining her footing and stopping only a step or two away. The two women stand, eyes locked, until Ottavia decides to bolt, breaking the stare and pulling the door open.

"No! Hey, wait!"

The local girl's hand reaches toward her but she doesn't advance. Ott looks up, not meeting the blue eyes, as she tries to discreetly slip past the half-open door. Although impaired by frost, the car's interior light bathes the woman's face and Ottavia falters, reading something new in the look that she'd originally mistrusted. What she sees now is benign, almost forlorn. The big girl turns aside and looks down, the toe of her boot begins to trace patterns in the snow, childlike.

"I just...uhm..." The brilliant blue of her eyes is misted, from cold sure, but maybe something more. "...well, I almost forgot... Merry Christmas, miss!"

Ott pulls out too fast and the Volvo loses traction, but rights itself as she eases off the gas. The girl's indicated sidestreet is barely discernable in again intense snow as she follows the advice and turns. The car slides before the tires find purchase on a narrow road, deep in snow but still passable. Ott drives on for several minutes, grasping the wheel tightly, fiercely concentrating on the whited out tunnel ahead.

The road borders the western edge of the vast sod farm, with no houses visible to her right. Ott tries to relax as the Volvo plows along, undeterred by the accumulation, but her own laugh startles her; an unfamiliar, relieved cackle. She tilts her head side to side, loosening the tension that burns her neck and something catches her eye in the process. She snaps her head toward the passenger seat and confirms what she'd found amiss. Her purse is gone, no longer in its place beside her book bag. Alarmed, she stretches, fumbling to see if it moved out of place on the seat. Her eyes flick back and forth, from cushion to almost invisible road.

The light of the dash doesn't reach the floor and Ott hopes that the purse fell there. She's anxious about steering with only her left hand and keeping one eye on the road but the missing cash, credit cards and credentials take priority. She reaches for the overhead light but feels the car drifting and returns both hands to the wheel. Ott cranes her neck, but can't make out anything below the dash. Still focused down, she lets off the gas and gently taps the brakes. The car slows. She leans toward the passenger floorboard to feel for the purse. Her fingers find only air. She straightens, glancing back to the road while reaching again for the switch above her head.

The car slows to walking pace as she flicks the light on. The floor space is as empty as it felt. Ott grabs the book bag and shifts it to the floor but still no reward is revealed. She slaps her hand on the steering wheel, looks forward in anger, and sees a diamond shaped sign, caked with blown snow, the message barely visible:

EAD

ND

~~~~~~~~

FREDDIE THE FLUFFER

JOYCE deCORDOVA

Freddie the Fluffer was really good at what he did and he was very much in demand. He worked long hours, sometimes seven days a week, rain or shine. At times he even worked nights, but that was usually outdoors, and until 2 or 3 in the morning. It was quiet at that hour, and he could work in peace without people bothering him or staring at him or calling him names. Horrible names. Freddie the Fluffer was an American in his late 20's and living in Rome. He was working there illegally because he hadn't bothered to get working papers when he arrived in Italy as a tourist in the late 1950's, which was four years earlier. He had been in a hurry, and he was escaping. No, he wasn't a criminal, well, not in any real sense, but he had taken flight and left his family behind in New York.

His family. He grew up in a rough Manhattan neighbor-hood where it was dangerous to be a peaceful and somewhat vulnerable soul. There, beatings and killings were common occurrences. His male cousins, however, belonged to a gang, and were very protective of him. It was "Hands off Freddie!" That was basically how he survived, not really through any cunning of his own.

He loved and hated his parents. He was the only son of an Italian family and, as tradition dictated, destined to carry on the family name. How lucky they felt. He was tall, very handsome and healthy, and girls were attracted to him. There would definitely be a good match out there for their boy. And so, when he was in his early twenties, they began to parade them in front of him. "Fred, this one really likes you" they would whisper. "She told me so. Look at how lovely she is! And her father! He owns three dry cleaning shops and is opening a fourth. He is interested in you coming into the family business. Your life would be set!" That was why he loved them. They thought so much of him, they were proud of him. They adored him and wanted only the best for him, and that was why he also hated them. They were choking him, so he would escape to his room at night, feigning fatigue or a headache and taking big gulps of any air still left in the room.

We should be clear on one thing. Freddie loved women. He loved their clothes, their long shiny hair that bobbed and shook when they walked; the high heels that made them look taller and more regal than what they were. And oh, the make-up. He loved the transformations that took place. A pale, mousy-looking woman with small beady eyes would be turned into a beauty with the right colors and chemicals and eyeliner and lashes. But he didn't love their bodies. Of course he went to bed with them, but mainly to keep his parents happy and unaware. And, they were there, so why not? Going to bed with a woman was like going to the gym. It was an exercise, and he did it faithfully, but it gave Freddie no real pleasure.

He had started to feel more and more like a schizophrenic. He was leading a double life. He was two people. One was this nice Italian boy, and the other was this gay man. He felt as if he were cut in half, and he was in agony.

Freddie tried to escape and soothe his soul and satisfy his cravings as often as he could by going to the Village, strolling along Christopher Street and picking up men in bars. He had sex in cars, trucks, alleys, bathrooms but was always fearful of being caught in the many surprise raids that the police made. He would shudder at the thought of his father coming to bail him out of jail because he committed 'lewd' acts. But even though there was that fear, he still continued.

He heard through the grapevine that there was going to be an Italian ship docking in Brooklyn with a whole bunch of Italian sailors. *Fresh meat,* he thought. He told his parents that he would be staying at a friend's house and wouldn't be home for the entire weekend. They kept prodding him.

"Which friend? Where will you be? At a party?"

"Imagine," he said to himself. "Here I am at twenty-four, still having to check in and out."

Freddie was not disappointed. The gay Italian guys were all over the Village in uniform, with their tight white pants, dark gorgeous skin and beautiful accents. Oh how he loved it!

And that is where he met Giovanni, and his whole life changed. As luck would have it, Giovanni's ship was going to be in port for repairs for a month. There was an instantaneous attraction, and the chemistry between the two of them was palpable. He knew he had found someone special, a true soul mate. Giovanni was an actor in Italy, but was forced to give up his somewhat fledging career and serve his mandatory two years for his country. He was not only physically beautiful, but he had a sweetness and a kindness that Freddie loved. In all his escapades and encounters, this was the first time this had happened to him. He had never imagined that being with one person could give him such complete happiness. For the first time in his life, he felt happy because with Giovanni he could be totally and utterly himself. Freddie had found his soul mate, and he was in love.

Giovanni was being discharged from the Italian navy in three months and they made plans for Freddie to go to Italy. He had no idea how he was going to pay for all of it. Because he so desperately wanted to be with Giovanni, and because he so desperately craved freedom from the shackles and chains his parents' lovingly bound him to, he did something he would never ordinarily have done. He asked his parents for the money. He told them that he had always wanted to see Italy, get in touch with his heritage in the country where his parents and grandparents were born. It was always difficult for them to say no to Freddie, and so they gave him the money for a round trip ticket. Freddie bought a one way ticket to Rome.

He wasn't coming back.

How would he support himself? He didn't know, and really didn't care. Something would turn up. Giovanni told him that he was in porno films because that was the only kind of job he could get as an actor, and being on stage or in film was his dream. He had heard of other men who went on to play legitimate roles and he knew that someday he would be one of them. So he did what he had to do. Giovanni also said he had friends in the theatre and he assured Freddie that he would make the contacts so Freddie could get a job...any job.

Freddie shared Giovanni's tiny apartment in Rome, a six story walk up. His bathroom at home was probably bigger, but they didn't care. They had each other and, for the first time in a long time, Freddie felt he could breathe. One day Giovanni came home very excited and told Freddie that he got him a job in a movie where he worked! He didn't know exactly what it was, but who cared? At least it was some-thing, and it meant that he could start paying some of the bills. His parents' money was critically low, and besides, he was determined to make it on his own. Living in Italy with Giovanni brought him the freedom he needed to be himself and that was what he would be. Himself. Living two lives was history.

Although he knew he would be trying out for a role in a porno film, it was still quite a shock for Freddie when he visited the set where Giovanni had a bit part. It was a huge warehouse and there were four porno films being made at the same time. There were gorgeous men and women lounging about half naked waiting to be called for their five minutes of fame. The costumes, or lack of, glittered. His critical eye told him that the jewelry was fake glass, but the effect was one of being surrounded by a kaleidoscope of color.

Freddie was nervous and excited. Giovanni introduced him to Dan, the set manager, who spoke English, and then he left for a call.

I wonder what part I'm going to have? he thought. *So it's porn. So what? It's money, and besides, some of these guys are so very hot.* He was getting hard just thinking about some of them. *But suppose I have to do it with a girl? It'll be okay. I'll just fake it. I've done that before.*

Dan's voice brought him back to the moment. "We want to see how you work out, Freddie. On a set, delays cost money and we can't have that. You and the weather are crucial to keeping our film on budget."

How about that he thought. *Me and the weather keeping a film on budget!*

"Okay Freddie," said Dan. "See that guy over there giving the other guy a blow job? Well, he is leaving us tomorrow; he got a part in a film, so we need a replacement. Hopefully, you are it. We are going to start shooting in fifteen minutes. Are you ready?"

Timidly, Freddie asked, "I'm sorry, but shouldn't we have a rehearsal first? You know, a run through?"

"If you need a run through, then you're not the guy for the job, Freddie, and maybe we should look for someone else."

"No way! I'll be fine. I'll know what to do. I'll figure it out." He was beginning to sweat at even the thought of failing!

"Okay, let's do it. Time's money, and it's money we don't have!" Freddie quickly stripped down and stood naked before the other actor.

"Freddie, you didn't have to take your clothes off for this, but it's okay.

"Well what are you waiting for?" asked Dan. "Shooting starts in only fifteen minutes. That's all the time you've got."

"Don't I need a cue?" said Freddie

At that, they all started laughing and telling him he was a good one and he would work out. He was so relieved! He'd be okay. He would just take his cues from the other actor. *The other actor*, he said to himself. *That's me! I'm not living off of anyone any more. I'm an actor! So what if it's a porno film? It's a start. I'll get to meet people. I'll network. I'll make something of myself...finally!*

"Okay, now to work." Freddie looked at the other actor, patiently waiting...for what?

"Come on Freddie, get on your knees and do your thing. Do you want a cushion? All quiet on the set, Freddie needs to concentrate."

And that's how Freddie the Fluffer came to be.

~~~~~~~~

BEING THE *GOODBOY*

DAVID PORTEOUS

They called me *Sparky* when I was too young to know my name. I thought they said *Spah-ki-i* to get my attention, and *Dah-ki-i* to my big brother. We were mainly white, but unlike our gray patches, his were black, so he got noticed first and was the first of us given to a stranger. I still remember my mother's whine when he was handed over. I didn't see it then, but later felt that she knew she had lost him. He knew it, too; he smelled of fear and his eyes darted about. I sensed his dark color got him taken, so with my coloring more silvery than the others' gray, I worried about being next to go, and a fretful day later I found that I'd been right to be concerned.

Two strangers with silver hair like mine came to see us, and pointed at me. They did happy noise, but my mother cried when I was given to them. I probably looked as scared as my big brother had, but not for long. They smelled kind. Before I grew to know better, I feared my life would often be upset by strangers coming to get me. That, and missing my mother and fearing that I'd never see my family again, made life daunting, but I soon learned that *MyPeople* wanted me to feel at home.

All we pups shared my mother's bed, but I got three for just me. *MyPeople* put one by their *BigBed*, and in the *TeeVee* and *DinDin* rooms. They gave me a *SqueakyToy*, and I saw I made them happy if I put it in a bed after playing with it. They said *GoodBoySparky*, so I knew my name. I'd already learned their point at the floor with *SitSparky*, and hand held up for S*taySparky*, with *DinDinSparky* my call to eat. I could see their pride in my learning *PeopleTalk* when they spoke about words I knew, so I learned even more to thank them for making me feel safe. It was the sense of safety they gave me that made me love them.

I learned *MyPeople* were *Dada* and *Mama*. Both told me *LoveYaSparky* in a way I sensed meant the speaker wanted me to think he or she loved me more than the other. But both made me their family. I sat on the *TeeVee* couch with them, slept up on their *BigBed* on cold nights, and rode in *Dada*'s car with my head out a window to catch the smells. I saw that they were old by how they got up slowly, did not walk steadily, and couldn't get down on the floor to play. They kicked my *SqueakyToy* and told me to chase with *Sparky'sToy-Run*. I knew what to do from *Walkies*. They said *RunSparky* to cross roads, and *Car-RunRunSparky* to go fast if a car was coming, or they held up a hand for *StaySparky-Car*. I learned *Walkies* from their holding up my *Leash*, and when they said words I knew and *Sparky'sSmart*, I knew I was their *SmartGoodBoy*. Sometimes *Mama* told me her best loving word, *SoAdorable!* That was usually after a day's visit to *GroomerLady.*

~~~~~~~~~

I learned it all before I grew-up, which took until cold days turned hot and then cold again, but kept learning. After I saw that showing I knew something made them happy, it was all I wanted to do. For five hot seasons we lived in our home, and my only concern was if I'd meet *BigBrownDog* when *Dada* took me *Walkies.* He showed he was a *ToughGuy,* as *Dada* called him, by snarling, and one day he bit hard into my front left leg. *Dada* kicked him until he ran off, and I stood on my good legs, barking, but feeling pain in my leg and not knowing why *Dada* hadn't noticed that *BigBrownDog*'s tail didn't wag. After I had my leg wrapped and could do *Walkies* again, if he came with no tail wag, snarling to say he was doing *WatchDogJob,* I'd growl and he'd go home, with life as it should be. Until *Dada* saw that *BigBrownDog* and I had that deal, he used to lift me up. Still, other than that, to this day I walk with a painless limp, I had a safe home, food and kind *MyPeople.* Life was perfect, but it didn't last.

In my sixth cold season, *Mama* got sick and *Dada* got sad. She barked coughs, and had to force words out. The worse she got, the more he sat and sobbed. I tried to cheer him up, but all I got was *ScramSparky* and kicked at. I knew *Dada* never meant to hurt me, so I had to accept that he was showing his need to cry alone. *Mama* never sent me away. She had me on the *BigBed,* where she then lay day and night, lying close so she could pat her *GoodBoy,* or do hand signs if she couldn't talk. It was early in our days on the *BigBed* that I smelled her neck and *Mama* laughed at my nose tickling her, but smelling death was no fun for me. Somehow knowing I would lose my *Mama* scared me. After then her loving *GoodBoySparky* did all I could to be soothingly cheerful with and for her.

~~~~~~~~

We lost her next cold season, when she was a tiny ridge in the *BigBed*, barking more, talking less, a tube to her nose from tanks on wheels. She kept me close, but touching her caused pain, and if she cried I felt helpless, worse if *Dada* thought I'd hurt *Mama*. I knew his shoving me aside was just anger about also feeling helpless. I'd seen him break *DinDin* plates, yelling at someone named *God* to help *M'darlin'*, as he called *Mama*, and I felt sad for both of them. When *Mama* told him that I didn't hurt her, he'd sob and slink off as she slumped back to suck tank air, beckoning me back close to her on the *BigBed*.

Life changed when ladies smelling of *WashTime* soap and dressed alike came to help *Mama* eat, wash, *Tinkle* or *Poopie*. She got up only for that, so never saw our home getting filthy. The soap ladies had *Dada* tidy up, but he mostly sat watching *TeeVee* through wet eyes. I could not comfort him, but our walks got him out of the sad home, and he'd usually remember to feed me. He'd just drink sour-smelling stuff *Mama* called *YerBooze*, seemingly so he'd fall asleep watching *TeeVee*.

One night, when *Dada* was on the *TeeVee* couch and I was on *Mama's BigBed*, I sensed a change in her. She was on her back, wheezing, and turned her face to me. Her hand moved in the *BigBed*, but she had no strength to get it out to pat me. Smiling lovingly, she shut her eyes and stopped the wheezing. I knew I'd lost her. I ran down to the *TeeVee* room, barking for *Dada* to come up, but he growled like a Rottweiler. I kept barking and circling to the stairs until he got quiet, eyes wide, and rolled from the couch to stumble to the stairs. I ran back up them, hearing his cries of *WaitM'darlin'* behind me.

Mama was still smiling, but after *Dada* saw her he ran to the phone, wailing like a siren. Soon real sirens wailed to our home and men ran in, some smelling of *WashTime* soap, the others of coffee and man sweat. While the coffee men talked to *Dada*, the others took *Mama* out on a cart. It was the last time I ever saw her, and the start of the worst time of my life.

For days, strangers came to talk to *Dada* and clean our home. It took days because *Mama's* daily soapy ladies tidied only the *BigBed* or *WashTime* rooms, and *Dada* had let trash pile up everywhere else. I hid in it from his angry-sad moods. Cleaning ended the day before people came for *YerBooze* and *DinDin* at a party *Dada* had for them to be sad for him. I was sad for me. The cleaning people had given me *DinDin* every day, but after *Dada's* party he'd forget to feed me, so I had to do *SitUpAndBeg*. If he forgot to walk me and I had to *Tinkle* or *Poopie* inside, he yelled and kicked at me, but I was lucky that his *YerBooze* made him fall down. No, lucky would be if he still said *LoveYaSparky*. I still had *Dada*, but missed him like I did *Mama*, missing their love.

115

Until the hot season after we lost *Mama*, people came to see *Dada* and point at trash, yelling words I didn't know. I'd growl to defend him, and so they'd yell at me. By then I was filthy, with bloody patches from scratching out hair knots, not *SoAdorable* – my *GroomerLady* visits ended when *Mama* got sick. Since then, *Dada's* face got thin and hairy, and as dirty as his clothes – a scary sight as he pushed people out the door. I couldn't help him in our sad time, as *YerBooze* and *TeeVee* kept me out of his life. I got weak, and had toothaches, so I wondered if I was going to lose me, but who would help *Dada*? He had no one else who cared about him.

~~~~~~~~

On what became our last day together, a man came to yell at *Dada* and tried to grab him. *Dada* swung a fire poker until he left, but he brought back coffee-smelling big men, who put *Dada* in a car. All I could do was growl, but the man *Dada* had run-off patted me, and gave me his sandwich for *DinDin*. It had been so long since I had felt kindness that I stopped growling and, for the first time in too long, I wagged my tail.

He took me in a car to a place with dogs howling to be let out. A lady I'd later know as *BossLady*, put me on a cold table like one at *DoctorClaude's SickDogPlace*, and a man felt me and my bent front leg, then looked in my mouth. I stayed still, as I'd learned, but he pushed a sore tooth, so I growled. He stopped, and I heard *GoodBoy* before I felt a sting just like *DoctorClaude* did to me every hot season, but it didn't end the visit, as it always had, because I felt myself going to sleep.

I woke in a cage, feeling as shaky as *Dada* with *YerBooze*, tasting blood, and hearing dogs' cries of fear. I found eating *DinDin* hurt, as I'd lost teeth after the man's sting sent me to sleep. Later, a lady took me to a room of pens, most with dogs my size, not the ones I heard barking. I went in an empty pen, which had a bed and a water bowl. She hung my collar and its name tag on the door with a card that must have had words about me, because people who came looked from it to me.

As people came to our room next day, some got noisily happy if dogs could go with them, I hoped to good homes. The work people were kind, but that scary place didn't make us feel safe. No one took any notice of skinny me, with bald patches, dirty hair and bloody mouth, but that changed the next day. I got taken to a room like *GroomerLady's*, and made *SoAdorable* again. I was still thin with sores under lost patches of hair, but people started to smile at me after I was clean.

A young couple patted me that day, and wrote on a paper for *BossLady*. I'd loved old people, but I'd go with anyone who could get me out of there. The man wrote, and I tried to look *SoAdorable* for his lady as *BossLady* put a sticker on my pen. I'd seen dogs go just days after stickers went up, so I was sad when they didn't come back, but an older couple talked to me.

They weren't as old as *Mama* and *Dada*, but I sensed a love in them like I had once known, and felt sad as *BossLady* pointed to my pen's sticker to show the young couple wanted me. The man patted my head, as if so I'd know I wasn't being rejected. His lady turned to a Pug in the next pen and pulled the man's

117

arm, but he just glanced at it before turning back to me. I did *SitUpAndBeg*, wagging my tail to show that I liked him, and then I heard him tell her I was a *SmartGoodBoy*.

When the place shut and dogs' dejected howls got loud, I thought about the next day, and the young couple taking me. I hoped they'd tell *BossLady* they wouldn't, and she'd let the nice older people have me. I could do nothing, no matter what happened, and would have to go where life took me. My seven full cycles of the passing seasons had taught me that wisdom.

Next morning, the young couple hadn't come after we'd been in the *Tinkle* and *Poopie* yard while our pens got cleaned, but the older man and *BossLady* came to my room. He looked glad to see me, but *BossLady* showed that she knew he'd be a good *People* for one of us, though I couldn't be the one. He squatted by my pen, talking to *BossLady*, but often reaching in to pat me, as if he wanted me to know that he'd take me to a safe place if he could. I think *BossLady* liked our contact, because she looped a *Leash* on me and led us along a hall. I knew this wasn't how dogs went to people, so I could only turn my hopes to the *Walkies* ending at a happy place.

It wasn't until I was let off the *Leash* to explore the scents of many dogs in an empty room that the man clearly saw how I walk. I knew his pointing meant he and *BossLady* were talking about my leg, so I ran around to show that it didn't bother me, but they laughed at my limping. It had been many season cycles since *BigBrownDog* bit me, so I'd forgotten that I didn't walk as neatly as I had. Now confused, I wondered if I'd misjudged the man, so I listened for words I knew as they talked. She said my name at times, and he did once, but also said a word I didn't know but it sounded like it was a name. It made *BossLady* laugh, and he then said it to me with his arms out to hug me into them, like *Mama* and *Dada* used to. Of course I ran to him, whatever name he was calling me.

BossLady gave him a rope toy and we played until she pointed towards my room and spoke seriously. He must have said something funny, because she laughed and left, brought back a *SqueakyToy* for him and left again, still smiling. He squeezed it, as if to show me what it was, and I showed I knew by doing *RunRun* when he rolled it on the floor. He laughed as I made it squeak and sat with it in my mouth. I must have been *SoAdorable*, because he hugged me like *Dada* had until *Mama* got sick. I hadn't felt so happy since before that time.

That didn't last. *BossLady* came back and, after talking to him, looped a *Leash* on me and they led me back to my pen. I was surprised when she didn't lock me in, but left us in the room, and I was glad the man had time to pat me. Surprise turned to joy when she returned with a paper like she'd given the young couple for him to write on. I didn't know what could come of it, but had high hopes after he left. They faded that night as dogs' howling to be free of misery got loud, and I knew I'd be joining in the din if someone didn't take me away soon.

Early next day, *BossLady* came to look at me while she talked to a flat phone like people all seem to have. She put it in a pocket, got out a comb and groomed me, I hoped to make me *SoAdorable* for someone to take. I knew it might not be the man I needed, and had sensed that he also needed me, so imagine my joy at seeing him and his lady that day. I was too excited to stay still as *BossLady* let me out of the pen to put my old collar on me, but the man handed her a new one and pointed to its name tag. She laughed, and said the word like a name that he'd said the day before, but said it like a question. He nodded, which I'd known since a pup was *Yes*, and said the word to me, to teach me my new name: *Gimpy*.

As soon as I saw *MyPeople's* home I knew I'd be happy there. While they got from the car *GoShops* bags that they'd had before we left the *SadDogsPlace*, I stayed in a fenced yard, where I knew I'd be able to *Tinkle* or *Poopie* on days too rainy for *Walkies*. I stayed by the yard's gate, so when the man said *ComeGimpy*, I ran to him, my wagging tail making him smile.

We sat on the *TeeVee* couch with the *GoShops* bags, and they talked to me while showing all they'd bought, so I sat and listened to show I'm *SmartGimpy*. I didn't know many words, but I heard he was *Daddy*, not *Dada*, and she was *Mummy*. New names for new *MyPeople* felt right in my new life. Seeing that they had beds for me in their *BigBed*, *DinDin* and *TeeVee* rooms, I felt at home, and when *Mummy* held up more than one *SqueakyToy*, I knew I'd always be happy and loved.

I also knew that I loved *Daddy* for coming back to ask *BossLady* to let him get me out of a room of scared little dogs hearing unseen big dogs howling in fear of ending their lives there. I'd seen grim life in *Mama's* illness and *Dada's* sadness, so my love for *Daddy* was endless. I soon learned *Mummy* is lovely, and checks me for ticks better than *Daddy* does. I love her for it, but I always know that I owe *Daddy* my life.

~~~~~~~~

For three cycles of the seasons, I felt more blissful than even in the best times with *Mama* and *Dada*. *Daddy* took me *GoForRide*, and told me *No-SorryGimpy* only on hot days or if he and *Mummy* were going out for a long time. In those times, I'd lie in my *DinDin* room bed near the back door until they got home to get the happy greeting they deserved, loving how it made them as happy as I was to see them. Life was good. I had a gentle new *GroomerLady*, another lady named *DoctorJan* to do my *DoctorClaude* check-ups, and the most loving and caring home any little dog could imagine.

I still have it all, but a change in me last year makes it hard to be *MyPeople's* attentive *GoodBoyGimpy*. I first knew that I couldn't hear when I saw *Daddy* talking and frowning at me for not doing what he said. It was embarrassing, but watching closely I saw he was saying *GoForRide*, and it puzzled me. I love car rides, and hoped I looked excited as I wondered what was wrong with me, but my worry must have shown, because *MyPeople* hugged me, and next day took me to *DoctorJan's SickDogPlace*. She looked in my ears and I watched her talk to *MyPeople*, hoping to sense what had made me deaf, but she didn't know, and no one was happy about that.

~~~~~~~~~

All the seasons have passed since then, and *DoctorJan* still can't fix me. I'm in no pain, like when *BigBrownDog* bit my leg, but I live with not hearing what *MyPeople* want me to do by staying alert for any hint of them trying to get me to do something. It's hard, and challenging on *Walkies* when I can't hear *CarComing-RunRun*. I've had to learn to stop myself at roads to look for cars, and when I do, *Daddy* does the smile that goes with *GoodBoy*. I sometimes see the face that goes with *SmartGimpy-GoodBoy*, and I owe them my extra efforts for giving me this life. I try to not show I get scared when they go out and I lose the security of seeing them, and to not react if I'm unexpectedly touched, which I also had to learn. In my early deaf days I'd instinctively snap, often finding that I did it to *MyPeople*. I loved that they instantly knew I was sorry.

I now know that the problems I've faced taught me to be grateful for all I have in life. For instance, I owe my ability to understand what *Mummy* and *Daddy* want of me to the grim time when my sick *Mama* couldn't talk, so did hand signals. I had to learn to be alert for that, and to see her meaning so I could be as loyal as she needed me to be. It's like that now, but with me deaf instead of *MyPeople* being silent, and though it's an effort for an old dog to stay alert, I know I must.

I've come to see that a dog's job in life is to give all we can to support our *MyPeople*, and to accept whatever we get back as our due. I am content to lovingly dedicate my life to being the *GoodBoy* for *Daddy* and *Mummy,* and always grateful for their tender care and acceptance of my limitations now I am old. I've wondered if that role was meant to be my destiny, and if maybe it's a role that *People* should take to help make life better for all the *People* they know. Maybe they already do, but we dogs don't see it. I can only hope so.

~ ~ ~ ~  ~ ~ ~ ~

THE LODGER

ANDREA RHUDE

I like it here, it is so warm and holds such possibilities, but it is a little too bright so I choose small shady places to live in now. Things are being built around me, tall proud things that I will be able to stretch myself into, but for now there is time while the foundations are being set, to sleep and wait.

Every bright room that is made has its shadows, even the newest, and these rooms are so new and warm. I have been cold for so long and I can hear what I know are words shaping my new rooms, even if I cannot understand them yet, and they are such warm things building my home. If I stretch I can touch them, hold them in my cold hands and I drink them down, but soon enough the cold returns and I'll have to stretch further next time.

I can feel the *Other* waking; it's always there, all around me, in the walls, and the floors. It changes my home, gives new texture to the thickening air and brings the warm, warm words closer to me, lets me understand them even as the light grows brighter. But the shadows have also changed, they have not just gotten darker and deeper, they have spread their grayness into the light so I do not have to risk the empty pain it gives to shed my chill. I can ease into the gray and warmth, and explore.

As I pass from room to room I drink in the warmth, and glory in my new home. The *Other*, that has begun to build new larger rooms using the warm words, hides from me and closes off the darkened cold rooms I leave behind me, but they are small enough not to diminish my home, and the new wonders the *Other* has built for me now makes me yearn to swallow them down. I follow the *Other* as it slowly builds great rooms full of warmth with shockingly vibrant colors and more complex angles that produce a new variegated light. It has begun watching me; I can feel its fascination and its warmth as it comes nearer. I have grown stronger and can tolerate even the brighter light now, and just as the *Other* let me understand the words, now I can see faces in the light; smiling, kind faces. Faces that I know hide teeth. The *Other* welcomes them as I try to warn it, but it doesn't listen. So, I wait and know soon the cold words will come and bite the *Creature*, then it will turn to me. And it does, and as it does it opens new rooms to me I never knew were there. Warmth pours into me.

"Try harder, you can do better." I hear the warm song in the words but the *Other* turns to me with a sudden shiver, the light dims and I drink the song as I listen and hear the cold sting under the warmth. I understand what the *Other* cannot; those words came from someone like me, someone who knows the cold of a winter looking into the glow of other homes, they know the true meaning of 'no' and 'can't' and that knowledge frosts every 'yes' and every 'you can'.

I feel the *Other's* confusion from the cooling space behind me, "but I tried so hard." Again the warm words ask for more, and the frost begins to lace the walls. I tell the *Other*, "they are right, it is cruel out there, you must be better," because it is true. We both want warmth but the chill begins to creep into the new constructions. The *Other* listens to the warm words but then it waits for me to speak, and I rage at the cold under the words that try to enter my warm home. The *Other* is safe and can build more rooms for me as the warmth fades from the closed and darkened ones; I will keep it safe, I will keep me warm.

Change is coming again, the shadows strain at the light and warmth, I can wander freely and the *Other* turns to me again and again. There is always something new to build, but the words coming in are brittle despite their warmth, with barely enough heat to chase the chill from the shadows. The *Other*, the *Creature*, builds and builds, frantically, and I try to help. I push along with the words, but none of the rooms have the warmth we need, despite their vastness and we are so cold.

The *Creature* no longer asks me questions or listens to the warm words; it is too cold in my home now, and the shape of my house has changed. I can feel its skin enclosing me, giving me sensations I never knew. I feel things brushing against that skin and they pull at me, some of them are warm.

I run to that warmth, bask in the new driving heat against the living skin of my house, and new words breathe through my home's darkened halls like a thaw. The old words speak with icy gusts warning the

Creature of storms and icy teeth, but we don't care. The *Creature* doesn't need to ask anymore, I rage back at the old words. I chose the icy words that I know would bite their warmth and chill them as they have chilled my home. My words scorch with cold so strong and fierce that my home feels warmed, but it doesn't last, shortly after my words have found their mark the cold intensifies around me. Only the new words give any lasting relief.

The *Creature* clings to me now and builds no more. The new words have grown cool, colder than the old words, they send frost back into the old closed rooms and the cold behind me intensifies. The heat I could feel through the skin of my home has become tainted; once the contact is over the warmth it gave drains away and takes more of my precious heat with it. The skin deadens and I rage at the thief until finally the new words are gone and it is colder than ever in my home.

The old words are still here and I can hear them with their warmth and concern, but the *Creature* no longer listens; it clings to me and I try to warm it but I have nothing left. All I can do is rage and try to keep hold of the incandescent ice that burns, so briefly, from my words. I will have to move on soon, but I cannot leave my home, the *Creature* holds me. The *Creature* is cold and no longer builds my rooms. I can release it. It asks questions, but I don't reply. It howls at me and I drink down the last of the fragile and flimsy heat. I pull back and leave the *Creature* to its darkened and cold halls; let it decide what to do with our shell.

I hear something new; a faint rasping noise that repeats and grows more frantic until with a soft poof and a new sulfurous scent that flowers with heat, delicious heat that spreads and eats at the shell of my home. The *Creature* wails, and as I revel in the heat of my burning home I remember; this has all happened before. I play in the flames and drink down the possibilities of all that could have been from the *Creature* as it dies. I need it all. I have to conserve it until I can find another home and another *Creature* that will build for me. Until then I will cling to the warm words and let them hide me as I enter my next small room and can grow again.

~~~~~~~~

THE MATTER AT HAND

SUSAN ROSENSTREICH

He didn't mean to turn right. His next sales call
was thirty miles up the road in Cottondale. The car just
turned on its own. A fine red dust rose up from the
road, unpaved after all these decades. The tires fell into
the deep striations left by successions of washouts; he
struggled to control the steering wheel. A gap between
the road and the driveway of the Yankee family's old
cabin caught him by surprise. He swerved, but too late.
The car teetered for a second or so, then jarred him as
it landed with sudden finality in the ditch by the cabin.

The Yankee had been a book man, not a farmer,
come south after the war to teach with buddies from his
army unit at the university in nearby Tuscaloosa. The
family had come to tiny Peterson, bought the cabin
from a gambler in town who had grown too old to tend
his stills and carouse at poker on the weekends. The
place would house the family that had outgrown the
Yankee's pay. Joe Boy had loved the Yankee girl
completely. At seventeen, he'd thought he might marry
her, and sat one day with her mother, talking about
how you would go about farming in these parts, how
they could make a life of it, adding the wood-and-water

capital of his daddy's acres to the fertile but unexploited flatland of the Yankee's acres. Corn and cotton, Joe Boy had told the mother; it'd just take a few seeds and their willing bodies to make a living. The wonder of those dreams. Even greater wonder that he had dared talking about them. But the girl's father had balked. His daughter would not wrinkle and fade like a woman's dress. And soon, the Yankees were gone, headed west for more pay and more excitement in California. Joe Boy had finished his last year at Holtsville High, assaulting southern boys rib-cage-skinny like him on football fields still scarred by the ancient furrows of cotton planting.

That was what he saw as he looked back toward the cabin from the ditch. The red dust blew up from a late afternoon blast of air, the daily but brief cooling of the fields in early August. Was it worth asking for help at the cabin? A figure appeared at the top of the drive, Joe Boy could just make out the white shirt, the slacks. "Hey!" A wave. Joe Boy waved back, the figure made to walk down the drive to him.

The place was now a weekend retreat. The new owner – he was solo, like Joe Boy – had left the layout of the cabin as Joe Boy had known it. The kitchen and dining areas were still on local flagstone, but it bore a load of waxen polish. The expansive fireplace, its hearth extending far into the dining area, had once warmed the Yankee family's life first thing in the morning, last thing at night. It now served to support an elaborately carved oak garniture. Here was where he had sat with the mother.

The men headed down the drive, a few tools in hand. Joe Boy pointed out the promontory that, years ago, offered a view of the lake. It was now drained. The man had not known the lake. He had come south from the Carolinas, a band saw engineer for Gulf States Paper. Joe Boy tried to make a joke about his own migration in the opposite direction, up to the Carolinas, rising from a tire manufacturer's factory floor to its regional salesman. But the irony provoked only a slight shrug and snort from both men. What can you do? They turn the world, you follow the turn.

Or you don't. As they neared the ditch, Joe Boy was able to show the man where the Yankees had grown watermelons, you could still see, all these years later, the outlines of the corn patch and the circular herb garden the Yankee girl and her siblings had worked year-round. The tools the men had with them were useless. The car spun its wheels a bit. The men rocked it for a time, Joe Boy pushing each time the vehicle reached its forward zenith, the cabin owner gunning the engine. The cabin owner's car was too puny to haul Joe Boy's truck out of the muck. They needed traction. More muscle.

"You know them Browns up the road? Past the curve yonder?" Joe Boy waved toward where he remembered Fred Brown's cabin had stood, just across the road from his own home. You wouldn't see the cabins beyond the curve from where he and the man stood, dirty in the ditch by the car. He turned his body to point out where the cabins stood as the crow flies, but was stunned to see that now, the curve had disappeared. And the bridge was gone. You could see

133

the Browns' cabin, after all, even through the dusty haze. The two trudged up the road. Suddenly, Joe Boy couldn't place where his own cabin had once been. He and his daddy had torn it down after Joe Boy finished school and went north. His daddy would move in with cousins in town.

They had long ago buried Joe Boy's mama; it had just been the two of them, Joe Boy and his daddy for years, living off their poor wages from seasonal crops and the kindness of the church ladies. They didn't beg; they just didn't need. They liked their hunting. And Joe Boy's daddy was skilled in the herbs. People came from all over these parts, asking for the potions and unguents his daddy knew to concoct from black walnut and sassafras, boneset and pine tar. All Joe Boy could do for the pain-twisted bodies that came to their door was hand them the tiny bundles his daddy would prepare, usually after hearing just a few words from his supplicants. They would offer their chickens or some butter or eggs in a cloth, and Joe Boy watched as they hobbled back down or back up the road, resigned, bent in strange ways.

The men stopped short of the Browns' yard. "You Fred Brown?" Joe Boy called out. The man in the rocker held still a moment, rose up and came toward them.

"Used to be. You after Fred?" The yard was barren, just packed earth, as had been the floor of the Browns' cabin. But Joe Boy, looking beyond the man who answered him, now saw that the cabin was gone, and instead, he could see a dog-trot structure, planks overlapping in neat rhythm, the porch raised well above the earthen yard, white-framed windows. Joe Boy stepped closer to the man before him.

He took in the full body and its place in the yard. The new house fell further and further away, more and more distant; the man from the Yankee cabin breathed faster and faster beside him. There was a haze. The pecan tree was gone, it no longer stood in the Browns' yard, but Joe Boy thought he could see, still inscribed in the dust, the marks of the rattler's body that had lay twisting there that day, agonizing under the heavy branches of the tree. Joe Boy looked toward the site of the old cabin, saw Li'l Tommy strolling out its door, and with the business end of his .22, poke at the dying reptile. Joe Boy saw himself standing in the road, barefoot, balancing his own rifle on his shoulder. He and his daddy had gone hunting, now his daddy was up at the cabin waiting on Sally Mae, the dark-skinned woman from the cabins down by the railroad tracks. Joe Boy's daddy had told him freed slaves built the cabins after the War Between the States. But Joe Boy didn't believe a word of it; Sally Mae's cabin would have to be a hundred years old, too long a life for a cabin in Peterson.

"He gonna die at sun-set, Joe Boy," Li'l Tommy said, great triumph in his voice. "Let him be," Joe Boy had called out from the road. "Just let him die, don't be doing him like that." It irked him that the skinny Brown boy would torture a rattler who was no more than an hour short of death. But Tommy snickered and threw stones at the writhing animal. Sally Mae came down the slope from Joe Boy's cabin, a small bundle, no doubt some herbs, in one hand, biscuits she had brought his daddy, still in their cloth wrapping, in the other hand. Joe Boy did favor Sally's biscuits, but he reckoned his daddy had let Sally keep the biscuits for her babies.

He felt the air swirl softly at his back as Sally Mae passed behind him. How could so small a woman raise a breeze? he wondered. He turned to her. Even if she came from the slave cabins, even if she took the bus into town three days a week to clean houses of white people who would forever be strangers to her, even if she didn't know the whereabouts of the father of her children. "Good ev'nin, Sally Mae," he called out, softly.

"Good ev'nin, Sally Mae," Li'l Tommy mimicked, pitching his voice high and nasal, wagging his hind quarters as he spoke. Dust rose up from Sally's soft step. Joe Boy coughed to clear his throat. Li'l Tommy faked a cough in answer. The sound jammed Joe Boy's thoughts. His ears rang. Tommy lifted the .22, and with the butt of it, lit into the snake. It arched, a single muscle, now in its final flex, fighting off the terrible darkness coming toward it. The animal snapped against the packed earth of the yard. Joe Boy heard himself roar with rage. Sally Mae froze.

Joe Boy was on Li'l Tommy in a single leap. He flung the boy face down onto the hard earth, pulled his head up and then forced it down, smashing it onto the ground. He turned the boy, stunned and open-mouthed, face up, pummeled his abdomen, kneed the soft tissue between his legs. He was deaf to the screaming, alone now in the universe, its law-maker, its ruler. His fury fueled itself clear of the horizon, reached the ether and was flung on the power of its decibels into some infinite system, forever reverberating everywhere. The snake, the woman from the slave cabins, the dusty road held off, moved beyond the world, witnesses until the cosmos would collapse. "Don't. Be. Doin'. Him. Like. That." With each word, he jammed his fist into Li'l Tommy's bloody mouth.

Joe Boy studied the figure in the Browns' yard now before him. "You ain't Fred Brown?" It seemed impossible that the pasty-skinned unmuscled body wasn't Fred Brown. Time had surely stopped, that's what it was. No, this figure was Li'l Tommy's old puny-brained daddy Fred Brown in front of him.

"Naw, he died. This here's his old cabin. I done fixed it up. We got us some trailers out back, rent 'em for the folks workin' at the Warner mill." He stopped short, face to face with Joe Boy. "Hey, now, don't I know you?"

Joe Boy rocked from one foot to the other. "Okay, look here, now, you Li'l Tommy?" he asked, his voice small. The two men stood, inches apart; the man from the Yankee cabin moved closer. But Joe Boy took a step back, enough to stretch out his right hand toward the man in the yard. Joe Boy could see now that there were children playing out back near the trailers, women in jeans and men in boots, carrying groceries, watering geraniums in planters by steps to their trailers.

"That you, Joe Boy? Why, you ain't changed one speck. 'Ceptin' you ain't no younger." He didn't smile. He couldn't smile; he was missing some upper teeth. His breath was even, calm. "What you doin' in these parts, boy?" He held out his own right hand.

"I got me some car trouble," Joe Boy said, hooking his thumb back over his shoulder toward the car in the ditch.

"Well, if that don't beat all," murmured Fred Brown's boy. He didn't offer the men a drink, didn't turn to the woman watching them from the door of the house. He ambled beside Joe Boy and the man from the Yankee cabin. They walked around the car some, the man revved the engine, Joe Boy and Li'l Tom shoved it hard. Once they got the vehicle out of the ditch, they worked together with a few tools from the Yankee's cabin to change the driver's side tire, then took turns running the car up and down a few yards before folding their arms on their chests and allowed as how the vehicle was ready to roll.

Dusk had fallen on the valley. The day had cooled down some. Li'l Tommy strolled on up the road toward his well-built dogtrot with the rows of trailers unfurling out back, over the old cotton field; the man turned up the drive to the Yankee cabin carrying the tools. Joe Boy drove on toward town, past the Brown house, past the slope his daddy had run down when he'd heard the ruckus, past the bare patch where his daddy had strapped him good and hard after the fight, past the middle of the road where his daddy and Fred Brown had stood face to face and his daddy had forbidden any Brown to set foot on his land ever again, past the Peterson railroad tracks, the slave cabins, the graveyard where his daddy and mama lay side by side. The car drove fine. He went on into Cottondale.

~~~~~~~~

AT THE CHAPEL IN THE WOODS

KIT STORJOHANN

I went to the old chapel in the woods most days after school as a boy. At first, it was mainly because I couldn't think of anything else to do. After a while, however, the crumbling way station for pilgrims in the old days became sacred to me in its own right, both as a haven for a social out-cast and as a mirror of the world around me. Large portions of the wooden roof had caved in, leaving just a few spots protected by time-hardened slats and shingles atop the rectangle of stones of similar dimensions to our living room. A moss-laden statue of a robed and bearded figure stood in the center of the chapel, heedless of the rain that poured down on an ever-thickening spongy carpet of lichen. The relics were old, harkening back to a land of missionaries, Indians, and the homesteaders my father revered and secretly envied.

Interloping houses from the last century, like ours, had been built alongside the time-crusted holdovers, corralling them into rough rows along the roads. Bands of pavement ranging from single lane streets to busy highways ran up and down the county, but there were still plenty of stretches of wild trees that shed their leaves in early October to stand bare through April. Mountains climbed into skies that seemed, to my young eyes, to be perpetually gray. All had proper names none of us knew, having been rechristened by custom or habit with monikers like "Rabbits' Hill" and "Old Man Cremmons". We had neighbors on either side it would have been difficult to hit with a stone. Little bridges of logs spanned the creek, held together by the sheer will of aged wood.

One might toss around labels such as rural or rustic, but the area's charm had already dissipated for me by the time my mother left, when I was almost too young to remember her. My father never tired of it. If he were still alive, I have no doubt he'd eschew the comforts of assisted living and haul his centenarian bones across the grounds to weed his gardens. For me, the only worthwhile thing in the place was the chapel in the woods, a marker of hope from a bygone era. I took it as a sign that the place where I felt trapped was only a short stop-over, provided one had the proclivity to wander.

My mother had sought her own path, leaving my father with a toddler and a vague explanation of 'finding herself.' In light of that, perhaps, he did her the favor of erasing her old self. A furious bout of *damnatio memoriae* had fed all the old pictures and documents to the fire. Entire swaths of relatives got lopped from the address book. Only the most stalwart still sent Christmas cards, which my father burned unread in our little wood stove. For all he knew, or cared, my mother could have been dead. I have no doubt that he often wished her so.

I, on the other hand, admired and envied her initiative. I had long abandoned the image of her walking in the door again. My hope was to leave town as soon as I could, and meet her on the road somewhere when our respective adventures happened to cross paths. Tales I read in books and magazines told of glamorous cafés in Europe or dusty deserts in Arab lands where reconciliations between long-separated relatives resolved tortured plots into happy endings. Although I knew she wouldn't approach the house, part of me imagined that she might linger by the chapel in the woods. I would arrive on an afternoon walk, and she would greet me, slyly asking personal questions to make sure it was me—like a queen ensuring that the boy left on a mountainside and reared by a shepherd was the true prince. Any time I pictured that scene, she was glad to see me, but had no regret about leaving; she would often take me to her next glamorous destination.

Whatever path through the trees and hillocks I began to follow, the old chapel always became the default destination of my wanderings, a huge part of its appeal coming from the fact that it was nearly lost to local memory. I encountered so few people during afternoon refuges there that I could count the number of conversations I'd had without running out of fingers. The area belonged to no one in particular, and few made use of it. Once in a while I'd see a neighbor wandering through, shotgun under an arm, on his way to the deep woods where deer and moose could be found. I saw two classmates there once when I was about eleven. They saw me, and looked embarrassed. I realized they'd been trying to smoke cigarettes they'd found or stolen, both coughing too violently to pass themselves off as old hands at the habit. Their expressions carried both worry that I would tell their parents, and the implied threat that they'd know it was me if I did. But they were gone a few minutes later, finding some other tree-coated nook in which to practice their new debauchery. By the time they unveiled their vice behind the school one afternoon, they had stopped coughing altogether. Most afternoons, however, I was alone with chipmunks and crows, with only the wandering hobo taking up any appreciable real estate in my memory.

The few friends I could claim were boys I knew well enough to play football with during recess. Inviting anyone over to my house was unthinkable, but I never lamented the lack of companionship. Loneliness, along with the cardinal sin of boredom, was something my father would never have tolerated in his house. He found company enough in any task to which he turned his mind. I envied his ability to focus on the intricacies of constructing a piece of furniture, or to let the world fall away as he aimed one of his rifles. I hoped that, in time, this would prove to be an inherited trait. Not that I had any proficiency with tools. In fact, I was strongly discouraged from even touching them after clandestinely borrowing a bow saw and accidentally leaving it out in the rain had wrought a particularly harsh whipping. Until the day I encountered the old hobo at the chapel in the woods, I had not been invited to touch my father's guns, and I knew from bitter experience that attempting to sneak around that particular taboo would have dire repercussions.

I battered down any residual resentment that churned in me whenever I overheard some clique at school discuss weekend or summer plans. Walks in the woods—tormenting insects by shifting their world's landscapes and waterways like a whimsical god, jogging as fast as I could to see how far I could make it before I tripped in the underbrush, or standing absolutely still in winter to listen for any sign of movement on windless days—were enough for me. My days were my own; my father had less and less use for people as time went by, barely keeping contact with anyone, save for a few friendly words now and again with the neighbors.

My father underwent a daily transformation into a dignified, besuited man who sat behind a desk at the county clerk's office talking about permits or ordinances. His accent softened to something blander, and he held his formidable anger in check. He would smile politely, shake soft, pampered hands without bristling in disgust, and pepper his speech with more bland courtesies in a day than he'd use in a year at home. To him, 'please' showed a lack of gumption; 'thank you' was toadying servility. "Just say what you want," he would say to my pleading gaze at the dinner table when it fell on the butter or dish of meat. "Or stand up and take it. Don't sit waiting for the world to notice that you want something. No one cares."

Farming was all but extinct in the area, but men who grew at least something on a plot of land they hadn't surrendered to some real estate developer were the ones he respected the most. Our little home was riddled with patches of garden, and tending them filled him with stoic joy. The house itself was quite new in the area, a short-sale from some tree-besotted soul who built it as a 'rural retreat' and then decided that it was 'too rustic.' The wood paneling coating every surface in the house was solid, but too sleek and immaculate to have the centuries-old character my father craved. In his opinion, objects should either tell a story or make room for others that did. His father had died when he was young, unintentionally bequeathing his tools and guns to my father. His unspoken disappointment attested that I had not yet earned my place in the sacred chain of ownership.

From an early age, I suspected that my path lay in the footsteps of my mother, not my father. The few memories I had of her were as murky in my mind as a film I had seen once and then almost forgotten. My father very rarely mentioned her, and the few sparse allusions were cautionary examples. Any questions I had were always answered with: "It doesn't matter. She's gone, and good riddance." I learned to stop asking, and eventually to stop even mentioning her.

The few photos which survived my father's purge showed the house had once been a haven of warmth, with pictures, a china hutch, decorative plates, trinkets, and bric-a-brac sitting smartly on every available shelf and tabletop. The home my father had sculpted from its ashes was strictly utilitarian, little more than a warren of sturdy, home-built shelves that stood almost empty. His guns were in the wall rack and, to my eye, he took as much joy from cleaning them as he did from bouts of shooting at cans in the property's vast grassy expanses. The only other items on the wall were a framed picture of him with his college hunting club, and a yellowing newspaper article about some other town, the purpose or relevance of which I was never able to discern. My bedroom was as stark as his, with nothing that might distinguish it from a hotel room. My father built my bed and desk, hewn from ash or walnut trees he'd felled in the woods, and were likely sturdy enough to survive a car's impact without losing more than a splinter or two.

Although he frequently chastised me for being too timid, my father enjoyed the silence my meekness imparted to the house. While watching television, he would station himself on the couch, engross himself in a program or football game, and then turn it off. There was never ambient music or anything on 'in the background'. "Just do one thing. Do it right," he was fond of saying. Despite his faults, his way of life was admirable, his philosophy consistent. He paid his tithe to financial exigencies in a suit and tie, but kept that walled off from his home life. His neglect of me was a salutary lesson that I welcomed and appreciated more and more over time.

The lesson of the hobo on that fateful afternoon was much more poignant and immediate. I met the tattered prophet when I was twelve, during one of my meanderings amidst the ancient stones after school. Between my arrival at home and when my father got in from work, I had the run of the woods. If I was at my desk working on my homework when he got in, he tended to not even ask about what had transpired before I got there. As I edged towards my teenage years, his hands-off approach to parenting began to allow traces of begrudging respect. His attitude evolved from a typical "Suit yourself" to add a silent coda: "You probably know best what you need."

When I reached my normal haunt, I did so in a loping stride, something more akin to a ridiculous dance than a useful gait. Grabbing the side of the chapel with one hand, I pivoted on one foot, making a huge loop through the air with the other and landing in a crouch—only to see an old man sitting braced against one of the stone pillars.

The vagrant's eyes were as smoothly closed as those of a corpse. I gave an involuntary jump as they flew open a second later, perfectly trained on me as if he'd been looking through his eyelids. But my customary fear did not build on this initial shock to compel me to flee. His aspect was that of a shabby, unkempt, yet kindly grandfather who'd wandered off. White whiskers seeped out at wild angles from his tan, wrinkled skin. His eyes were a very light blue under a cloudy sheen with gobs of bright white creeping across the surface, rendering the irises a mottled patchwork. They quickly jumped by me and darted around, scanning for others in the area. When they resettled on me, they had surrendered their wariness—and had been the only part of him which had moved at all.

"Don't worry," I said to his silent question. "I live here."

"Here in the woods?" His voice, puzzlement tinged with admiration, wove itself into the stillness of the day.

"No." I gestured vaguely towards home. "Up the path."

Although later years have revealed that his affliction was likely cataracts, and that he probably ended his days blind, my younger self was hypnotized by the milky gaze that hinted at a touch of the mystical. I convinced myself that he saw beyond the awkward boy, an outcast from every social group and his own family, perhaps viewing great deeds and adventures that lay in my future. One of his hands vanished into his coat and fished out a bottle filled with something whose pungent scent, when the cap was unscrewed, wafted unpleasantly over the afternoon in mere seconds. "So, young buck," he said as he took a sip. "What brings you out here?"

Trying to feign nonchalance at his presence as though I were no stranger to fellow wayfarers, I casually answered "I come here sometimes." I tried not to hint at the fact that this little oasis was the only pocket of peace I was liable to find in the world, and that I treasured it accordingly. "And, uh," I asked, trying not to force the question, "why are you here?"

"Just passing through, young buck," he said with a smile. He turned his face to the cloudy sky, drinking in the pleasing coolness with a sigh. "So," he said, still gazing heavenwards, "do you come here to look at dirty magazines?"

"Just to think," I said, my tone level and guard unraised.

"Yes," he conceded with a thoughtful nod, his clouded gaze meeting my eager one. "A man needs a place to think."

"What do you do?"

"I wander the world," he said. "Finding employment as necessary. I see corners of the country that have been just about forgotten in these changing times. I stroll, hitchhike, or ride the rails in my eternal pilgrimage."

"That's what I want to do too," I said.

"It's a good life, if you keep your wits about you."

"How many of the states have you been to?" At twelve years old, I imagined that question to be a fair gauge of a person's worldliness.

"Most," he replied cryptically. Sitting up with a start, his eyes scanned the trees again, wary lest some unseen brigade materialize from the autumn-stained underbrush. Satisfied that we were alone, he settled against the pillar again.

"Which state is your favorite?" I asked.

"Hmm," he said pensively. "Well, I loved it out west. Perhaps the forests of California. No," he corrected himself. "Washington. The forests of Washington."

"I've heard," I ventured, "that there are trees you can drive a car through."

"I've done it," he said, his milky eyes looking past me as though he could see them out in the expanses of maples and comparatively paltry pines. He took a sip from the bottle. "Hell, I've climbed a few of them."

"Really?"

"Well," he conceded, "not the same ones you drive a car through. But I've managed to mount some sky-scraping trees. I worked as a logger. For a time. A man earns extra as a topper, so I volunteered any time I could."

"Why do toppers earn more?" I asked, happily

trying out the word as though I were an old pro with industry terms.

"Hazard pay," he said with a sad smile. "Things happen up in those branches. Not always the safest place to be."

"People die?"

"Sure do. It's more common to see a comrade be terribly hurt than to die, but I've seen both. I've watched men die in boxcars and in jungles. On back roads and in cheap shacks. In sun and shade. I've seen men die of thirst, and watched them drown. Most don't mean to do it and try to avoid doing it, but I've seen men die on purpose from time to time."

"Like in war?" I asked.

His face twisted into a semblance of a smile, undergirded by sadness that was apparent, even to me. "Well, I have seen men die in battle, but they never meant to. I've seen some drink themselves to death, and watched others get too tired and worn down to do anything else. One day, a buddy of mine and I were in the desert, out southwest. We watched the sun go down, paint the whole horizon in brilliant colors as we passed a bottle back and forth. He told me it had been the best day of his life. Then he walked off into the darkness. He never came back. When I found him the next morning, I saw his body lying on the sand, his throat cut out."

"Who did it?"

"He did it himself. Still had the knife in his hand, blood all over his fingers."

"Why?"

He shrugged. "Wish I knew. Men can do strange

things. Drink?" he asked, his tone wavering between question and command. I had never touched alcohol, due to my father's decree and my own lack of curiosity, but I took the proffered bottle without question, telling myself it signified fellowship and acceptance. The crows barked from the spare-branched pines as though to encourage me as the bottle's moist glass touched my lips. I sipped tepidly, expecting to recoil from a vile and harsh sting. Instead, the whiskey slid over my tongue and down my throat as gently as water. The man did not seem to mind that I took another swig before giving it back to him.

As I handed it over, I asked "Do you remember everyone you've lost?"

He shook his head while drinking long and deep. "No. I used to keep a running ledger of faces, names that went with most of them too. But time goes ever onwards, the numbers of the dead climb, and my mind is starting to...mix things up. Things blur."

"I want to leave," I said wistfully. "I don't know how."

"You're young yet," he said. Having decided that he was not some ranting or delusional killer, I entertained a brief hope that he would ask me along on his adventures. An old man with magical far-seeing eyes walking the Earth with his young acolyte. He made no invitation, however, but stared at the darkness that was swallowing the afternoon.

"What do I do?" I asked him. "How can I leave?"

"Just..." In the silence that followed, I feared that he had either dropped off to sleep or forgotten the question. Finally he said "Just don't forget that you want to leave. A lot of folks think they want to leave. Almost all of them forget." He drank deep and then handed the bottle to me. I followed his lead, grimacing slightly this time as the liquid threatened to rumble backwards out of my mouth again with a bile sting that I only barely choked back. The chapel in the woods danced a bit in my eyes, almost merging with the dawning darkness. I stood to hand him the bottle, but felt myself wavering.

"I want to leave," I said. "My mother left."

"How many folks live around here?" he asked as he gave the bottle back. My next swig was as smooth as the first.

"A few. But we have some space. Between neighbors." My voice was slow and syrupy.

"Nice," he said admiringly. "How many people come to these woods?"

"Just me," I answered proudly.

"Mmm," he said, glancing around as nervously as when I'd first encountered him.

Within a few moments I was sitting beside him, propped against the ancient statue. When the bottle returned my way I waved it off. He accepted the refusal with aplomb. "You're a good kid," he said slowly. "Maybe...I don't know. Maybe you should stay put."

I leaned back on the moss-fuzzed stone robe of the statue. The hand that found my face was akin to the sand-paper my father used to shave splinters off his creations, but it was not unpleasant. Nor did it linger. "What's your name?" I asked when I opened my eyes, but there was only the thinnest trace of deep blue hugging the outline of the mountains. He was gone. I found that I could stand easier, that the effects of the whiskey had been somewhat tamed by my nap, but the walk back to the house in the dark was still slow and treacherous.

"What the hell is wrong with you?" my father asked as I tottered in the door after the wake of dusk had faded to night. His beer was set down on the table and he'd crossed the room in a few brisk strides, shoving his face into mine before I had any idea what was happening. His nostrils flaring he pulled his face back and stood at his full height to glare down at me.

"You've been drinking," he said coldly. Though not overly given to caring about what I did in my own time, there were a handful of activities which were, for his son, explicit taboos. He frequently and preemptively reminded me that he knew the exact level of each bottle in the liquor cabinet, and how many beers he had in the fridge. Whenever he spoke of one of the men in town as 'a drunk', his voice would curl into an intense timbre of hatred.

My ear was ringing along with a sting to my cheek before I'd even seen him raise his hand. Instead of crying or looking around, however, I raised my gaze to meet his; courage might dissuade him from striking again in a way that cowering never would. "Just a little bit," I admitted.

"Yeah, a little bit is how it starts. You want to become a worthless drunk like your fool of a grandfather was?"

"But your father wasn't—"

My face was stinging once more and I couldn't help the tears creeping out of my eyes when the force of his next blow, doubled by anger, caught me again with blinding speed. "You're damn right he wasn't, you little sonovabitch. But your other grandfather was a drunk. Used to get himself liquored up every night. Then he'd laugh, yell, start crying, and start hitting. I had to lay out the worthless bastard a few times. He couldn't hold down a job. Even his children hated him." This oblique reference to my mother was more mention than he'd given her in years. "Is that what you want?"

"No," I mumbled.

"I can't hear you."

"No!" I all but shouted.

"Good. Then tell me where you got the stuff."

Exhaling deeply, I felt confusion and alcohol causing me to waver on my feet. I tried to stumble towards the couch, but my father's hand grabbed my shoulder and pulled me back to face him. "I...um," I offered helplessly.

"Don't 'um' me, boy. Where did you get it?"

"I was walking in in the woods, and I met a guy out by the old chapel."

"A guy? Friend of yours from school?"

"No. He was like a hobo or something."

"What?! Some bum in the woods got you liquored up?"

"I just had a couple of sips," I said, expecting the mask of anger he stared at me from to be accompanied by another of his lightning-quick slaps. Instead, he grabbed my shoulders.

"What the hell did he do to you?" he said, shaking me as though he'd caught me stealing from his wallet again.

"What? Nothing. We talked about stuff."

"Yeah, what kinda stuff?"

"He told me he rode the rails."

"Betcha he did," he responded through clenched teeth. "Where'd he touch you?"

"He shook my hand," I replied brusquely. It seemed unwise to mention his leathery hand's gentle touch on my face.

"Drop your pants."

"W-what?" I said.

"Now!"

Terrified, I undid, my belt, drawing out the process in hope that he'd lose interest or his anger would abate before he started on the whipping I was sure I was in for. His glare sped me up, however, and I bent over to present my bare backside, gritting my teeth against the pain of the wallop I was sure was coming. I thought I'd outgrown these disciplinary sessions, and steeled myself to keep silent when the blows came, as a way of earning back whatever respect I'd lost. Instead, he spread apart my buttocks and started probing around. "That hurt?" he asked as his finger prodded the edge of my anus.

"N-no," I said, confused.

"Lucky boy," he said, letting go. "If that sonovabitch is lucky, he'll be gone by the time I get to him." He had already gotten the shotgun from the rack, and was busily loading shells into it before I could tell him that the hobo had already moved on. "Pull yer damn pants up!" he barked. "Now listen. I'm going to lock this door, and I don't want you to open it for anyone. The only one who comes in here is me, and I have the key. So you do not touch this door! Got it?"

"Yes sir."

"When do you open this door, boy?"

"I don't."

"Good boy," he said with a scowling nod. "Stay put."

The song of the robins had not abated in the darkness, and I listened to it as I lay on the couch letting the room swim around me. The crows too had clung to the last few threads of light in order to bellow out their demands into the woods. Owls and night peepers were already making their songs heard, and I tried to imagine the sound of trains rattling along tracks nearby. One empty boxcar would be all it would take. I had no desire to end up a bum in the woods, but I knew there was only so long I could stay put.

My mother had shaken off my father's yoke and walked away from everything she'd known. The troubling image of her as a bag lady in some city, a filthy creature begging for nickels as she pushed her filthy life around in a shopping cart, found its way into my mind, but I batted it away. I tried to replace it with one of her standing at the edge of a forest whose trees were large enough to hold up the sky, but fell asleep on the couch unable to focus on much of anything.

When he finally returned, my father shook me awake and told me to get the hell to bed. "You're getting up at dawn," he said. "It's high time I taught you how to shoot."

The next morning was the first time he let me handle his guns. The only other time I'd taken one from the rack, just to hold it, prompted a beating so merciless that I was dissuaded from even going near them, lest I bump one out of place. Oddly enough, as he held the .22 rifle, a greater calm came over him than I'd ever seen. The tension dissolved, creeping through only when we stood facing the line of cans he'd set up.

"Every time you squeeze the trigger," he said, "I want you to imagine that pervert bastard's face in your sights." I tried to follow his instruction, but found that the milky eyes and their sad gaze were hardly an inducement to fire. But I found an acceptable substitute. The method of shooting I developed that day would carry me far away from the world where I grew up. I would pull the triggers of many rifles, sometimes with a human being in the crosshairs. Each time I sighted a target—whether it was hunting squirrels near the chapel before I left home, in combat, in competition, or the peace of the woods in a deer-blind—I used the same technique to summon traces of anger just long enough to focus on a single point and send the round home. Daylight crept across the first morning I spent shooting with my father, narrowing my aim even further until I was knocking the cans over more times than I missed, a ratio that would reach the level of mastery in the coming years.

My father clapped me on the back. "Good shooting," he said, with unprecedented pride. "You really gave it to that sonovabitch!"

"Yeah," I said. "I really did."

~~~~~~~~

Going Home

Joyce deCordova

It was a smooth flight. That was good, he thought, as his stomach was unsettled and he had slept poorly. In spite of the almost weekly short hops he took managing his clients in the northeast, he never had a restful sleep the night before he traveled. There was always the anxiety of not waking up in time (he set three alarms), or getting stuck in traffic (he lived half an hour away, but always allowed three hours to get to the airport). But today was different. He was going home for the first time in twenty years.

He started to reminisce and thought of the day he set foot on US soil when he was 21. He had a tourist visa, so he never suffered the horrors of the undocumented coming from all over the world. Of course he had read about them crossing waters in rickety boats, burrowing through tunnels, climbing walls, crossing deserts, braving bombs and mine traps. He was grateful to be one of the lucky ones. All his papers were in order, so he sailed through customs and never looked back.

Until now.

Before he came to the States, he remembered his grandmother telling him stories of those that had left more than a generation before him. They knew they would never see one another again, but they lovingly lied, hugging and caressing each other, willing themselves to stamp the memory of each other's face into their very being. They took photos, trying to hide their grief by standing tall and determined. In spite of promising to come back, most never did.

The world is different now, he thought. We have email, iPhones, Skype; we stay connected. Every week for the last twenty years, he saw his mother on Facetime or Skype. He was sadly aware of the wrinkles becoming more embedded, her hair grayer and thinner; her body rounder. He saw the funeral held for his father...his idol, and the family giving him a virtual hug with an anguish that they all felt and crying tears he could see but could not taste. He saw his brothers and their wives and children growing older. They showed him images of the cows they bought and the houses they were building with the money he was sending faithfully every month. There is a family compound now thanks to him, they said, and they are grateful and he feels proud.

His family chose him to come. He would have stayed in his country. It was familiar to him, and he'd never liked change, nor did he have that sense of adventure of the young. That need to "spread his wings" was not part of his DNA. So why him? He was the youngest and had no wife or babies and, most importantly, the family felt he had the most saleable skill. He was a carpenter, having been one of the fortunate ones who learned the trade from his father as well as from a vocational school. So, like Moses, he was chosen to go to the Promised Land.

But it wasn't a land of milk and honey, and there were no streets paved with gold. It was a land of strange foods that made him vomit and gave him diarrhea off and on for months, and the streets paved with blacktop asphalt lasted only one or two winters before the snow and ice made them crack, only to be tarred again.

Life was hard. But his family was counting on him and even though he was homesick, he had to succeed for their sake, if not for his own. He rented a bed from a fellow countryman along with five other men who were also struggling. He felt lucky to get a job as a dishwasher for $6 an hour, saving every penny and working as many hours as he could. Imagine, he would muse, in my country I used my hands to make fine cabinets and furniture and now, here I am with my hands in harsh soap and scalding hot water for 12 hours a day. But he took solace in the fact that his situation was not unusual. Among his roommates was a fellow who, in his native country, was an accountant and now was mopping floors at the local bank.

The immigrant network is a beautiful thing. It is universal. Every nationality has it and it would be difficult, if not impossible, to survive without it. It is quiet. It is oral. Many come with the attitude of every man for himself, but then each realizes that they need the connection of one person to another, so they share what they have because, if for no other reason, they know that they need each other to survive. It's not necessarily because they are kind and altruistic; it's usually because they are in survival mode.

So, a word from one led to another and his dishwashing days were over. He started working for a local carpenter in a small town. He was doing all the grunt work, but didn't care because anything was better than washing dishes. Gradually the boss recognized his talent and, more importantly, how much profit he could make. For a few years, he felt good about the fact that he was responsible for his boss' wealth. In fact, his skills were what built his employer's new home, and he was proud of it. Between his meager salary and the odd jobs he found on his own, he kept his family out of poverty, and he was proud of that as well. He was fulfilling his mission.

But, as time passed, it wasn't enough. He wanted to go home, but knew he couldn't. He had set up a pattern with his family and now he was responsible for them as well as responsible for the isolation he now felt. He was alone and in limbo. He couldn't go back, but could he go forward? He thought of himself as a money machine, an ATM that his family relied on. Was this his future? He was uprooted at 21 and now, at 28, his roots had to be replanted somewhere, otherwise they would wither and die. He needed to belong and he needed to feel safe. He needed to be able to hold his head up, walk the streets, get rid of the rickety bike and drive a car and get rid of the fear that his deportation was just a matter of time and would happen when he least expected it.

So he went back to the network and was introduced to a 30 year old Puerto Rican woman who would marry him for $20,000. "Here is the contract, and this is how it works" she said. "You give me $5,000 now; $5,000 when we marry at City Hall. We stay together for three years until you get your green card, and then I will divorce you and you will give me the other $10,000."

So that was the plan. At first, she wanted no part of him and he felt the same. This was a business arrangement. He moved into her tiny one bedroom flat and slept on a pull out couch. They wore wedding rings. They had a joint bank account and religiously put in the same amount each month so all expenses were split down the middle. Their interviews with Immigration went well. Time passed and his green card was issued. He was safe and, unexpectedly, he was happy with his wife.

Oh, she was no beauty; far from it, but her body matched her personality. Even though the rice and beans had thickened her middle, she was solid and strong and they both felt safe and secure with each other. They decided to stay together and to put the balance of the $10,000 that he owed her towards opening up their own carpentry business, buying a truck, tools and machinery. They thrived. And, somehow, amid all the frenzy of coping with unexpected success, the uncertainties of making payroll, and meeting impossible client deadlines, they also managed to have two sons.

It was the beginning of their virtual reality family. His sons knew their cousins, grandmother, aunts and uncles not through Sunday meals (although they were 'present') but rather through technology. When they 'visited' the family, they were all cleaned up and of course on their best behavior. But it wasn't genuine and it wasn't real. This bothered him so much so that his wife encouraged him to go and visit his family. He needed to touch, smell and embrace, and Skype and Facetime were just not enough.

So there he was, on a plane going home.

Upon arriving, the weather gave him a kick in the chest. It was oppressively hot and humid; he could hardly breathe. The small airport had no air conditioning, and his clothes immediately became damp and stuck to his skin as if they had been glued. But that was quickly forgotten when he saw his family, except for his mother who was too frail to travel, all waiting to greet him and take him home. They ran towards each other and hugged and caressed and looked into each other's faces, touching and feeling skin and hair...all denied them for over 20 years.

During the bumpy two hour ride to his home, they spoke of the feast they were planning that night in his honor. They were disappointed that he could only stay for three days, but they understood that he had to get back to his work and his family. Finally they arrived at the house, so much smaller than what he had remembered from his youth. There was his mother. His first thought was that she had shrunk. She was no longer the proud straight-back woman he had left 21 years ago. Even though he had visited with her on Skype, he had failed to notice how much shorter and more frail she had become. She caressed his face and he was ashamed of himself for feeling a sense of unease. Her hands were rough and smelled of foods and spices tucked away in his memory and, instead of finding comfort in them, he found her smell to be strange and his reaction was somewhat disconcerting to him. How interesting, he thought, that childhood memories he had treasured and coddled and gave him comfort all these years no longer did.

She wouldn't let go of his hand. She was afraid that if she did, he would disappear and never come back, so she held on. He endured her touch.

He asked his family to describe a typical day of living on the compound, and it seemed they were all supervisors. With his money, they hired their friends and neighbors to tend to the cows, plow the fields, reap the harvest and build their houses. Gradually it dawned on him that his brothers had become overseers. All these years of imagining them toiling in the hot sun with their hands becoming calloused, weathered and gnarled, was changed as he felt their hands, which were smoother than his own.

The next two days were full of people, relatives and friends hugging him and thanking him for all he had done for his family, and in turn, for them. Each night, he would crawl into his lumpy bed and, in spite of the comfort that the foods gave him, his unsettled stomach churned. His departing there couldn't come soon enough, and a wave of guilt came over him because he couldn't wait to leave. He had to put on a mask of sadness and distress that he was going back to the States. They begged him to stay longer and he made believe that he was torn and was seriously considering staying a few more days, but how could he? His wife and sons were waiting for him (how he missed them!) and his business would suffer if he didn't get back.

His business would suffer? That they understood. After all, he was their cash cow. So, amid tears and hugs, he left.

On the flight back, he went over the trip in his mind. He now realized that for years, he had been living in two time zones. Throughout most days, he would look at his watch and visualize what his family would be doing. They would be having lunch; they would be going to bed; or they would be out in the fields. Visually, he had each foot planted in two different lives. He needed to put them together and walk firmly and solidly on one path instead of two.

He now knew how to handle the future with his family. It was so clear to him. He likened it to a divorce. There is a marriage, and there is a history in that marriage, and then, for a myriad of reasons, it ends. Even when it ends amicably, there is a price to be paid. It is called alimony, and that is what he would pay for the rest of his life.

As the flight continued, he slowly began to feel like himself again. There was the down pillow for his head and the soft blanket to wrap himself in. There were the flight attendants with familiar foods and drinks. There was music he could listen to (he loved smooth jazz). Yes, he sighed, he was going home.

~~~~~~~~

Bar Association

Gerard Meade

It's Friday, crowded as usual with end of week revelers. I'm familiar with most of them, at least by sight, but new faces constantly pop up. If they hang around for a while, which many don't since the place is kinda quaint, I'll come to know them well. Keeping up with the demands of a thirsty crowd is second nature for me, so I can stay on top of things, yet still manage to be conversational. I usually spot the newcomers straight off and make a point of welcoming them. Tonight there's a few, hooking up late with co-workers or meeting friends for drinks.

The old school juke box is cranked, voices are necessarily raised in order to be heard. This is the crescendo that leads to the evening's climax. It won't last all that long. I know, I've been here for years and seen it many times over. A couple of folks I don't recognize enter separately and squeeze their way through the crowd to join a group near the end of the rail. Filling orders and refilling empties, I work my way down to this gathering of regulars as introductions are made. There's some shuffling of chairs as a few of the group depart and the new ones snag stools two apart.

Their orders are as different as their appearance, one requesting 'beer and a shot', the other a Sazerac. While constructing the unusual cocktail I ask for preferences, which brew, shot of what? That answer and the orders will be the last words exchanged directly with these two for the majority of their stay.

As predicted, and is fairly typical of this last workday for most, the crowd thins early. Eventually the juke goes silent and one of the suit-types requests that I tune to CNN on our lone screen. Not being one for that stuff, I comply but leave the sound muted. My environment will provide all I need, my preference being the entertainment offered unknowingly by my clientele. A cluster of ladies will soon need to be cut off at one end of the bar, the remnants of a boisterous group of male regulars hover nearby like wolves over a lamb. The two newbies remain in place although the crew they joined disburses, Sazerac nursing the initial cocktail while the other is far more ambitious in consuming tap Bud and JD. While straightening and cleaning, my attention keeps drifting back to them. Sazerac: nerdy, with the big black specs to prove it: and Bud: long haired, kinda scruffy—hippy style, do speak occasionally but not directly to each other. Saz focuses the bulky spectacles on the silent talking heads and speaks out loudly every now and then, not to anyone in particular but rather as if addressing the tap handles. Bud, seemingly more intent on the cash still before him, does the same just after, not in response to what Saz has voiced, but instead he delivers commentary from left field, entirely unrelated. I find the non-conversation quite interesting.

The two had been casually introduced by mutual friends when they joined the crew of regulars. The post-work party then resumed and I noticed no further interaction between them and their new acquaintances; they'd simply taken their stools and basically kept to themselves. At this point in the evening, with much of the crowd gone and the din slowly diminishing, their intermittent blurbs are clear; distinct, disjointed, unexpected, and often quite revealing.

Apparently Sazerac knows technology like Greeks know diners. Bud can name the guitarist in that band who had one hit in '72 and knows who produced the record, he's blurted similar tidbits about performers from Judy Garland to Mylie Cyrus. Unable to help it, I'm captivated by the duo, and strain to hear details in each unpredictable outburst. Thoroughly enjoying it as I work, my eavesdropping spares me the flashes of alleged breaking, or fake, news and breaks the monotony of the never-ending tedious maintenance. Polishing glasses, it occurs to me that these two portray the unique, diverse, and eclectic style of not only the bar but the collection of tracks in the old Rock-Ola as well.

I finally give the ladies in the corner the boot, the pack of wolves follow in hope, and the vast majority of stools now lack partners. Saz and Bud stay put until they're eventually the last to leave. They rise to settle up almost simultaneously and depart in similar fashion to how they earlier non-conversed: together but...not. My contrived, yet authentic, 'convivial host' thing seems to fall flat when neither really responds to my thanks and well wishes, but both leave very generous tips. I find myself smiling for quite some time after locking the door.

Eight years later, still standing behind the stick, I shrug off the last of that reverie. Many have come and gone since, but Saz and Bud are still steady customers. I've been told, of course, that those aren't really their names. When they come in, they still sit two stools apart, as close as possible to their original spot on the far side of the taps. One of our usual suspects long ago clued me in. It turns out that Sazerac is actually Sloan, but Bud? Well, guess I nailed that one, but I don't call them by name since they've never mentioned them to me personally. I did once say: "What's up Bud?" but that was before I'd been schooled. The drink orders remain the same but Sloan now picks up the check for both. The reason, the same knowledgeable source also informed me, is that Sloan and Bud were married just last year...go figure.

Over time there have been many who questioned my perceived underachievement, my family had expressed their concerns rather vociferously, but I'm really quite content. It seems to me that many, if not most, who take issue with my lack of professional progression are miserable in their own pursuits. Not me. I like Fridays. I like my customers. I love my job!

~~~~~~~~

JUST DAYS

WILLIAM RUE

In two days Cordie would be jetting off with James. Over the past week Paul had discovered (from cryptic notes on the downstairs phone's message pad, scribbles on scraps of paper left in the shed, favorite websites on her laptop) that they were off to Bermuda. He still didn't know where they'd be staying or for how long, and she wouldn't tell him.

"What if I need to contact you?"

It was near dark and they were standing in the kitchen, Cordie by the side door and Paul at the stove where, wooden spoon in hand, he waited for a pot of water to boil. The twins were in the living room tuning out to a Nickelodeon sit-com. He slammed the spoon on the counter and spun to face her. "What if something happens to the guys and I need to reach you? Did you ever once consider that?"

Eyes edgy, she took her phone from her purse, carefully pressed a button and the cellphone beeped. "Of course I've considered that," she replied indifferently.

He tore open a box of macaroni and cheese, and with shaky fingers fished out the foil packet, shook it, and ripped it open savagely. A puff of Day-Glo orange chemical powder drifted up into the still air. "So you're just going to disappear with this asshole indefinitely..."

"He's not an asshole," she snapped. "And stop using that word in front of the guys."

A long, silent staring match ended when he turned from her and blindly dumped the noodles into the boiling water. A few missed and scattered on the stovetop. He didn't bother to pick them up. Posture hunched, he nodded. "So you're just going to run off and not tell anyone where the hell you are, or how anyone can reach you in an emergency?"

"Laura knows how to reach me."

"And what if I can't reach her?"

She slowly placed her cellphone on top of the dryer; a tiny red LED light blinked. A smirk tilted the corner of her mouth as she said: "Laura's a damn shut-in...never goes anywhere. Don't worry: you'll be able to reach her."

An uneasy silence. Just the television sounds drifting in from the next room.

"Why don't you tell me where you're staying, at least?"

"Because I don't want you calling us."

"I know you're going to Bermuda. Just give me the name of the hotel, so I can at least leave a message at the desk."

"No. Call my cellphone."

"It's out of the U.S. It may not work."

"Bermuda's just off the coast. It should work," she said. "Or you can just call Laura."

He smiled to himself. "So it is Bermuda."

After hesitating: "Yes. James is taking me to Bermuda," she said proudly. "And he's paying for everything."

He busied himself stirring the pasta which bubbled away, didn't need stirring. "What does Laura think about all this?"

"She thinks I should have dumped you years ago."

He vaguely doubted that. He'd always gotten along with Laura, always sensed that she liked him, and his company. They had an easy rapport, enjoyed much of the same music, many of the same films. Cordie had once (years ago, just after Laura's divorce from Clayton) told him she suspected Laura had something of a crush on him. And Paul had been, deeply (and secretly) attracted to her. For fifteen years. Ever since that first night on the deck of his parents' house on Captiva... and the window that looks out on Corcovado.

His words came slowly: "So Laura knew all about this guy. The whole time."

She smiled. "I think she's actually a little jealous. I don't think she's had a boyfriend in, like, two years, or something."

"I seriously doubt anyone's jealous."

"A lot of my friends are."

"Of some old souse you met in rehab?"

"He's not a souse," she said. "He has a disease."

"He's a drunk who is as old as your dad."

Her nostrils flared almost imperceptibly, but she ignored that. "At least he's making an effort to get better. James is making a concerted effort to beat his disease. Which is a hell of a lot more than I can say about you and your depression," she spat. "He's taking steps."

"Taking steps," he repeated. "May be a little unsteadily, but hey."

"You're just angry and you're jealous and I get that," she told him haughtily. "I totally get it." She stepped away from the door, moved closer. "And you know what, Paul: I feel sorry for you." Her familiar smirk. Then after seconds of dramatic pause, she repeated her assertion.

"I feel sorry for you." His voice had risen, the words were peevish and immature. He now regretted saying them.

She laughed. "Sorry for me? Why feel sorry for me?"

He had no answer to that. Stood there dumbly at the stove, stirring pasta that didn't need stirring.

"In two days, I'll be on a pink sand beach. With another man," she crowed. "And you'll still be here. Wrapped up in your miserable, pathetic little life."

"My miserable, pathetic life?" he threw back at her. She smiled, saying nothing. "Taking care of our children in their home. While you are off on some beach fucking some guy as old as your dad that you just met in rehab." He pulled the pot of boiling water off the stove and slammed it down on a large, tarnished slab of butcher block. "You met in rehab! Doesn't that register at all with you? The very...absurdity of it?"

She edged back to the door. "You don't understand the disease," she said, fiddling with her cellphone. He wondered if she wasn't somehow recording their conversation. "James does...and understands me in ways you never can, or will."

"This isn't about your disease," he said. "This is about responsibility...your obligations as a parent. It's about your children. Hoyt and David. Remember them?"

She held her cellphone out and he noticed the LED now stayed lit, no longer blinking. He thought of grabbing it from her and hurling it against the wall.

"I'm a good parent," she said quietly, evenly. "Don't you ever question that or try and throw that in my face."

"Abandoning your kids for a vacation at an undisclosed location is being a good parent? Since fucking when?"

"I am not abandoning them."

"Oh? And if Hoyt wants to say goodnight to you, or have you read him a story?" He yanked a pair of oven mitts off a peg by the stove. "What's he going to do, huh?"

She stood there leaning back against the dryer, arms folded across her chest, jaw working silently.

"What can he do? Call Aunt Laura?" he pressed. "Ask her to pass along a god damned message to mommy?"

A long, silent staring match. She turned away, nodded, and said: "I'll check in every night. That make you happy?"

"Don't do it for me," he told her quietly. "Do it for your children."

As her cellphone's red LED stared him down, he drained the pasta into a colander in the sink and said calmly: "And another thing... Do you really have to talk to this guy in the house? Can't you take the phone outside or something? I mean, that's just being obnoxious." A gust of vapor rose off the slippery pile as he shook the water from the colander.

She smiled. "I thought you said you didn't care."

He put the empty pot in the sink. "In front of them," he hissed, jabbing a finger toward the living room. "They don't need to be exposed to this."

She reached out and began distractedly fiddling with her phone. She seemed to be reading a text message.

"This is all very confusing to them," he stated, as if that was a news flash. "Don't you see that?"

She didn't respond, didn't even look up from her phone. He let out a deep breath, carried the colander over to a large china bowl on the counter, dumped the steaming noodles into it. "I'm going to fight for the guys, you know."

"Sure. Good luck with that."

She put her phone down on the dryer. He sliced off a too thick slab of butter and dropped it carelessly into the bowl. "I spoke to Barry about all of this," he said, stirring the bowl with unnecessary vigor. "About your latest trip, recent behavior... your drinking, which has accelerated. Got provably worse." Pause. "So we're filing a motion seeking full custody."

"You won't get it."

"We might."

She leaned back, glaring at him, eyes unblinking. After a shake of her head, she grabbed her phone, slipped it back in her purse and replied quietly, smugly: "Have fun trying."

"The court date is one week from Thursday," he said, then smiled. "You may be flying back early." A bellowing silence engulfed them; he shrugged. "Sorry."

"We'll just push it back until we return," she retorted. "Nice try." After a tight-lipped smile, she turned and walked out the door in silence.

Paul waited a few seconds before following to stand at the open door and watch her get into her car. He then went back to the stove and took a bite of the pasta. Undercooked. He scraped the greasy heap into the garbage, refilled the pot with water and had just placed it back on the burner when he heard the car thunder to life.

Hurrying back to the door, he leaned against the jamb, shoulders slumped, as Cordie still sat in her silver Mustang convertible out there. He watched her light a cigarette and roll down the window, watched her reach into her bag, grab her cellphone (with its still glaring red demon's eye) and tap some numbers on its keypad. He watched her smoke and talk and laugh into her phone for minutes. She was still smoking and talking and laughing when she jammed the car into reverse, backed out of the driveway and happily drove off, music blasting, her wind-blown hair flying wildly behind.

~~~~~~~~

Cordie had been in Bermuda for four days when the letter of termination from one of her clients arrived (giving him the excuse he needed to call and perhaps put a little damper on her honeymoon with that old drunkard). He found Laura's number scribbled on a pad by the kitchen phone. He'd come to believe Cordie, that Laura was somehow in on this; that in her loneliness, her constant need for drama, she'd egged on her friend to pursue this extramarital affair; that perhaps she got some sort of twisted, vicarious thrill out of it all. Two of her marriages had failed and, just maybe, she had secretly, or subconsciously, wanted his and Cordie's to fail as well.

"Hello?"

"Laura. It's Paul. I need to contact Cordie," he said in a quiet, neutral voice. "I need her number in Bermuda."

He could hear television noise in the background, then: "Oh my God. How are you?"

"I've been better," he said coolly, staring down at a thin black thread of sugar ants marching across the countertop. "Do you have her number?"

"I have it here somewhere."

A long pause. He imagined her there in her apartment in Jacksonville, alone and watching TV. He tried to recall the last time he'd seen her, at least two years ago, late spring. That night, just an hour after dinner, Cordie abruptly excused herself, staggered upstairs and passed out in their room, leaving Laura and him downstairs watching Mystery Science Theatre. They'd sat on the couch, just inches apart, uneasily parroting snippets of the godawful dialogue, laughing a little too hard at each other's remarks and *aperçus*. It was humid, so all the windows in the house were wide open, and he could smell her fragrance. He watched the screen's bluish glow play over her face; sensed in her sly, playful smile that she was well aware he wasn't really paying all that much attention to the movie.

"She called me that morning from the airport."

"You knew about this guy for a while, didn't you?"

"She'd told me about him, yes."

"And you knew she was planning this little trip?"

"I had no idea."

"You had no idea," he repeated tonelessly.

"I had no idea she was going to do this."

He sipped his wine and vaguely watched the ants. The protracted silence got awkward.

"That Saturday," he heard Laura say. "She calls and tells me 'here I am at the airport...guess what I'm doing, honey? I'm getting on a plane and flyin' down to Mobile!'."

He swished his wineglass violently before tipping it back and draining the entire glass. "Interesting."

"I told her not to do it. I swear."

A thin black thread vibrating. Alive. *I need to buy more of those fucking traps.*

"I had no idea she was involved...romantically with him."

"Really?"

"No idea."

He went to the fridge and poured another glass of wine.

"You must be so hurt. I'm so sorry."

"Has she lost her fucking mind?"

"Yes. She has," she said. "She's lost her mind."

There was a drawn-out, staticky pause.

"I can't be her friend anymore. She has gone crazy. And she's toxic," Laura said. "Completely toxic."

"She called you from the airport?"

"I really tried to talk her out of doing this. She's gonna lose those boys, that's what I told her."

"I'm filing for divorce."

"She told me."

After a pause, "I've already hired a lawyer."

"Good."

The ants were moving in a line right around the traps. "And you really didn't know."

"She'd talked about this guy. They didn't hook up down there. This all happened after rehab. She was drunk one night and feeling sorry for herself and this lucky loser just happened to answer the damn phone when she was drinkin' and dialin'."

"She had me convinced you were somehow behind this."

"She said I was behind it?"

"Yeah."

"That's a damn lie."

"That's what she implied."

"Hell no."

He paced around the kitchen. "Bermuda?"

"Yeah. She's staying at the Hilton. I may have her room number. If not, it's under his name. The room."

"And she's with this guy right now." He turned his mind to distorted voices in the background. He could have sworn he heard a laugh track.

"She called me the other night. And I almost called you. I wanted so bad to call you and talk to you."

"Is she alright?"

She didn't reply. A plucked banjo. Canned laughter.

"Is she alright?"

"And you care?"

"What happened?"

"I swore I wouldn't tell you."

"Did he hit her? What?"

"No. He didn't hit her."

Silence. Just faint, churning TV sounds. "Tell me."

"No. I can't tell you, because I swore to her I wouldn't," she said. "Don't ask again, or I will hang up on you."

He recognized Don Knotts' voice. *Barney Fife.* After a long silence, "I just need the number."

She gave him the number and they hung up. He dialed the hotel. The woman at the desk had a delightful, plummy British accent and she connected him to the room. Cordie picked up the phone on the fourth ring. Paul pushed random buttons on the microwave panel.

"Having fun?"

"No, it's Paul," she called, while covering the mouthpiece. Bile rose from his stomach to his esophagus. His wife was at this moment sharing a hotel room with another man and he was talking to her. To them.

"As a matter of fact, we are."

"That's nice."

"So how are the guys?" she asked him, her voice breezy, uninterested. She was drunk.

"They're fine. But I'm not calling to chit-chat...and I really hate to interrupt your little tryst, but you got a letter today from Sylvia Mosbacher."

"Oh, Christ. She is such a pain in the ass," Cordie said. "What does she want?"

"She's firing you."

A stunned silence. A sound of flowing water. Distortion on the wires. "So, you open my snail mail now too?"

"You asked me to contact you if something like this came in," he told her. "You think I want to talk to you right now?"

Another brief silence, then: "Just hang onto it. I'll call her tomorrow and deal with it. This is the second time she's fired me from this job... It's bullshit, because she's not even paying me...her publisher is. She's nuts. She'll probably e-mail me tomorrow to rehire me," she laughed.

These ant traps are fucking useless. He watched the thin black thread stream around them. "So, how's the weather there in Bermuda?" he said, taking a healthy swig of his wine. "I heard it was raining."

"Yeah. Well, there's lots to do indoors."

He could just picture her smirk as she said that. He let out a breath. "Okay. Well. Have fun."

"Oh, we are."

"And I guess I'll see you in court."

"Good line," she cackled. "Wow! Very original!"

He slammed the phone down in its cradle, and paced the kitchen. After a few minutes he went to the refrigerator and pulled out the now half empty magnum of Pinot Grigio and poured another glassful. If he weren't drinking alone, he wouldn't have poured quite so much. He picked up the phone again and dialed. Two rings.

"Laura. It's me Paul, again."

"Hey, Paul again."

"I just spoke to Cordie," he said. No television sounds in the background. "What do you know about this guy?"

"C'mon. Don't do this."

"You have to tell me. I'm going crazy here."

"No."

"Why is she...fucking this guy?"

"You're just torturing yourself. Stop it."

"She told me...she told me he has a big cock."

She was silent. He gazed out the window. His old white haired neighbor—the ex-cop Dave, burly and red faced—was out there running a ridiculous oversized dust mop over his gleaming, bone-white Camaro.

"Is he good in bed?"

Laura stayed silent, but he could hear her breathing. He turned from the window and paced about. The peel-and-stick tiles he'd laid down so meticulously just a few months ago were already cracked and curling up darkly at the edges.

"Please," she finally implored.

"What has she told you about this guy?" he pleaded. "I need to know. I just...need to know."

"I can't talk to you about this."

"Tell me."

"I swore to her I wouldn't."

"I'll call her brothers," he said. He began to pace again. "Do they know about this?"

"I'm sure they know all about it, yes."

"Unbelievable. It's unbelievable. So she's really fucking this guy."

"I'm telling you: don't go there."

"Is he any good?"

"I'm going to hang up."

"No, no. Don't go." He ran as hand through his hair. *I do need to get a haircut, don't I?* "I'm sorry. I'll stop."

"Thinking about it'll just make you crazy. Don't."

He walked to the side door and opened it. "So they have fucked... Often?"

He looked out the door. Neighbor Dave was now giddily demonstrating his big dust mop to a hapless passerby, a young woman pushing a large stroller.

After a long, crackly silence: "What do you think?"

He felt bile swell higher inside him. "I don't want to."

"No, you really don't," she assured him, her voice calm, but a trace of impatience creeping in. "Don't think about it. It'll just make you crazy."

He just wanted to hold someone right now; he wanted to hold her. "They're probably fucking each other right now."

"Turn the bus around."

"What?"

"I said 'turn the bus around.'"

He cracked a smile, took a slug of his wine. "I like that expression." He repeated it, she said nothing. "Still there?"

"I'm still here."

He drained his glass, walked to the refrigerator, took out the large, sweaty bottle and poured another one, right to the top. "Where'd you get that expression?"

"It's my mom's. She always says that."

They were both quiet. There was a cricket somewhere in the house. *Must be behind the dryer.* He set his wineglass on the counter and slid his finger though the condensation, then ran his wet finger through the trail of ants, which sent them scattering, but only momentarily.

"Don't tell her we had this conversation."

"Paul. I'm not talking to her."

"I don't want her knowing how upset I am about all this. It'll just give her more satisfaction."

"I'm not taking her damn calls anymore. I've had it with her calling me, all drunk." There was a long crackly pause. "Hearing about him."

What the hell is she telling her? He held his tongue, ran his finger over the counter. Another long silence. He closed his eyes. *That damn cricket.*

"Thank you for listening," he said finally.

"I'm not gonna poke the bear."

"Poke the bear..." He opened his eyes.

"Don't go poking the bear."

"That another one of your mom's?"

"Yes."

He could hear late summer insects sawing away outside in the yard. "Does she love this guy?" he asked. "Is she in love with him?"

"Turn the bus around," she urged him. "Turn it around. C'mon."

"Okay. I'm turning the bus around." He smiled. "A big wide, slow turn."

"I care about you, Paul. A lot. And you don't deserve this," she said. "And we never had this conversation."

"Of course. Never happened."

"We haven't spoken. Got that?"

"Got it."

"Good."

His wineglass dripped tiny pools onto the counter which he rubbed with his finger. He absently drew a heart, then scribbled through it, erased it, as he said: "I'm sorry, Laura. This is just all so weird. So sudden. I didn't even ask you how you're doing."

"I'm good."

"How do you like it there in Jacksonville?"

"Hot as hell right now. But the job's great. Challenging, but the people who work there are wonderful and I have this neat little townhouse," she said. "I have it all set up with my tiki stuff and my little Elvis shrine."

"You out near the beach?"

"Not too far. A fifteen minute drive. But I have a pool...a community pool. It's a good size, and I swim laps every morning before work, so I'm in pretty good shape."

It seemed like a gratuitous detail, and he couldn't think why she'd mention it, unless... *Captiva...bright cloudless day. Laura's aquamarine one-piece gripping her curves. Her dive into the pool, then gliding up to him, smiling, hair wet, eyes shut. Laura at the steps, dripping water, her body shimmering with bright points of light.* The wine and sound of insects buzzed in his mind. He cleared it to ask: "You're happy?"

After a pause, "I suppose so, yeah." Another pause, "All things considered."

She stayed silent as he repeated uncertainly: "All things considered." He had to add: "That's... Well, good. It's what matters. That you're... That you're happy. Right?"

He didn't know what else to say. He didn't want to hang up. He sensed that she also knew that they'd pretty much run out of things to talk about, but didn't want to hang up either.

After a long, awkward silence: "I love you, Paul." She said it playfully, not really meaning it. Just so he'd feel better.

"You know—that's an easy thing to say—"

"—but can I prove it?" she laughed. Southern accent. Low, throaty. Musical. Another drawn out silence. Just that damn cricket behind the dryer.

"Pretty stale joke."

"It's from that movie 'Serial', right?"

"I just knew you'd remember that."

"Christopher Lee playin' a gay biker," she said. "I adore that movie. And you're the only straight man in the world I know who would actually get that. Who'd know what the hell I'm talkin' about. And I just love Martin Mull. God, he's just so damn funny." Her words slowed, quieted. "He reminds me of my older brother, Will, kinda."

He stood listening to her lovely, honeyed voice from the phone. His mind drifted again to that weekend visit over two years ago. He'd picked her up at Islip airport, driven alone, and on the hour-long car ride back to Southold, he'd felt an intense sexual tension. He often wondered if she'd felt it, too. He recalled the moment he first saw her standing there at the curb, arms up, elbows jutting out awkwardly, shapely breasts pulled taut as she tied her hair back in a ponytail...recalled how, as they hugged, she'd made an express point of leaning her shoulder into him to ensure there was no full frontal chest-to-chest contact. ("I knew you were only tryin' to cop a damn feel.") The way her ear had softly brushed his cheek. The way she smelled.

"Thanks for listening to me," he finally said. "And keep me posted, would you?"

"Paul. C'mon," she chided. "You know I can't do that. I shouldn't even be talking to you. You need to just do what you have to...focusing on your wonderful boys has to be your priority. You can't think about her. You have to let go. Put it out of your mind." Pause. "I'm glad you're divorcing her."

"I have to," he said. "I offered to reconcile."

Silence, then: "You must protect the children." She didn't see him nod and rake fingers through his greasy hair as she said: "That girl's a fall-down drunk...total mess. Abandoned her kids and husband to run off with some nasty redneck..."

"He is, isn't he?" he said quietly. That was good to hear, oddly reassuring. He sipped his wine. He already needed to pour himself another glass.

"...some...nasty drug addict," she was saying.

"Wait. He's a drug addict?"

She went silent.

"What sort of drugs?"

"...Paul."

"Coke?" he said. "Are we talking about meth? Heroin? Pain killers? What?"

"I can't go there. I'm not going to," she said sharply. "I've already said too much and you'll just use it against her. And I could get in trouble with her. And God knows I don't need her on the warpath coming after me. I've got a lot on my plate right now. Okay? You understand?"

"I understand. But now that you've brought it up..."

"She's in no immediate danger. It's just..." she faltered. "She really shouldn't hang around this guy if she's serious about getting better." Pause. "And that's all I'm gonna say."

"Come on—"

"No."

"You can tell me."

"Goodnight."

"I need to know what's going on. Please tell me."

"I'm hanging up now. Goodnight."

A click and then after a few seconds the dial tone. He thought of calling her back, but didn't.

It was dark in the house. And it was just 8:00. He left the side door open and let the cool wind continue to blow through. He walked to the fridge and poured himself another glass of wine. He could hear the katydids in the tall trees behind the house.

Five weeks until frost.

~~~~~~~~

Excerpt from William Rue's novel '*Last Tango In Jacksonville*" Published in 2010 and available via Amazon.com

KNOW THYSELF

DAVID PORTEOUS

He felt anxious about being conspicuous signing in at the desk for the Historical Fiction Authors Association seminar. His last HFAA event was five years ago and, as he'd published nothing since, he'd be asked when the next book will come out. If truth be told, which he had no intention of doing, in all that time he'd written only a few notes for a rehash of the Titanic tale, now starring underdeveloped fictional characters. He'd have to lie to deflect the queries, and to fake being a fastidious researcher; if nothing else, he now lied creatively.

Adam Mott woke in a sweat from that nightmare arising from fear of not meeting his last book's sales. He'd uttered the fear to his agent recently, and could again hear Mo Grinberg's attempt at an avuncular tone: "Not to worry, m'boy. Writers can't always line up words right. They...you know what they... you want to write, but unconsciously fear that you...they didn't think it through. See? Your mind's got in its head that there's a plot flaw you didn't spot. It's writer's block, and it'll pass. Like a kidney stone, maybe... But it will pass."

Adam's response: "Does Simon Winchester's agent

say that? No! Simon puts out nauseatingly well researched books every few years! And Bill Bryson did...amid his travel books... A History of Every damn-thing... And a dictionary for writers! So why can't I be like that?"

Rather than relive Mo's agonizingly astute answer, Adam focused on the bedside clock. Seeing 3:45, he grimaced about facing three more hours of restless distress until he thought: *No, it's a...whaddayacallit? Omen... Symbol... Something. A reminder that, back when I could write, I got up at four to do it in the quiet. That dream waking me now is telling me to get back to my writing ritual. Yeah, must be.*

Adam glanced at his wife, Myra, and feeling benevolent now that the message had given him hope, he gently slid out of bed to not awaken her. After complimenting himself on his thoughtfulness, and success, he bypassed his study to make coffee, and a celebratory breakfast seemed appropriate while the coffee was brewing. Making toast added delays as his search for taste-tempting toppings belatedly found the bread burning and he had to reload the toaster. As tardily, he came to recognize his mind's malevolence in finding distractions from sitting down to write, so he went off to do just that.

At his desk, he masterfully kept his reading of Facebook posts to an hour, but then wasn't sure what to do. His skimpy notes offered no encouraging clues, and the creative spark he expected to flare had dimmed. He couldn't keep a word on his computer screen for ten seconds before deleting it and, after a pensive pause, trying another. His buoyant mood was sinking as rapidly as doubts bubbled up in his mind. The computer's clock told him he'd sat there for another hour, so he made a bold new start; he typed a heading:

THE TITANIC: AN ADVENTURE

An hour later it was still all he had, except for a fifth mug of coffee and a looming headache that, with luck, would let him retreat to bed. But a nagging notion that he might need self-discipline was being amplified to inner screams, and that got Adam pompously deciding: *"I must get my writing back to its best before I can be all I was."* After pondering that, he wistfully added: *"If I can remember what both of those were."*

"Can't sleep, honey?" Myra asked through a yawn from his study's door. "Got a flash of inspiration? I'm glad."

"Yep...got it now." He hoped she was too sleepy to hear that ring hollow, but had to add: "Now I'll get its flow going."

"That's nice, hon. Like to hear more, but have to shower and go. We're pitching for Chanel's ad campaign, and the..."

Adam heard no more; he waved, hoping it looked like considerate respect for her need, saying: "You'll hear tonight." He then gazed at the boldly titled screen, its blinking cursor a vile reminder that he had nothing yet, and sought help in memories of Creative Writing classes. He recalled hearing 'nothing is written until one writes', and advice to 'just let first drafts flow and reshape it all later'. It inspired him to release chain thoughts for his fingers to artlessly impress on the keyboard.

~~~~~~~~

It seemed just hours later, but he saw it was 7:10 PM when he heard Myra drop her briefcase, a familiar sign that she was cranky, so he had to quickly evaluate what he could say he'd done. Scrolling through thirty pages on the screen had him sitting mute with shock when Myra's high heels click-clacked into his study, bringing a curter than usual habitual greeting.

"How was your day?" Without pausing, she added: "Mine was *merde*! Chanel hated our..." She stopped, mouth open; she'd seen Adam scroll over pages of text and her tone turned gleeful to say: "Your day rocked! I'll get wine so you can read it to me." It was only then that she misread his dazed look. "My honey-bun has worked his butt off! You need the wine!"

After his first sip of Medoc, even before Myra was settled in a chair, Adam was reading aloud, a hand aloft to fend off interruptions. Thirty pages later, he turned to ask: "So...?"

"So... No iceberg? The Titanic actually hit a spaceship from a galaxy far, far away?"

"Umm... I think I was going for a metaphor, but it didn't quite work. So, I know I'll have to change all that, and –"

"Change nothing! It's brilliant! More so as a first draft... your best writing ever. And so...fucking...funny, honey!"

He hated Myra for ending the most lavish praise she had ever given his work with that slur, but said only: "No one will like 'funny' linked to the Titanic tragedy."

"Are you mad? Everyone's going to love how your

little spaceman just clicks his fingers to seal the hull's hole, and to make the water in it vanish! And everyone will get your satire in how the rich people on board whose lives he's saved get him elected President. But your finale...them making him Planet President, and his finger clicks end wars and eradicate cancer, religions...all the world's blights... It's brilliantly funny!"

He tried to sound calm. "But not historical fiction, which is what I write... Who I am. And a short story, for Chrissake, not a real book! Am I reduced to writing in some Sci-Fi genre? Jesus, Myra... What about my stature as second runner-up for historical fiction author of the year, six years ago? That is how people know me... And like me!"

"No, Adam... Absolutely no! Now you've mastered this genre...whatever it is...you can write in its style and get rich on the results, because people will love you for stories like this. It's just way too brilliant to even think about changing, and..."

Again Myra's mouth froze open, but this time in horror, as Adam jiggled the mouse, clicked 'Select', 'Select All', and then tapped the 'Delete' key. She was almost too numb to hear him mutter: "A man needs his standards."

~~~~~~~~~~~

Originally published in in the antholgy '*Strangers In My Mind*'
by The New Atlantian Library / Absolutely Amazing eBook
(2017)

THE PRINCESS AND
THE TURNIP EATER

HELENE MUNSON

As a child I knew both of my grandmothers, the princess and the turnip eater. I inherited some jewelry from them.

My princess grandma left me bangles of sparkling, shiny glass, but never gave them to me because they had broken long ago. I got them in her stories. They played a prominent role in my favorite tale about her enchanted childhood in Burma. In my childish imagination, those bracelets were the most beautiful things I had ever seen. I became determined that, once I had grown up, I would travel to the places where they could be found...

From Mumbai I had taken a regional flight to the town of Cochin in the South Indian state of Kerala. It had been an important trading post on the spice route for centuries. The historic streets were inviting visitors for a stroll to explore the town and its twin city, Mattancherry, so I looked around. How magnificent this town must have been a hundred years ago, when its spice merchants invested their riches in the town's architecture. Now, still beautiful, it is a shadow of its former self. I assumed that there must have been a war. In Germany, a country wedged between the power struggles of Eastern and Western Europe, there had always been a war. I started listing them in my mind: *'The Unification War, the Peasant Wars, the Thirty Years War, the Seven Years War, the Austrian Succession War, the German-French War and of course the two World Wars.'* I was sure there were more, but those were the only ones I could then recall.

But for once, a town's demise was not due to a war. This city had been proof that all ethnicities and religions can live together in peace and thrive for centuries. Ruthless antique dealers had plundered it, stripping almost every window and door of the delicately carved, hardwood panels. I looked at an empty doorway and wondered: *'Are the antique carvings that once graced this entrance now mounted on some living room wall in an estate in the Hamptons?'*

Tired from walking, I went to a restaurant; I was its only customer. This was July; the air smelled tropically wet, the rainy season was here. While I lingered over a cup of overly sweet milk tea, I looked out at the delicately fabricated, iconic Chinese fishing nets in the harbor. With every sip of my tea, sparkling glass bangles jingled on my wrist. I had bought them earlier in the day at a local street market.

The stall owner had asked: "Why don't you buy metal ones? Only poor people buy glass. Glass breaks easily and you can cut yourself".

"I want glass. My grandmother wore glass," I insisted.

"But your grandmother was not Indian" he dismissively told me.

"No, but her Indian nursemaid used to give them to her when she was a little girl in Burma," I said enthusiastically, ready to tell him my family's story. But he had lost interest in my patronage and wrapped my purchases in newspaper.

When I arrived in Southern India, I was ecstatic to find there was an abundance of glass bangles in every color of the rainbow – some iridescent, others decorated with sparkles. Their delicate beauty was everything I had envisioned them to be, but it was also disappointing to find out how common they were; in my girlish fantasies they had been so precious. A dozen cost 50 cents if I haggled hard, or $1 if I coughed up the tourist price; I bought a dozen in every color and felt rich.

I had imagined these bangles as rare and hard to come by, and they had been when I travelled to Burma, now Myanmar, a few years earlier. I had found none in the local markets. Indians who had been invited to the country under the British Raj but were forced to leave the country in the 1960s, had taken more than their glass bangles with them.

My princess grandmother's stories were like fairy tales: happy, full of adventure and mystery. Her two sisters and she had lived like little royalty in an enchanted, exotic world, doted on not just by their parents, but also by the entire household staff. She remembered: "Timber elephants did all the heavy lifting in those days. There were hundreds of them. When the elephant cows were working in the forest, Mahouts would sometimes bring a baby elephant to our garden and we were allowed to play with him."

Another time she told me: "My mother was a lady, a true Grand Dame of Rangoon society, always impeccably dressed in starched, white linen dresses with lots of fine lace. She never did housework and certainly did not cook, but once she got curious and ventured into the kitchen wing. There she saw a boy in a loincloth sweating heavily. Under his arm on his naked torso, he held a large piece of meat that he was pounding soft with his elbow." She laughingly added: "But none of us ever got sick from food poisoning!"

The story I had liked most was about my grandmother's Aya-nursemaid. As all children do, I asked her to tell it to me over and over again, and she began: "We had fifteen servants, but the one I liked best was my Aya. She was kind and gentle, and taught us girls how to speak Hindi. But she was also vain. Indian women's long, black hair is a source of great pride, and she gave me a glass bangle for every grey hair I found and plucked from her head. But she got sick, and my mother offered her medicine, which she refused to take. Her relatives brought her herbal concoctions and traditional foods, but she got worse and then just disappeared. Other servants told us that her family had taken her away during the night, because they were afraid that my mother would take her to a British hospital...and then one day she was back again."

My turnip eating grandmother gave me a small, black, scratched-up metal locket when I went to live with her. Like my princess grandmother, I had been raised overseas and I adored my Baba, my Brazilian nursemaid who had taught me Portuguese. But for better schooling, I was sent to Germany to live with my turnip eating Grandma and Grandpa Fritz.

It was as though a grey shadow had come over my life. I resented how strict she was; I had to eat whatever was served up to me, even though I hated root vegetables. How I missed the mangos and green coconut water! Grandma was appalled that I did not know how to clean my room, nor my shoes, and she taught me how to do that without wasting any polish. She was so frugal; lemonade was mixed with water, and gift-wrap paper was ironed and reused.

She was a World War I war child, and told stories from her youth: "Before the war our lives in Mülheim were happy. I remember one Christmas my brother and I got an orange each. We had never tasted such a fruit before. The *Kolonial-warenhandel*, a shop that specialized in goods imported from the colonies, sold them. But with the trade embargo against Germany when war began in 1914, such delicacies became unobtainable, along with lots of other foods. The German farmers being away in the war made the lack of food imports even worse. By the start of 1916 we were living pretty much on potatoes. But worse was to come! It rained so much that the 1916 potato harvest failed. We had not seen meat since the beginning of the war and now we were eating the turnips that we had fed to the cattle before. We named the winter of 1916 the Turnip Winter. Then in 1917 they started rationing turnips, and it was the coldest winter we had ever known!"

I interrupted: "But there are lots of coal mines around Mülheim."

"Yes, but the coal was used to keep the furnaces burning day and night to make arms. Then they ran out of metal. I remember one mild day in June 1917; we woke up to hear all our church bells ring at once. It was a glorious sound coming from all around us and for a moment gave us hope. We had grown up with their sound, and so had our parents and their parents. But this was the last time that we would hear them. Men came to dismantle them and melt them down to make into cannons and gun shells. It was such a shame! We saw the bells stacked high in scrap metal yards that we called bell cemeteries," my grandmother added thoughtfully.

Only when I was older did I understand the true loss of the bells, and what it had meant to my grandparents. Since the Middle Ages, church bells were important to European communities, and originally were only cast by monks who knew how to use the right alloys. Just like people, they had names like *Big Bertha* or *Gloriosa*.

She continued: "When things got better after the war, churches collected money and bought new bells. But we had them only until 1940, the second year of the Second World War. Then Hermann Goering founded a company that made him money by melting bells down for arms and we lost them again. He even stripped graveyards of wrought iron metal decorations." With a sad smile she added: "Not even the dead were exempt from doing their duty for the war effort."

After a moment of silence she continued, remembering: "The bells also rang when Johann marched into war, my only brother. He and his friends were so excited. He was nineteen and had just started University when he became a First World War soldier. He never came back. So many of them did not come back, and we who stayed behind also died...of hunger, malnutrition and the Spanish Flu."

My grandmother went quiet. She walked over to her desk and took out a small, black iron locket, all scratched up. She opened it and inside was a tiny faded photograph.

"This was Johann. I have worn the locket many years, you can have it now." She offered it.

For a High School project our history teacher suggested that we ask our grandparents about the time when Hitler had come to power. When I asked my turnip eating grandma, her memory was already fading and she had to think a while: "It was winter...1933, and I had just given birth to the twins, who needed feeding around the clock. Your aunt Marlene was a toddler and Uncle Ludwig was five. Opa Fritz had to help me; I could not keep up with four children...after all, I had no washing machine or refrigerator in those days. Later that year Ludwig came home from Kindergarten with whooping cough and infected the other children. Little Erika and Hilde fared the worst. We thought that Erika would die, and her grandmother took her away to make it easier on us."

"But my mother Erika did not die," I interrupted.

"No, but her twin sister Hilde did. I could not save that little girl...not even a year old," she said mournfully. Only then remembering my question, she added: "No! It wasn't the Fuehrer's rise to power that kept me awake those nights."

Alzheimer's struck my turnip eating grandma in her old age. Her husband, Grandpa Fritz, could no longer walk, so he wrote her long to-do lists, and joked: "I am the brain, she is the legs." In the end she could not recognize any of us.

My other grandmother, the princess, remembered everything. She had been fortunate to miss the First World War in Germany. By the time the Second World War broke out, she had already emigrated to South America. She had never felt hunger or seen death. But by the time she had retired, she was destitute. In contrast, my turnip eating grandma had taught school for decades and secured for herself a modest, but adequate pension. Princess Grandma had nothing to fall back on, as there were no public pensions in Brazil, so my father brought her to Germany to care for her. But the experience was not a happy one. She had difficulties relating to Germans her own age; she saw them as dour and perpetually depressed. What she found particularly annoying was how they greeted each other. If you politely asked an older generation person "Good day, how are you?" the answer was invariably a sigh of "Oh, it has to!" meaning that one had to continue living as though it was our moral duty, but life had little joy. Germans, in turn, considered Princess Grandma's perpetual Pollyanna good mood annoyingly superficial.

In the years of the post-war German economic miracle my father was able to provide well for her. But that did not hold her for long. She eventually fled Germany, to live out her last years in her beloved Brazil, where everybody was desperately poor, but the skies were always sunny and blue.

My turnip eating grandmother died blissfully, forgetting everything. When her beloved Fritz died after 70 years of marriage, it did not register with her. She could not remember anything -- including the hardships of two World Wars, the loss of a brother, and a dead child.

~ ~ ~ ~ ~ ~ ~ ~

SHADES

JOYCE DeCORDOVA

She was the color of chocolate, but not quite. There was a hint - a tinge - of cream blended into the mix. And any time she looked in the mirror, which was not often, she was sadly reminded of her father. His color was his only legacy to her. He was white and her mother was black. She felt sad that the faint blush of whiteness of her skin was the only tangible thing she had from him. There was really nothing else, except for the money he faithfully sent to her mother for "my daughter's care" as he put it. Really? It was a pittance, and she believed the paucity of money reflected how little he thought of her.

Isabel was bitter and sad - and yet, she longed for him. She wanted him to live in the apartment she shared with her mother and her grandmother. The three of them living in a fifth floor tenement in Manhattan in the 1940's; sharing beds and smelling urine behind the stairs where the drunks would sleep and pee. Three females. No men. She wanted to see him shave and she wanted to feel the roughness of his beard and to soak in the smell of him. A male smell, she decided, was so different from the smells that came from the perfumes and powders worn by the women in her life. She wanted him to embrace her in a strong hug that took her breath away.

Although he lived in the same neighborhood, he visited her about once a year. He would pat her head and tell her how much she had grown. *Of course, she had grown,* she would think to herself. *Thank God at least being a midget wasn't in her genes!* His eyes would make little contact with her, but would longingly go to the door, looking at it as his escape from the "mistake" he had made. She, Isabel, from the time she was born, into adulthood and probably forever, was his mistake. She was his albatross.

While growing up, the kids at school, especially the girls, would tease and shun her. "Make up your mind, Isabel," they said. "Are you black or white? You can't be both...nobody is."

"But I am both" she would say. "Mulatto, is what I am."

"Oh yeah?" They would snarl. "I told my momma what you said you are and she told me what a mulatto *really* is. It's a cross between a donkey and a horse and it's called a mule. You're not a donkey and you're not a horse. You're no one, Isabel, and belong nowhere except as a freak in a circus."

"That's not true. My family says I have the best of both!"

She really didn't know what that meant, but they said it so it must be true. It wasn't. What was true was that although she was living in a sophisticated town, Manhattan in the 1940s and 50s, Isabel just didn't fit. The perception was that blacks were dumb. Isabel was smart. Blacks looked and smelled like monkeys, and they had that kinky hair that was rough to the touch. Isabel was beautiful. Her features were chiseled and she carried a refreshing, faint scent of lemon. Her hair felt like a soft brush that entwined your fingers when you touched it. She was tall and had a sophisticated walk that her mother and grandmother encouraged. "Don't look down like you're ashamed of yourself. Hold your head high and look people in the eye Isabel. That shuffling 'no ma'am, thank you ma'am' look is not for you. Be proud of who you are child."

But who am I? She mused. *I feel as if I am on a river with each foot on a separate log going downstream, trying to keep my balance before the water swallows me up.*

Life and relationships didn't get better as she got older. There were rejections everywhere. "You're great Isabel and I wish I could invite you, but..." That was from her white friends and then there was "Just who do you think you are? You may look a little like one of us, but you're not. I've seen your Daddy around, and he's as white as cream. I guess that explains the color of your skin. You're not a real black. You're nice enough, but you're not black enough."

It would have been comforting if she could say she was a diagnosed schizophrenic, living in two worlds. At least that was an identity! But she had no identity. She lived in limbo where nothing was happening and, aside from her mamma and grandmother, no one really wanted her. She was waiting. She was in a holding pattern, just like a plane ready to land and smooth out and be safe on the ground.

Her life began to change after her grandmother died. She was 17, in her senior year at an all-girls Catholic high school. It had been her mother's decision to send her there. She believed that the nuns and the other girls would practice what they preached and be kind and accepting towards their fellow man. They weren't. They were mean, in an insidious sort of way that made their rejections somewhat confusing and even more painful and hurtful. Isabel had begged her mother to send her to the local high school where, because of the huge numbers of students, she would blend in and be less noticed.

"That's what I want, mamma. I just want to be a number, and I want to be like everybody else."

"But you're already like everyone else, Isabel! Remember what your grandma used to say when you were little? If you look at the bottom of everyone's feet, they're white, and that makes us all the same."

"So when I meet someone, mamma, we have to compare the bottoms of our feet so they see we are the same? That won't work, and you know it." And she would storm out and go to her room that she had shared with her grandmother and cry in frustration and hurt.

Aside from her grades, which were impressive, there was nothing really positive in her life. Even having high grades did nothing to raise her image of herself. *Of course they're good. I have no friends, no social life...all I have is school, then back home and study. If everyone did that they'd all be scholars.*

If truth be told, Isabel *was* a scholar. She loved to learn, had an unquenchable thirst for it. The adage

'Don't judge a book by its cover' didn't apply. Before she opened her mouth, people had formed an opinion of her, usually a negative one. But books were her true and only friends. Books didn't judge your looks. They couldn't see you! They were generous and just poured out what they had, be it good or bad, and they let you be the judge. She had no control over her color, but she did have control over her mind, and she saw that other girls in her school grudgingly respected her because of it. In her senior year, Isabel decided that her destiny was to fill that cavernous hole called a mind with knowledge. And knowledge was power, wasn't it? And with power came control. Over what, she had yet to find out.

She didn't apply to Ivy League universities, even though her grades were competitive. She knew it was a waste of time and money that her mother didn't have. So she went to City University and the four year experience changed her life. Her dream came true. She was just a number! One of thousands that came in all shapes, sizes - and yes, colors!

Even though tuition was cheap, she still had to work to help at home and pay for her clothes and some of her books. There were really no other expenses. She led a meager life...in every way.

Isabel found out about a part-time job as a phone operator at a local hospital. It would mean working alone as a night operator on weekends. Not exactly what she wanted, but the money was good, so she applied and was hired. Of course she was; the switchboard was in the basement next to the laundry room! That meant no visibility, which suited her just fine.

One night, a caller asked for the emergency room. He sounded stressed and began to tell Isabel about a friend, who had been injured in a motorcycle accident and taken to the hospital. The phones were quiet at that hour and she just let him talk. His voice was beautiful. It was deep and warm and it intrigued her. He told her his name was Dick and he was a musician living in the West Village. She expressed sympathy about his friend, then connected him to Patient Information. After a few minutes, she noticed a disconnect on the call and felt disappointed that she didn't get to speak with him more.

The next night he called again. She asked "How is your friend doing?"

"He's much better, and they sent him home today."

"Oh that's great" she said. "So why are you calling? Is there something else I can help you with?"

"You know, last night when I called, your concern about my friend sounded so genuine. It made me feel good that a total stranger, like yourself, could reach out and understand how stressed I was and offer some comfort. That was so nice of you and I wanted to say thank you for that."

Isabel smiled. Aside from her mother and grandmother, no one ever complimented her, and it made her feel good. Imagine! All she did was be herself and he was thanking her for it! How refreshing, she thought. There she was, just being Isabel, albeit on a phone, but nonetheless, his thanks warmed her almost as much as the sound of his voice.

"Do you have time to chat a bit? Are the phones busy? I figured they wouldn't be at this hour and that's why I waited until now to hear the sound of your voice again."

Oh my, she thought, *we are intrigued by each other's voices!*

"Actually, it's a good time. Hardly any phone calls at this hour." She tried to keep the excitement out of her voice, but he caught it!

"So you feel like I do! I'd like to know you better...what's your name?"

Where is this going? she wondered. *But wait, this is harmless, right? I'm only on a phone for god's sake. He can't see me. It's just one voice talking to another.*

"It's Isabel...and yes, I remember your name. It's Dick isn't it?"

And so it went. At first, she resented her work schedule because it tapped into her free time from school. But now, she couldn't wait for the weekends to come. She gradually came to feel that Dick was her date for those evenings. Sometimes she would dress up and put on makeup and "good" clothes to start her shift. Her mother would ask her if she was going out after work and she was always elusive.

"Maybe, if I'm not too tired mamma."

Her mother was delighted. Isabel had made friends! But she dared not ask too many questions. She might spook her. And besides, she seemed so happy.

Isabel told Dick the nights she would be working, and he would call and they would talk, minus some interruptions, throughout her entire shift of three to four hours.

Talk about what?

Everything! Her hopes, ambitions, her fears. The books she was reading. The poetry she wrote. His music. He was a clarinetist and he would play some of his recordings for her. He'd describe the other musicians, their talent, or lack of. His love of the classics.

At times, she asked him where he was playing, but he was always evasive or he would say that it was out of town. There was a period of two weeks when he was traveling with a band through Europe and it was difficult and expensive for him to call. That was when she felt lonely and also when she realized how much she depended on him and cared about him. He was now woven into the fabric of her life.

She was falling in love with a guy whom she had never met, never touched, never kissed and never did all the things she had read about, but had never done.

He didn't ask to meet her. He said the relationship they had was special, almost sacred. That made her suspicious, and yet she was intrigued as well. Suppose he was a monster? Ugly? Disfigured in an accident? A fire? All these thoughts ran through her head. If truth be told, she was afraid to meet him. Isabel had never told him that she was mulatto. In all the conversations they had, she never once mentioned it, and it had begun to bother her, because her color and all that came with it, was part of who she was.

After a few months, she decided she was strong enough to tell him the color of her skin and if it turned him off, so be it. But she wanted a face to face meeting and she believed his reaction would tell her everything she needed to know.

"Let's meet tomorrow night. You had mentioned that you were free...no gigs, and it's Monday, so I'm not working and my classes end at five."

He hesitated. "Why, Isabel? Everything's going along so smoothly. You know how I love our talks, how much I look forward to them. Why spoil something that's so special?"

"Why? Because honestly, Dick, I want more." And then it hit her. He was unhappily married! He had kids and she had become a pleasant and gradually a necessary diversion from his own miserable life! "Wait Dick, I'm beginning to get it now. You're married aren't you?"

He laughed. "No, I'm not."

"Well then, why not meet?"

"Because, Isabel, I'm afraid it might spoil, or even ruin what we have."

"Dick, would it help if I say that I am afraid of that as well? But don't you think our relationship is strong enough to go the next step? And, if we meet and it's not, then isn't it better that we know it now rather than later?"

She couldn't believe how aggressive she was. But she so wanted him!

He sighed, and then there was silence on the phone. She thought he had hung up.

"Isabel, are you sure you want to do this?"

"Yes, where?"

"I think it's best to meet here at my apartment. I'll have dinner ready. Say at about seven?" He gave her his address.

"I'll be there." She hung up quickly. She didn't want him to change his mind.

The day was a blur. She kept going over all the possible scenarios in her mind. Maybe he's short, fat and ugly. But would that matter? No, because I know the *real* him. I know how big and kind his heart is. I know his passion for his music and how talented he is. I know his ambitions. Actually, I know every nook and cranny of his life, and I am falling in love with the essence of him. That's the truth.

But then came a dilemma. She laughed. What would she wear? She rummaged through her sparse choices of clothes, trying on one thing after another and chose a red wool dress that had a slim skirt and a low-cut top. She looked great in it and red was her favorite color. Would it be his, she wondered?

Usually when she went out she put on a base makeup that would lighten her skin color a bit, but she decided not to do that tonight. She was a chocolate color, that was fact, and she decided she had to be loved for who she was...warts and all.

"Dick Grant" said the sign on his door. Her hands were sweaty. She hesitated. Maybe he was right. Why possibly spoil a good thing?

Before she lost her courage, she knocked. Then she heard his voice telling her the door was open and to come in. That gorgeous voice!

She walked in. The apartment was dark and her eyes had trouble adjusting and then she saw him standing there with outstretched arms beckoning her to him.

He was blind.

She thought "why did I wear wool! It's so scratchy." But all he could feel and taste and love was the softness of her skin.

~~~~~~~~

GLORY

GERARD MEADE

The cab dropped him downtown, not exactly the address specified, but on the avenue at the intersection of the street he'd given. It's Monday and it's late, the only soul in sight is struggling with an over-filled shopping cart, forcing it farther south. Turning left from the bright thoroughfare onto the connecting lane, he passes quickly into deep shadow. A dysfunctional streetlight on the opposite curb starts, offers a brief bluish flicker before failing its task and returning to sleep. Adjusting, he clings to the dim bloom of a distant working beacon; its minimal glow reveals the profile of litter congregating in the gutter. Under their cloaks of shadow, few addresses are discernable and doorways, scattered amongst a complex array of storefronts, loading docks and residential portals, are recessed; details of their depths not revealed by the distant lamp's frail light.

Glimpsing a number whose stainless steel finish reflects the slight luminance, he strains, but reads it and knows he's close. Focused on the numerals, his toe snags the edge of an unnoticed shift in the aged, concrete sidewalk's plane. Off balance, he stumbles toward the curb, colliding on the way with a large metal can of putrid, discarded trash. He remains upright, only barely, but the container surrenders to gravity. The resulting cascade of shattering glass and bouncing cans fractures the silence of the deserted block, echoing off the façades of the stone structures lining the urban canyon. He follows the receding glissando of an intact bottle as it rolls along the potholed asphalt. His attention's diverted from the bottle's retreat by a boom that sounds from an undisclosed recess in the attached row of buildings.

"Yo! Evan! Dat you?"

The baritone voice resounds as if God's to Moses, its echo overshadowing the last of the dispersed trash's clatter. Evan stumbles again, this time without collision or collapse, and turns toward the sound. His voice in response is mouse-like, a stark, unimpressive contrast to the roar he'd heard. Unseen critters patrolling the surrounding debris might have voiced it more convincingly, if capable of such a feat.

"Uhm, yeah...I'm Evan."

He squints, pointlessly, trying to locate the source of his summons. Another false start of the overhead lamp briefly reveals a silhouette, ebony against dark ash, in a doorway behind him to the left. The fleeting light intensifies for a second, before it eclipses with an audible snap. The image that remains post-sight is that of a stocky, box-like male—he conjures the famed Chicago Bears' 'Refrigerator'. With his retina slowly adjusting, he carefully navigates a path.

"Over here, man! C'mon yo—what you dawdlin' 'bout?"

As the distance closes, a crack of fragile light escapes from the jamb of a still mostly invisible doorway, providing a better target. Inches before he'd be stumbling over another obstacle, he's rescued when the door opens part-way. Dim, yet bright in contrast, the light reveals little beyond the jamb. As Evan climbs the three steps to the platform, the door swings open completely, blocking his view of the man now behind it. The deep-toned voice rumbles once more but it's muffled by the door's steel mass.

"Damn boy, c'mon...inside, downstairs!"

He hesitates—duh, of course—considers bolting and just forgetting the whole thing, but finds that he's already beyond the threshold. The thick slab slams immediately behind him. A narrow, check-patterned, steel-stepped staircase is vaguely discernable in the only light, thrown from an unseen fixture at its base; friggin' creepy. Evan spins back to the door and pushes the panic bar to open the latch but feels no resistance from the lever, the door won't budge. He shoots a quick look over his shoulder and down. He's spooked, yet curious and undecided nonetheless. He turns back, attempts a hopeful knock, and receives the response one might expect...from a refrigerator. With no other choice, he cautiously takes the first step down.

"Move it kid, we ain't got all night!"

The voice has an edge, it's older and authoritative, and comes from somewhere beyond the tight space at the foot of the stairs. Startled by the man's bark, he pauses on the first tread before reluctantly resuming his descent, gripping the rail like a lifeline. Reaching the end of the staircase, the indirect light vanishes as his toe touches the floor. Unsteady in sudden darkness, he pulls out his phone and scans its tiles for the oft-neglected flashlight app. The dry scuff of a sole precedes just a glimpse of a shoe, barely visible in the screen's muted pastel glow. Before he locates the app a firm grip is on his forearm and the phone is gone from his grasp.

"Let me hold that for you."

Ok, I've ventured beyond creepy. His curiosity takes heel as panic takes hold.

"Oh man, listen, you want the phone...fine! I don't have much...money or anything, but take my wallet, it's yours, just please leave me alone and let me outta here, ok?"

"Easy kid, this way."

The grip on his arm slides up to his bicep, still firm but not overtly violent. The tone is the one he heard from the top of the stairs, a cop voice. The hand prompts him along for a few blind steps then pulls him up short. Something rustles behind his back and it's followed by the squeal of reluctant hinges on his left. A door's been opened but nothing beyond is visible, all is nigritude. A nudge from his escort urges him forward and Evan slip-shuffles like a prisoner in a perp walk, fearing the unseen obstacles that might lie ahead. Although their progress is slow, it's less than a minute since the lights went out. Evan's eyes have yet to adjust. Uncertain of its intent but strangely grateful for its guidance, he obeys when the hand pulls back lightly, signifying another stop.

Thoughts and images ricochet in his mind like atoms in a collider until one breaks free to the fore.

How can this guy be leading me in total darkness? No 'special ops' green glow is evident and he isn't tapping along with a blind man's cane. As he ponders, the hand on his bicep turns him, holding firm while the opposite hand pushes down on Evan's shoulder.

"Sit."

Evan's rapid breathing and the elevated staccato of his pulse resound in his ears, and both seemed amplified by the surrounding nothing in the wake of that command. Evan holds his breath and eventually wills his knees to release. He freefalls backward toward what he prays is really there. His butt hits the chair, inciting a racket from some mechanism or component as a support breaks his momentum, preventing a farther fall. The seat's firm, but not without give; he exhales.

"Stay! I wouldn't advise wandering around...that could be quite dangerous."

His captor's determined footsteps recede at a tempo that was lacking in their approach. Two things simultaneously strike him. First, he thought of the man as his captor; second, he isn't physically restrained. Stumbling about blind without direction would be foolish, dangerous he'd been warned, so he is bound by that. In solid blackness, with only these thoughts and fears, another anxiety looms: *I really have to take a piss!*

More hopeful than sensible, the embryo of an escape plan is aborted before having any chance to grow. In a cellar most likely ignorant of building and fire codes, he might encounter a labyrinth of unseen perils should he attempt an escape. He could wander in a maze before falling into an abyss—which wouldn't be out of context—resulting in his untimely demise. With his bladder expressing concern, he diverts his attention by revisiting the event that had inspired this nightmare...

The career expo had been well attended, more desperate and disparate souls had convened than he had anticipated. What didn't surprise him were the pitifully typical offerings from potential employers. He'd meandered and eventually came across a securities firm that he knew of. Their stellar track record and constant placement on 'The Best Places to Work' seduced him to join twenty other hopefuls, all waiting in line to talk with a recruiter. He was appropriately dressed and groomed, blasting heavy metal through his earbuds to help ward off the anxiety which always paralyzed him when interviewing. Lost in the music, he didn't notice her approach. He reeled when she plucked the bud from his ear.

"*You* listen to Slipknot?"

Evan was stunned. *She* was stunning, though he'd never be able to explain exactly why. She wasn't 'model gorgeous', but she was something, also extravagantly and provocatively dressed considering the surroundings. Combining the look with her brazen approach and the cocky smile she favored him with, he was instantly sold. She had 'It'. He didn't really know what 'It' was, but...she had it. Once, with a bit too much time on his hands, he'd tried to figure the 'It' thing out. He didn't, of course, but he concluded that maybe the Greeks offered an explanation. According to myth, Zeus originally created all beings half-man and half-woman. Realizing the magnitude of his blunder almost instantly, he promptly whacked everyone in two. As a result, we each have, and are constantly searching for, our other half: 'It'.

"If you like that kinda stuff, you should meet me later."

Along with the perplexing invitation, she provided a time and the fateful address he occupied. He'd fumbled for paper and pen, scribbled the street number, and looked up; more than ready to agree but suddenly lacking words. She'd met his eyes, offered up a sly smile, and pirouetted away. Forcing his gaze from the revealing swirl of her short, loose-fitting skirt, he called out after her, almost shouting the carefully crafted response. "Ok...yeah...great!   I'm...uhm, Evan."

Her laugh was musical and faded too quickly. She waved back over her shoulder without turning, Italian style, and replied to the sky, knowing that her words would carry back.

"Later then... Uhmevan."

He watched her go. Those who'd gathered behind him in line watched him. His enamored expression, a stark contrast to theirs, demanding he turn around and close the gap in the queue. Pleasantly distracted by the encounter and excited by its prospect, he nearly forgot to kill the raucous metal still blaring, tin-like, from his dangling earbud when he finally reached the reception table. The brief interlude had quieted his nerves, enabling him to confidently court the company rep as she reviewed his résumé. The matronly business woman invited him to sit at one of the desks behind her, someone would join him soon to conduct a formal interview. Lady luck, whatever her name may be, had smiled upon him, apparently just in time.

He'd assumed from her remark about his music preference that they'd meet at a club, downtown it appeared. He'd been to some bizarre ones there, and heard stories of others that put his uncomfortable experiences to shame. He wasn't one to seek out the strange but his exposure to it, albeit limited, left him unafraid when things began to get squirrely. He was blinded by longing and lust, unaware that figurative would become literal, and drew his courage from desire.

Sitting in the dampness and obscurity of the dungeon, trepidation had evicted longing, but acknowledging the damp alerted him to reemerging senses. His fear, elevated by the opacity, had stolen the majority of his perceptive capabilities. Smelling the must, however, brought awareness of recurring drips in the distance. Turning to follow the sound, he finds he can discern different shades within the umbra. Returning depth perception follows with renewed thoughts of escape, but those are short-lived.

Coinciding sounds from opposite directions shatter any plans. A skittering sound, unfamiliar but most likely a large rodent, and another that he can't identify. He focuses, sensing more than just the rat's presence, and his bladder reasserts its need. The rapid pounding of his pulse becomes audible once more, obscuring the faint sounds. In the minutes that were spent deciphering shadows, his scotopic vision has improved and he thinks he sees movement, but the minimal difference in relative shades is still misleading. External silence returns and his pulse continues to pound, several seconds pass.

The sudden explosion of LED light assaults what expects only dark and Evan whites-out like an old TV screen whose signal has been lost. Reflexively covering the eyes that he's already squeezed shut, he anticipates an impact, possibly an explosion, but none follows. He lowers his hands and steady pink light seeps through the closed lids, bringing along a dull ache. He remains still, not sure that he *really* wants to see, then hesitantly begins to blink his eyes open.

At first it's only the harsh, unforgiving light obliterating all. The pain, a reaction from his team of sensors, reflectors, and muscles within the eye, eases with the second and third attempt. His surroundings begin to emerge, blurred at first but more refined with each refresh. Slowly, he turns his gaze forward, concentrating on a shape that shifts restlessly, as though dancing uncertainly. He holds onto that image as it comes into focus.

"Hey Uhmevan."

As she becomes clear, he recognizes the smile. It quickly morphs into a frown of care or concern, but she resumes the undulation anyway.

"I'm Glory, glad you could make it."

Fully capturing her form he's almost willing to dismiss his detainment, thinking all had not been in vain. The pixie that had captivated him earlier is now a vixen in black; it's an outfit men dream of but rarely encounter. His fear of a premature release evaporates and he finds he's quite content with his restored vision.

The music starts, the eerie first notes fit the scene but also confuse him. Black Sabbath blasts out the title track of the eponymous first album—his ringtone, from somewhere to his right. He forces his eyes away from Glory to a sharp drop in the now-visible ceiling that casts a shadow to the farthest corner, untouched by the harsh LED's. A man, predictably dressed in a blue suit, white shirt and questionable tie, emerges from that void. The intense unison guitars grow louder as he nears. His head is lowered to the screen and his gray buzz cut picks up a halo of colors from its reflection. He steps close and extends the phone. The familiar cop voice: "Answer it."

Evan fumbles the handoff but hangs on to the phone. The surrealism mounts as he raises it to his ear, not thinking to check caller ID. His voice is unsteady.

"Hello?"

"Evan! Pietro Stamkos. CEO, Regent Secure."

Although he hadn't had the pleasure, Evan remembers the name, but doesn't immediately make the connection to his interview earlier in the day. His first thought's quick but disjointed; he's still dressed for business but more concerned with what Glory's outfit might suggest.

"I just wanted to let you know, you got the job."

The voice is deep, sincere but upbeat...maybe too much so. It was past midnight on friggin' Monday for chrissakes!

"Well...wow. That's great. I'm, uhm, a little surprised to hear so soon."

"Hey, I never like to wait on good news. Let's get together in the next few days to go over the details. My secretary will be in touch."

His head's spinning with events that seemed linked yet unrelated, common but beyond imagination, the logical and supernatural. Evan does his best to summon a professional tone, hoping to sound more confident than he feels. 'Salome' has stopped dancing and strikes a seductive pose that Evan can't disconnect from. He clears his throat.

"Sure thing sir, this is great news, just great. And I will definitely be looking forward to that call."

"Of course you will. Anyway, I doubt your attention is on business at the moment, but make sure it is when we meet."

A strange sound accompanies the last words and Evan's focus strays back to where it should be at this hour.

"Oh, don't worry sir, my attention will be where it needs to be."

"Alright then, sorry, uhm...Evan, later in the week then."

"Yes sir, I'll be ready."

"Good, good, oh...one more thing."

"Yes sir?"

The confident, overly boisterous tone is gone and the next words are delivered with serious intent.

"The girl, Evan. She's no perk...far from it. She is my daughter—my only daughter. It's true our company deals in securities, Evan, but *security* is paramount. Discretion is a valuable commodity son, something revered here at Regent Secure, and you'll want to keep that in mind going forward."

~~~~~~~~

RECONCILIATION

KIT STORJOHANN

Coming here was a mistake, Beth thought. Rather than the grim antechamber she'd expected, the hospital's "Family Room" was suffused with manufactured coziness. The round-the-clock presence of her estranged cousins further imbued it with a disconcerting degree of personality. This branch of the family, which had been rent from hers due to the baseless feuds of elder generations, may as well have been in their own living room as they lay draped in recliners in front of a huge flat-screen television. A quiver of cousins—whose dour, angular features she could not quite match to those of the jubilant playmates of her early childhood—stared meekly at her as though she might have arrived out of the shadows of the past with a miraculous cure for her dying aunt. All she had was a bouquet of white and yellow flowers, too late for any plausible get-well wishes, yet ghoulishly presumptuous as a memorial offering. The passel of weary refugees bundled in blankets had spread across all of the couches and easy chairs along one wall. Stacks of magazines sat on the table as placid as bishops, their traditional roles supplanted by tablets and phones beeping under the flicking of weary fingers.

They still had the same determined gawkiness, the same unsettling vertical visages Beth remembered, in contrast to her rounded features. Coming to life like flowers after rain they sat up, assuming the same formal postures as they would have under the gaze of a stranger. Half-smiles were forced onto dried, chapped lips. Clothes worn for the better part of two or three days were rearranged to a semblance of tidiness. Hands were coldly offered with a banker's formality. Beth was able to greet each one by name, her weak handshake timidly confirming friendly intentions. Introducing herself to a sullen teenaged girl she did not recognize—presumably the only one of the succeeding generation old enough to be present—she saw from the girl's glare that the family enmity had become a treasured inheritance. She sat with her shield of flowers in an empty wingback chair across the room. Her cousins remained in studious silence while nurses shot past the room like darts.

"Good of you to be here," one of the cousins ventured in a sympathetic baritone. "She'll appreciate it."

Beth tried to reconcile the voice's surety to the squeaky drawl of the boy who had always proven a gracious winner in every chess game they'd played, even before he'd lost his baby teeth. Since the 'falling out', she'd lost touch with all of them by parental fiat. Realizing that she'd receded into a murky and obsolete image in their minds, just as they had in hers, made the reconciliation process daunting. Lifetimes of experiences separated them, their common blood trumped by seething resentment that had, over the years, ossified into a dull hatred.

The others nodded silent assent, continuing to regard her like a panel of examiners. She longed for their collective gaze to dissipate, for their focus to resolve into chatter among themselves. She'd have preferred benign invisibility, her presence lost in a flood of banalities about who was feeding the cats at home, or who needed to call which office. Yet there was no respite from the silent scrutiny of the owl-like congregation on the other side of the sea of scuffed faux-wooden floor tiles.

Perhaps the pre-bereaved themselves were happy for the distraction. Perhaps they expected Beth to show contrition on behalf of the previous generation, to throw herself on their mercy and admit fault for unremembered sins. That might bring a comforting vindication to the old woman lying on the other side of the door being subjected to procedures and tests which extinguished any vague hopes one by one. Perhaps they half-hoped that stashed in her flowers was some marvelous new panacea, a fitting peace offering in recompense for the decades of injury. Yet none spoke, each content to be a single strain of the silent chorus of judgment until the doctor—a gray-haired woman even shorter than her patient's teenaged granddaughter—stoically entered to deliver her verdict.

The old woman's status, they were advised, was not good. Technical terms were coldly tossed around by the doctor as matters of fact, explaining reasons for each curative measure's failure. Her summation was that the limits of medical science had been reached, and a short period of stability was all that might be offered. They would be allowed to enter two at a time to see the old woman. Lucidity could not be guaranteed. It was understood, without needing to be directly stated, that the granted audiences were to be their farewell. Beth nodded along with the rest, deftly hiding her horror at having arrived at this inopportune, sacred moment.

She'd hoped to find a warm family in a sterile purgatory, hugging her across the gap of decades without judgment or anger. The scene that had played itself out in her mind many times in the preceding days was of a cheerful, dignified old woman holding court, laughingly admitting that she no longer had any idea of what had even spawned the old grudges. Beth would offer her flowers and gain back a family to help her assuage the loss of her own mother the previous year. Then a phone call some days later from a cousin would tell her that the old woman had passed peacefully, grateful to the end for Beth's olive branch. Instead, she sat like a plump aberration amid a sea of unblinking eyes that stared from faces like axe blades. An emissary without a message or proper tribute, she hid behind her flowers, losing herself in study of the bleary outlines of sailboats in the paintings adorning the walls.

Pairs of cousins disappeared with a nurse, only to reappear a short time later with tears in their eyes. Proximity to death had apparently brought the old woman the powers of blessing and benediction. Each supplicant received personalized absolution, tumbling forth into the waiting room flushed and dizzied with emotion as though they had just come from a holy site.

A tearful cousin—emerging freshly anointed—met Beth's gaze and said "She asked for you." Beth nodded, and walked alone with the flowers along the gallery of jealous glances of the pilgrims who had yet to see the old woman.

She entered the room to see a desiccated mannequin, a far cry from the dignified matron of old photographs and stale childhood memories. A few patchy strands of white were all that adorned the spotted head. If Beth put her hands around the old woman's sticklike arm, her middle finger would easily meet her thumb. Tubes blossomed from beneath blanket and gown, and the old woman was tethered by wires to a metal arm on wheels studded with machines brandishing flashing lights and rotating numbers. The patient gazed at the ceiling in self-conscious martyrdom, as though the act of breathing was a herculean agony suffered for the good of all mankind.

Beth clumsily offered the flowers to the old woman, who beckoned her closer and wordlessly bade Beth bow her head. Laying her hand on Beth's forehead, the old woman called Beth by her late mother's name.

"I forgive you," the faint rasping pronounced. Beth had no idea how to respond, and stayed half-crouched beside the bed while the old woman sank back on her pillow and sucked in her last attempts at breath.

These lapsed into the sterile hum and twitter from the machinery as the nearly fleshless husk awaited reply. Should Beth accept on her mother's behalf? Proudly refute the old woman's jurisdiction over her conscience? Try to correct the mistake, and offer her own name with an explanation that her mother had already died unshriven by her sister? She stayed crouched in indecision for so long that one of the instruments resolved into a steady beep and a flurry of nurses. Absolved of crimes that Beth was not sure even existed, she was gently hustled away from the body to face her bereaved cousins and explain why she had stolen the last breaths of the old woman with meaningless silence.

~~~~~~~~

GRANTED

ANDREA RHUDE

She had walked this way many times before on days when she had to get out of her apartment and couldn't think any more. This old part of town was being cleaned up and had begun to get tourist traffic, but not so much that they charged you to breathe, you could still pick up a fancy coffee for under four dollars. Not that she could; Jenny tended to simply walk, noting the slow process of gentrification clean and alternately condemn her favorite haunts. One or two of her favorite old buildings had been demolished and replaced with resin brick, and vinyl moldings; soulless studies of the lost original style.

Sometimes a lost treasure was uncovered, then quickly preserved or destroyed. Exploring them was one of few things that gave her enjoyment. The low arched alleyway, almost hidden by rubble and the next old building to be judged, was one she had not noticed before.

Jenny carefully made her way over and ignored the signs warning of instability and the requirement of hard hats. Once through the clutter and debris, she stopped and sighed. It was beautiful, the sun felt warmer in the alley and the street noises were diminished to something more like the lapping of distant waves. Loose cobblestones underfoot slowed her enough to notice the sun shining on the blankets of ivy clinging to the brick walls. It smelled old, but not stale, more like she had stumbled into a forgotten garden before the flowers bloomed; ancient and earthy with a touch of fresh green.

Someone's coming, perhaps a bargain can be struck. I can hear their steps tickle and trip in my dream...

The alley opened up to a small courtyard. Dried leaves crunched underfoot and skittered in small whirlwinds against the circular walls. In the center stood an old fieldstone well. The ugly slab cover, which must have been added to save some poor child from falling in, had broken and crumbled to bits around it. The water smelled clean and cool as she got nearer.

They are closer and the seal has broken. It's been so long since I've had company... Perhaps I should wake.

Something shiny caught Jenny's eye and she picked up an old worn coin, a penny. She smirked and leaned over the well. The coin was cold in her hand and ugly, not enough to solve anything, but just enough to remind her of all her problems. She laughed and looked down into the dark unseen water.

Hello, pretty maid. Now I can see your dark hair and sad eyes. Don't you have something for me?

"I wish my true love, my knight in shining armor, would find me and take me away from everything."

Jenny whispered into the well and dropped the penny, feeling silly.

A coin? Come pretty one, a better tribute is needed if... Oh. Something else? Yes, something precious, something personal...the tang of warm iron...

Her finger itched and she looked at her hand. Something had sliced neatly down her ring finger; she sucked it. That was what she got for wishing.

A proper invitation! One must not be rude...and I have my list to fill before I can dance free...so, now Puck shall play Cupid. But one must be thorough when one grants such a wish, let me check my list...Oooo! That would work nicely.

Jenny left the alley feeling the chill of the day more than she should have. She had to get back to her apartment but the worn clapboard siding of her favorite antique shop brightened her thoughts as she walked. Expecting a closed sign and the dampening of her brief optimism, she glanced at the door. It was open. Before more practical thoughts could dissuade, she entered with a tinkling of bells.

Inside, the lights shone softly through the multi-colored glass of old lamps and the floors creaked like the deck of a ship as Jenny walked. As usual, she took a wandering path through the curios and remnants of other people's stories without touching anything. Money was too scarce to be tempted to part with, but it was nice to look.

Yes, come look...

Something shimmered just behind a clock on an old table. She slipped by umbrella stands and followed the shimmer past rocking chairs until she found a strange oblong glass box about the width of her palm. Without realizing, she picked it up and held it to the light. The thick glass was so old and clouded in the soft metal frame she couldn't quite make out what was inside. She lifted the tiny metal latch but age had sealed it tight. The light shifted and she turned the box just a bit to see the smallest edge of its contents; something small and delicate but not much more than a wavy shadow.

It didn't matter; she couldn't just pick up trinkets. Jenny lowered the box and was about to place it back on the table when something shifted and flashed inside. She dropped down to stare at it without changing its position.

"May I help you?"

Jenny almost dropped the little box and stood to face the shopkeeper.

"I was just trying to see what's inside..." That was why she never picked up things in stores; it was an invitation to the shopkeepers to do their job and try to sell stuff. She blushed and put down the box. "I couldn't open it."

"It could be very old, from the medieval period." The woman was younger than Jenny, with a pen perched over her ear and an effortless smile. Jenny forced a smile on her own face and tried to figure out how to extricate herself.

"We just got it in from the estate of an old English woman, but we have no authentication. We can't tell if it's a really good reproduction, a well-made fake, or an intriguing original. It's not worth the extensive testing. Which is good news for you."

"Huh?" Jenny looked down at the table and realized she still had the box in her hand.

"The red tag." The woman pointed an ink stained finger. "We're trying to move some of the stock we can't authenticate. It's a sale."

"I really can't." Jenny tried to put the thing down again. It twinkled and she couldn't look away.

"No pressure, but do yourself a favor and at least look at the tag, it obviously speaks to you." She gave Jenny a nod and drifted back into her store.

Too bad she can't hear so well... What do you have to do to get picked up these days?

Twenty minutes later Jenny came out with a small paper bag stuffed with tissue paper and one glass box that she had no use for. The price was great, and the woman had taken an extra ten percent off when she couldn't find it in the store inventory, but she had spent too much. She'd have to cancel her data plan for at least two months to keep her budget. The whole thing made no sense, but it had been so fascinating. The weight of the box in its bag twisted a knot in her stomach. Would it still be fascinating now that she spent so much of her limited funds on it? She walked faster.

Her key clicked in the lock and she gave the door a hard bump with her hip to open it. Home was a small apartment that smelled vaguely of dust, not because she didn't clean it, but because most of her furniture had sat in second hand stores and 'antique' shops that never heard of authentication. Jenny navigated the labyrinth of furniture to her prolapsed sofa but the blinking light on her anachronistic answering machine dragged her over. She should just leave it, there was no chance what was on it would be good; the landline was for her personal calls. Her eyes traced sideways over the growing pile of needy mail from creditors, lawyers, and her mother. She pressed the button.

"It's your mother." Jenny groaned. "I wrote you a month ago! You can't ignore this and hope it goes away. I'm getting calls *here* from *your* creditors. I know it's not your fault, Jenny. It's that scuz you dated using your credit card, so it's *your* problem. I love you. Call me back this time." Click.

That's her mother? Oh, what a wonderful woman! To think of her daughter and leave so inspirational a message. I must thank her some day.

Jenny turned away from the phone, collapsed on her sofa, and drew out the little glass oddity to hold it up in the twilight. It absorbed the light and drew her attention just as much as it had back in the store. That was rare. Most things lost their glitter once you owned them – fiancées, for one.

She hadn't needed that reminder, and it was getting too dark to see the box. She had to put it down to light candles. The electric bill was too high, she owned the candles and could burn them without someone putting a hand out for money. She would have cut off service but for the need for refrigeration. Fortunately the gas, water, and heat were included in the rent or she would have turned them off. Well, the heat maybe. Her stomach growled and she took a candle the two steps needed to the small stove and cupboards that symbolized a kitchen. She stretched up and grabbed a can; soup, it would keep forever, it was on sale, she had coupons, she bought a lot of cans. She was sick to death of it.

The candlelight danced on the glass box and she ended up toying with it so much her damn soup got cold. There wasn't much to do after dinner had finished; she had sold her TV and her computer. The only things to do were re-read old books and burn her candles. She went to bed and was surprised she had absently brought the box in with her. It was a fine thing though. The first useless thing she had bought in a year.

Now the two of you have become acquainted, proper introductions can begin...sleep. Oh no, those dreams won't do at all. You cannot meet up while being yelled at by a grocer... Try these instead...

Jenny woke with a faint tune slipping away from her and still holding the curious box. For the first time in months she had a night's sleep that hadn't left her feeling tense and worn. A slow, sweet smile warmed her face as she stared at morning light shining through the glass panes of her box. Her dreams had something to do with what was inside, but as she tried to find a fragment of memory they evaporated from her mind. Her smile faded and she blinked at the stinging in her eyes; nothing pleasant ever seemed to last.

Time got lost in the shining watery maze of the box, and now Jenny had to run. Even if she hadn't sold her car and could drive, there was no way she would get to work on time.

Numbers juggled through her brain, figuring out how to make up for the lost time as she slowed her echoing steps on the marble tiles of the office's busy lobby. She had to find a way past Belinda; the secretary, and the dour glare she would send Jenny for her tardy arrival.

Someone waved covertly at her and she saw Cory give her a small nod. He sauntered over and grinned.

"I signed you in," he said. "Now we have to get you past the dragon." He was taller than Jenny by about eight inches. She smiled up at him.

"I just hide in your shadow?"

"If Belinda sees you she'll roast us both. She's worse than the surveillance camera." He raised his eyebrows and made a gallant gesture toward the supposed safety of the cubicles.

Jenny stretched her stride to meet Cory's, and he kept himself angled to block the dragon's glare. Jenny caught brief reflections of Belinda in the windows, relentlessly scanning the bright lobby for malefactors. For a brief moment, Jenny felt like she was back at her old summer camp, sneaking to the lake after lights out.

After they successfully braved Belinda. Jenny laughed and sat heavily in her chair. "You saved my butt!"

"Just a few dollars." Cory shrugged and smiled again.

She shook her head; there was no way he could know what those few dollars meant. Especially since she had no intention to let anyone at work know what kind of wreckage her love life had made of her whole life.

What? Oh no, no we can't have that. I was asked to unite the lovers, they are on MY list and I will see to this...

She absently hummed the half-forgotten melody from her dream as she scratched the cut on her finger. Her smile died. "I have to make up for my lost time."

For an instant Cory looked disappointed, then he smiled and let her get on with her work.

Before day's end she was called into her boss' office. He sat hunched over papers, his hair stuck up haphazardly as if he had been running sweaty hands through it. Jenny felt her throat tighten.

"Hi, Jenny. I know this is a bad time for you. I've been having some talks with HR." He looked up apologetically. "I know about the garnishment, and that makes this harder..."

Oh Shit! Images of stacked cardboard condos, Sterno can heating systems, and bathing in fast food bathroom sinks all cavorted in her mind.

"You are one of my best workers..."

Here it comes, 'I'll write you a glowing reference.'

"But I'm going to have to cut back your hours..."

She blinked at him. He gave her a pained look.

"We lost the McClure account, and this is the only way I can keep everyone on..."

"Just hours?" Jenny almost fell over.

"We have to cut everyone's hours..."

"I understand."

"Stick with us and I will make it up, promise." He sighed and gave her a wary smile.

~~~~~~~~

On her way home she picked up a newspaper, no more data plan for the cell and she had to check the want ads for part time work. Not that she had a car to get anywhere, or a computer to e-mail her resume out. It was always 'hold on just a little longer', but her fingertips were slipping before this. Did everyone know about her disgrace? Is that why Cory had helped her out this morning? A million small bites nibbled away at her and now one more big chomp...

She bumped open her apartment door and saw something shimmer on the coffee table; the box. Hadn't she left that in her bedroom? But a tightness released in her chest. With a sigh, the newspaper forgotten, she picked up the box.

Morning found her still on the sofa, in the same clothes as yesterday, and the face from a dream fading from her mind.

Lunchtime found her sitting at her desk, running her fingers lightly over the glass box. She felt better with it near.

"Jenny!" She looked up at Cory staring at the glass box.

Keep your eyes to yourself...

"It's nothing." She dropped her hand over the box, but he grabbed it and stared at her finger.

"What happened?"

"It's fine, nothing really..."

"It's infected, and swollen." He glanced up and frowned. "You're not looking great either..."

"Thanks." She took her hand back. It itched. "I'm fine."

"You look pale..."

"Cory, I have all of this work to do and half the time to do it." She turned from him and brought up the last document she was working on. What she really wanted was to examine the box again, but she couldn't while he was shoving his nose in her business.

"Will you get it looked at?"

Of course, she thought, I'll walk to the free clinic three towns away and have them give me a Band-Aid. It's just a cut. She scratched it and realized Cory was still watching her with that damn worried look. "I'll soak it tonight."

"If it's still bad tomorrow I'll take you to... What's that?"

She hid the box in her bag and found a smile to disarm him. "Just something I picked up." His attention followed the box and Jenny bit back her rising annoyance.

"Look," he sighed, shifted uncomfortably, and stared at her again. "I know things are hard for you right now, with the cut backs..."

"All our hours were cut back."

"Yeah, but you sold your car, and haven't been ordering out for lunch like you used to..."

"You've been paying a lot of attention."

"Not really." He dropped his stare but didn't leave. "I just notice things like that. Please... I know I have no right to, but if you need anything, even just someone to talk to... Well, I'm offering. Okay?"

She strangled her flaring temper, found another smile and a nod for him, figuring it might make him leave. It did and she pounded the keyboard as her mind tried to grasp wispy remnants of dream images until quitting time.

~~~~~~~~

That night Cory sat in his home office staring at the computer screen and felt a chill radiate from his spine. The way Jenny had tried to hide that creepy little box from him, it wasn't like her. He had tried to go on with the rest of his day, but the horrible old box had a death grip on his brain. The first thing he had done when he got home was run an Internet search; it was a reliquary, some part or thing of a dead person was inside it. Now an unreasonable anxiety rolled like a tide in his gut. How did you save someone from a box? He should call Jenny and tell her...what? That a trinket she'd picked up made him uncomfortable? She'd think he'd lost his mind, or he was some kind of domineering troll.

Mind your own business, it's your wish I'm granting too. A little late, maybe. Quit whining, my list is long...be glad I've gotten to it.

It was just a box. In the morning he'd make sure she had that cut looked into. That was real, that could be helped.

~~~~~~~~

Jenny woke the next day, staring at the box and humming the song that had hovered on the edge of her mind. Her finger was cold and white. It was Friday, supposed to be a half-day. She saw the bright glitter of morning light dancing around the box's wavy glass, and could almost see the small object inside. She lay on her sofa, humming, reveling in twisting patterns in the glass, and let the ringing phone go to the machine.

"Jenny?"

A small jolt almost roused her; it was Cory, she closed her eyes. What did he want?

He's not going to help...ignore it.

She let her thoughts return to the depths of the box.

"When you didn't come in today... We're all worried. I hope you're getting that cut looked at and forgot to call in... Give us a call, let me know you're alright."

She closed her hand over the box, sighed, and allowed her eyelids to lower into beckoning dreams.

The man she had dreamed of sat next to her. He watched her with sad dark eyes. There was a smell of rust, and sweat-stained leather. She tried to sit up but couldn't gather the energy, so simply watched the man. He was in armor; not shiny armor, the few metal pieces were dented, mud covered, and rusty. The rest was torn and damaged chainmail; blood stained the padded shirt that showed through the holes. A heavy riveted helmet sat in his lap. There was a familiarity in the eyes, not their color or shape, in the spirit that stared out at her. He shook his head and stared at her like Cory had; concern and worry mixing with some warmer emotion. She reached out and touched his hand...

Two who were meant to meet have met...the incarnation a bit premature but it is the only way I could get two names off my list. Don't look at me that way, I was asked after all. But there is one more part of her wish that needs to be filled.

The knocking echoed in her small apartment. The knob turned and the door opened.

"Jenny?" A cold draft raised the hairs on Cory's arms and brought the scent of rust. His throat tightened. "Jenny?"

Stillness.

His footsteps sounded muffled in the dusty air. The smell intensified and his heart raced as he reached the sofa. It was empty except for that little reliquary. A shiver shook his hand and, against his will, reached for it.

A sharp pain pierced the bone in his ring finger as his hand closed around the box. The world shifted and flowed around him making him sit heavily on the sofa. In his hand the box laid opened, presented to him on ancient velvet were two finger bones woven together by briar thorns. Cold and irrational certainly stabbed at him.

He closed the reliquary and caught the faintest scent of rosemary and lavender; the shampoo Jenny used. He was too late. The box felt warm in his grip. He stood and raised his arm to hurl the damn thing to the floor, but stopped as Jenny's scent hit him again. Something shimmered in the reliquary. He refused to look at it, but clutched it to his chest and left the dead apartment.

She's away!! The challenge met on all fronts!!! Still...

Too bad she could not wait. But mortals may confuse the plans of fate. It is their right. So, it is I who step in to facilitate. If I shorten my imprisonment with my service, I pray you, blame not this Puck! It is the list that YOU have made that keeps me in this watery vault. To be free is my goal, but no wish I make, for the grantor has the power...that must always be me.

~~~~~~~~

THAT SILK DRESS

HELENE MUNSON

It wasn't the distance still lying ahead that worried Ann, but the distinct possibility that she might not make it to her ultimate destination in time for the ancient, once-a-week Kashgar animal trading market. She had already travelled hundreds of miles down the Silk Road, crossed deserts, and had stayed in a former Soviet hotel that had no water; she had slept on villagers' floors. No host had a verbal language in common with Ann, but it hadn't been an obstacle so far. Still, it had not prepared her for the challenge she now faced in this god-forsaken Chinese provincial capital with communications broken down. She was excitingly close to completing a once-in-a-lifetime journey, but here in front of the train station in Urumqi it all seemed to unravel. She felt that she was treated like a rabid dog, so unwelcomed. Ann needed to concentrate, recalling memories and wondering: *Can anything that I've experienced and learned on this trip so far help me now?*

Her thoughts wandered back to earlier parts of her trip. She had traversed several hot deserts, the fiercest having been man-made. What was once the giant Aral

Lake, alive with sturgeon and vibrant communities on its shores, had shrunk to a large polluted puddle. Hulks of rusting ships lay in the sand, more than 100 miles from the toxic water. This gigantic, environmental catastrophe, little-known in the West, resulted from a wasteful draining of the lake to irrigate cotton fields, the Soviet's idea of progress. Making matters worse, they had stationed a laboratory for testing biological weapons on an island in the middle of the lake. After the collapse of the Central Asian segment of the Soviet Union, the local Turkic people had paid the price with major health issues, including multiple forms of cancer, and the evidently permanent loss of their fishing livelihoods.

In Samarkand, Ann had been invited to a bridal shower. While passing the open gates of one of the traditional, walled courtyards that had existed in Central Asia since antiquity, she had peeked inside. Food was being served on rows of tables at which mainly women sat. A small band played traditional music as a dancing girl in a rhinestones-embroidered, lime-green dress twirled her long, wide skirt. Seeing the delight on Ann's face, a man had motioned for her to come in. She had declined with a polite gesture, but he had insisted. Ann went in to find herself being seated next to the only woman who spoke a few words of English, the local school teacher. When the music stopped, a male member of the bride's family held up packages one by one and, microphone in hand, said a few words about each of them.

The teacher translated: "This is a dressing gown given by the groom's family to the bride's grandmother. The blanket is a present to the bride's mother."

The people applauded each item. After the presentations, the teacher took Ann to see the bride, who was hidden in a back room, as the few men in the audience, although from her family, were not allowed to see her. The shy girl of maybe 17 was dressed all in red, a fantasy in Chinese polyester lace and tulle, her future wedding dress. Returning from the bride to the courtyard, she saw most of the women were dancing, wearing traditional striped silk Uzbek national dresses with vertical patterns, a sea of vibrant colors. Ann joined in the dancing, but felt ridiculous in her Western attire of cargo pants and long sleeved t-shirt.

The next morning, her first project had been to go to the market and buy a traditionally striped, silk dress. Silk had been produced in the region for centuries, and was used not just for dresses but everything from home textiles to carpets. Unfortunately, the artificial fibers imported from China had begun to replace them. The national dress was usually worn with a pair of full-length bloomers made of a cotton material imprinted in a bright floral pattern. As the dress was three quarters long, Ann felt sufficiently covered for traveling in Muslim regions, and chose to forgo what she saw as hideously wide pants with a cumbersome drawstring on top.

It was a decision she was to regret on venturing into more orthodox Muslim regions of the Fergana Valley in eastern Uzbekistan and Kirgizstan. Ann's last stop on the Uzbek side was the sleepy town of

251

Margilan, its only official place to stay being a decrepit Russian hotel where no maintenance had been done since the fall of the Soviet Union, 15 years before. There was not a drop of water in any bathroom pipe, including the toilet, and it seemed wasteful to use her expensive, bottled Nestle water for more than cleaning her teeth. Unwashed and uncomfortable, she had headed to the market to get a shared taxi ride to the Kirghiz border.

Clearly wanting to help, a woman dressed in a fashionable top and jeans approached, asking in English "Are you lost?"

Ann responded: "I'm hoping to get a taxi to Osh, so I can then make it over the Irkesthame Pass into China. I'm on my way to Kashgar."

The woman smiled. "That's not as easy as you think. It is the most direct route, but dangerous...lots of bandits are in the pass. The Kirgiz Osh truck drivers go to buy merchandise in Kashgar, but only cross the border in convoys...they're afraid of getting robbed. But my sister, here, can help you."

With that she introduced Safranesia, a woman dressed in traditional attire, but with her hair covered by a full veil, not just a loose scarf as most Uzbek women wear. The sisters grew up on the Uzbek side of Fergana Valley. But while Amina, the English speaker, had moved into the capital, Tashkent, and worked in an office, Safranesia married a devout Muslim and moved to Osh in Kirghizstan, just over the border. Once a month the two women met in Margilan to chat and shop.

Ann shared a taxi with Safranesia and two other women, and put on a headscarf to blend in. At the border, they gave the guard some cash, and he did not check their papers, not even Ann's passport with the visa that had been so hard to obtain. When they reached Osh, Safranesia took Ann to her house, where three children and her husband greeted them excitedly, and invited Ann to stay. The older children, boys aged maybe eight and ten, kissed their mother respectfully, then continued with their chores. The younger one sprinkled the yard with water to keep down the earthen floor's dust, and swept it out with a homemade broom. Safranesia shooed the two boys and her husband out into the street, and boiled a bucket of hot water on the wood stove for Ann to wash.

She undressed in the yard, soaped herself and washed her hair in the half-emptied bucket, keeping some water to wash her underwear. Never in her life had so little water felt so good. Like all houses, Safranesia's had a courtyard inside tall walls, making them family compounds, often having several generations under one roof, but here only two rooms had been finished. Ann understood that houses were built for family needs, and this was a new compound with still young children, so the whole family slept on roll-up mattresses in one room. Because of her visit, the males were banished to bed down in the kitchen so Ann could sleep in the room with Safranesia and her daughter.

The following two days Safranesia took her to the house of the truck drivers' head honcho, but there was no convoy that she could join. The rest of the time was spent visiting women neighbors and, as rumors of a westerner staying with Safranesia had made the rounds, they all wanted to meet this strange being. Ann was served food and tea wherever she visited women, who shared their world with her and wanted to know about hers. During one visit, she learned that close together eyebrows were seen as a sign of great beauty, and she allowed a girl to draw a uni-brow on her with a kohl pencil.

She and Safranesia communicated in gestures and signs, but drew little pictures on pieces of paper when they wanted fuller conversations. Safranesia wanted to know how many children Ann had, and if her house back home had a garden. She'd already learned to pretend to be still married, and that her husband was back home waiting for her. It was especially important when speaking with curious taxi drivers to avoid obnoxious offers to become a second wife, which Ann quickly understood amounted to the role of a mistress.

She learned that from the taxi driver who had taken her across the desert to Aral Lake. He spoke exceptionally good English, having been a university lecturer, but found driving tourists a lot more profitable. He told her about his second wife while explaining that he married his first wife, also his first cousin, to make his mother happy by keeping her sister's only daughter in the family. After earning enough money, he had set up another woman, but his first wife found out and wanted to leave him until her mother-in-law intervened and said "You've done nothing wrong, if anybody is to leave our home, it will be my son." The man had yielded.

Ann thought: *The lesson, is that the society is dominated by men, but family comes first. A man who no longer has a family compound to return to after work is disrespected as an outcast, not just by other men, but the whole community.*

Safranesia confided in Ann that her husband, Ali, was a simple man who worked for his cousin and would never earn much money, but she was content with her marriage because he worshipped her and they both loved their children. It was while staying there that Ann realized how men avoided her, and became aware of the irony of how safe it was for a single woman to travel alone in the Muslim world. She was kept safe in people's homes, playing with the children and helping the women to cook. Had she been male, no self-respecting local man would have let a stranger see his wife and daughters unveiled in his home. One evening in Margilan, Ann formed an impromptu, brief friendship with a fellow English traveler. While dining in a restaurant, curious young men came up to them, but quizzed only him about life in the West, completely ignoring Ann, as though she was invisible. She'd learned that it was their way of showing respect for her.

On the third day in Osh she realized that she had to find another way to get to Kashgar in time for the famous, ancient Saturday market. The night before Ann left, Safranesia took a pair of her own bloomers from a closet and gestured for her to try them on, and then she adjusted the fit with a few stitches. As Ann dressed next morning, Safranesia appeared glad to be sending her on her way looking more decent with her lower calves and ankles covered. With her modesty restored, they went to the market square, where Safranesia negotiated Ann's ride in a shared taxi to Bishkek before an emotional embrace to say goodbye. Safranesia gave Ann her own Muslim prayer beads, a well-worn strand made from white glass, which Ann has owned ever since and cherishes as talisman.

Arriving in the Kirghiz capital, Bishkek, Ann realized that she no longer had the time to make an overland crossing via the army-guarded Torugart Pass, which was considered safe, so she took a flight to Urumqi in western China. In the taxi from Urumqi airport to a railroad station, giant sky-scrapers built of steel, glass and marble loomed over her on both sides of the newly built avenues. She wondered: *Where are the mud buildings with courtyards these people have built for centuries that I saw all along the Silk Road? China's Turk population really has been catapulted into the 21st century by Beijing's poverty eradication programs....though a better name would be heritage annihilation programs.*

At the train station, Ann found that she had missed the day's one train by half an hour. Now the only way to get to Kashgar in time was to take a 24 hours long bus ride, which meant that she had to get a taxi to the bus station in a hurry.

"Tenty dolla, tenty dolla" the taxi drivers shouted as they encircled her, grimacing mockingly. All were a head shorter than Ann, who felt like a tired old lioness surrounded by a pack of hyenas. By her calculation, the ride should be the equivalent of two dollars in local Yuan, not their outrageous cost. Feeling trapped and ready to accede, she searched her handbag to check if she even had a twenty-dollar bill. Taking out her wallet also accidentally dragged out her little digital camera, which fell to the ground, dislodging bits of the casing and its battery slid across the pavement. Embarrassed and angry, Ann kneeled to collect the pieces as the drivers howled with laughter, and a new refrain: "Money! Gimmie money!"

With rising irritation, she thought: *'These morons aren't dangerous...but so annoying. I've made it this far, and now they're making me miss the last bus of the day. I'm already tired...I need to concentrate and not let my guard down.'*

Ann saw a young Uighur man watching from behind the drivers, but he came closer, motioning her to stay put. After a brief study of passing traffic, he stepped to the curb to signal a private car driven by an Uighur to stop. They spoke briefly, and then he motioned for her to get in the car.

She saw seemingly sincere concern in the young man's face. Looking into faces and eyes was how she kept safe on this trip, as she could not verbally communicate with people and had to make split second decisions on whether to trust anyone. Again she was trusting in the kindness of strangers. Ann thanked the young man with a nod and got into the car.

The driver had her at the bus station in just minutes, but shook his head as she offered him some Chinese Yuan notes. Ann extended her arms, palms up, and shrugged in a gesture meant to convey: "Why don't you want money?" He smiled and pointed at her dress. She understood only as it dawned on her that Uighurs, Uzbeks and other central Asian tribes were

Turkic people who not only shared a religion and many traditions, but also a national costume. Wearing an Uzbek striped, silk dress with Safranesia's Kyrgyz bloomers was like a flag making a political statement, advertising her sympathy for the repressed, underprivileged Turkic minorities on both sides of the border, all dominated by policies of communist regimes in distant capitals that discriminated against local ethnicities. Dressed like an underdog, she had emboldened those taxi drivers to treat her like an inferior, but it also got two Uighur men, strangers to each other, to protect her from Han Chinese abuse in a small act of kindness and defiance.

More than a decade has passed since her travels in that silk dress. It served her well, but it was time to let go. The world had changed. The news reported ISIS had infiltrated the Fergana Valley and Osh was now a hotbed of terrorism. Ann wondered what Safranesia and her boys were doing now. She felt the heavy silk texture one last time before sliding it into the black garbage bag destined for the Salvation Army.

~~~~~~~~

What Good People
Do About Us

Susan Rosenstreich

Dorothy leaned in, struggling to hear Corinne. Noonday sun bounded off the wall behind her friend's hospital bed, setting Corinne's lips in a frame of light. "Phhah," is what she heard her friend say. But she knew what Corinne meant.

Dorothy took hold of her friend's hand. Death was close. "The deed's signed, 'Rinne, it's all set. Richie drove Lloyd and the governor out to the land. In the red Mustang, mind you! Miller Ranch Open Space Preserve, just like you wanted the sign to read. Great photo!" Both women snickered. Can you imagine bucking builders and bankers the way they had? "Hey, we done us a good job, 'Rinne. Long time comin', right?" She smoothed the hospital blanket over her friend's body, and felt mirth ripple through it. Dorothy giggled and hummed the tune off their favorite album. Other singers, younger ones, fingered melodies from Electric Flag now. But in her last moments, Corinne was sure that new audiences heard the same call she had heard years ago. How it had felt all those years ago, the fluid mixing of rock and blues and soul flowing through the high-ceilinged music halls and expansive parks of San Francisco, of Sacramento, signs, she believed then, that her country had finally found the right language for its history. It had seemed right back then. Which she under-stood now was true only to a degree, but still. Remember that you felt so sure?

Long time comin'. But for Dorothy, as she sat beside Corinne, it was not the same. Their songs, the ones they sang in private, or just with Richie their neighbor, these songs that big voices performed now, with three or four guitars, drums and mikes and all that, well, those songs for Dorothy came from way back, back in the world she had dreamt of changing, of such lives that she, small town daughter, would know how to champion. Even when she left that southern world, had become a pastor, a real woman of the Lord, found herself a church out here in California, she still thought of how she came from back there. And how music and song had traveled with her. There was nothing showy, nothing store-bought about music for Dorothy. No, for her, songs flowed through so much, the throaty plunk of the banjo her father had held close like a baby; the last light on music evenings in her small white house in Alabama; songs that were never the same twice. That was where songs came from.

"I purely don't know why you say 'that's not how this song goes, or that song sounds like this,' like there's just this one way a song is. What's this 'right way' you keep on about, Corinne? There's no 'right way', child." Dorothy had always been astounded at her Bay Area friend's inexperience with the world.

These West Coast folks carried on so loud, they couldn't hear the real world. When Dorothy and Corinne first met, already a decade ago, marching beside each other at the protest against an urban renewal project that would have destroyed the homes of Dorothy's congregation, the distance between the two women had drawn them together. "You people are plumb tone deaf. You think it all begins right here in the place where you're at. And you go leadin' the way somewheres where you don't have any idea of. Where d'you really come from, Corinne? You don't have no idea 'bout this country's past, how could you know, how you even see where you're goin' to?" Dorothy's exasperated return to the speech of her childhood was a habit that amused Corinne, but from the beginning of the friendship, she had known better than to smirk. Corinne knew Dorothy had something to say that Corinne would never have heard from anyone else.

That Friday evening after the protest – way back ten years ago, the newly raised Rainbow Flag snapping smartly in the San Francisco breeze – Corinne had sat in her bright yellow living room sipping scotch with Richie. At twenty-six, Richard Haines was more or less the neighborhood youngster, a blank-eyed Viet Nam veteran, still hesitant with strangers six years after coming home. The boy was motherless; thank goodness his father was enough of a parent who brought great gossip to Corinne's neighborhood scotch evenings. Tonight Dorothy was to join the gathering for the first time, and that, Corinne knew, would give Richie something to think about besides trying to stay off drugs. "It's not just some Alabama folktale, Richie.

She's a real pastor, not some southerner made up in a book. You think the professors are comic book characters?"

The professors, who lived next door to Corinne, and who themselves had 'come up', as they said, from Alabama some years earlier, called it the 'southern worldview'. When he had first heard this idea of a "worldview," Richie was a beardless kid, wandering around neighborhood living rooms where his father, a car mechanic, sat with adults who all had college degrees, and who, cocktails in hand, argued with each other over Bay Area politics and whether war was always inevitable, as Mr. Haines claimed, or whether instead war was the default state of the insecure, as the professors argued. Their palaver had pierced Richie's young universe. He had attached himself to the professors' book-filled household, had sat at their table for meals that fed his brain, and in a fast-firing spate of adolescent reasoning, had signed up to serve in Viet Nam. Stunned, the adults had regretted not having mitigated the heat of their discordant debates. Richie returned from Viet Nam drugged and defective, but Corinne was not about to swaddle him in pity. "You, young man, are not going to hell in a handbasket if I have anything to say about it. You're getting a suit and tie and going to law school. Dry out and I'll pay for it." She was as good as her word. Comfortably independent since her father bought off her share of the family land in farm country east of Berkeley, Corinne had provided the cash. An army of Richie's neighbors had done the rest, plucking the boy from the mud of despair sliding over him. Corinne had proven herself a good risk assessor.

The professors needed no scotch to warm to Dorothy, and winked knowingly at Corinne's new friend, a southerner like them, as Corinne described how the two women had met. "So I said to Dorothy, I said, 'Well, then, why'd you come all the way out here? Oakland's no place for Bible-thumpers.' And you know what she said?"

Dorothy broke in. "I said, 'The work I do, back home or out here, it's all the same to us. You folks don't go to church, Corinne,' I said. Well, it's the truth, isn't it? You don't know, when people like me preach, when we talk about things like the good road and the right path, we don't mean some made-up world in your imagination. It's a real world we're talking about. You folks bounce from one bonfire to another, wearin' yourselves out trying to do good. My people don't work on it that way. You can hate pigs all you want, but they're gonna be there every day of your life. You do more good if you help your neighbor than if you keep tryin' to get rid of that pigsty."

"Well, but it does sound like Corinne's hit the nail on the head, Dorothy." History professor, Samantha, wasn't worried about the so-called future; history would take care of that. "What are you doing out here, after all? Everyone in this town prays to just about anybody and the last thing they see is God in someone else's eyes. How do you even stand talking to us?"

"Well, it's enough to tire a soul to death, I can tell you. Corinne knows I yearn to turn tail and go back." She could go to her Alabama town, open the door to her mother's white house just down from the church, be the first woman to lead them all, dark-skinned, light-skinned, hick, city slicker, in the fight to right the world. But instead, here she was, ordained just a year ago in a small pastoral college in Arizona, leading an evangelical church in amidst Bay Area tumult, the most unlikely place on earth to spread the message. These protest people think they know better, but they got no idea how many wars and how many race riots there are in this world. You can't fight 'em all.

Corinne changed the subject. "You know what? Richie's gunna run for City Council, aren't you, Richie?"

Richie was stunned. "'Scuse me, Miss Corinne Buxton? I mean, you just got me in law school. How're Berkeley people gonna vote for a kid like me?"

But Corinne had her plans and, as the neighborhood said, Corinne knew a good bet when she saw it. "Dorothy, who's your speaker down at the church for Memorial Day?" The fact was that every Memorial Day, Deacon Matthews spoke on the unassailable dignity of those who died for a country that had once enslaved them. How would Dorothy's parishioners take to having this withdrawn, pale boy, a white boy with a father who owned car dealerships, speak on remembering heroes?

Well, they took to it fine. "See what I'm talking about, Dorothy?" Corinne wasn't surprised at Richie's power to move a crowd to dream. "You just don't know us people on the coast." You could have heard a pin drop when Richie spoke that Sunday. "We are guardians in this corner of the world. We need to rise up against those who favor darkness. It is up to us to save what others want to waste." Even if you didn't believe him, you could see a time when you would.

"You have done us proud." Corinne didn't hide her tears at the celebration for Richie's win in November. A few weeks later, as Thanksgiving got near, Corinne, Dorothy and Richie took their Sunday drive through the vast park between the Berkeley hills and the undulating hills so short a time ago devoted to ranch lands and fruit farms and walnut groves. Now, a checker-board of housing clusters, but still, it was Corinne's homeland. You don't drink the water of a place and not be from there, body and soul. Drawing near the acreage that had been in her family for a century and more, the trio sang along to the radio in Corinne's Buick, and for a moment, considered Electric Flag's 'Killing Floor' as their theme song. Richie darkened. "Okay, how about 'Over You'?" Corinne had moved to Richie's neighborhood before he was born, had known him from the day his parents brought him home, had mourned the death of his mother, though what good could have come of her, drinking like that and driving pickled with Richie in the car, to boot. 'Over You' was just the right choice.

"Here's where we had our horse barn." Corinne slogged through the upturned soil as if it were her favorite family room rug. "Over there we had walnut groves, plums and almonds. Hundreds of acres. Heaven on earth in February and March. My Grandpa Miller, why he let my mother take up with those banker Buxtons, I don't know. My father's clan, they all think in piggy bank clinks. If it makes money, they'll buy it."

Evelyn Miller, Corinne's wild mother, was of the earth her family had farmed since statehood. How did Grandpa Miller let her take up with the Buxtons? Easy. Evelyn, just a young teenager at the time, saw them circling the land, had even packed heat to keep the snooping vultures at bay. That had scared hell out of old Miller. Seeing his Evelyn turn vicious, he had wasted away with worry until his beloved daughter finally agreed to marry a Buxton. Miller felt he was brokering a diplomatic alliance. Nothing was diplomatic about Evelyn. Buxton's rage at this stronger and smarter wife was a trap. Evelyn showed her children how to buck the blows, then entrusted her land and her slow-witted son to her beloved daughter and ran off to hide on the northern coast of California. "Good riddance," snorted Buxton as he sank into indebted drunkenness.

"The man's a cruel joke, Dorothy. A rotten piece of padre. I don't know how my mother didn't shoot him into shreds."

"But, look here, Corinne, he is your daddy." Dorothy couldn't tolerate the outright condemnation of a father. Yes, there were failed fathers, but murder won't fix that.

"Oh, Dorothy, shut the hell up. That land was like his own body to my grandpa and my mom." On the Sunday drives out to the farm, they had watched as acreage was cleared, shaved of the groves, scoured of the nature that had fed the spirits of Corinne's mother and her family. Neat grids now hemmed in blocks and blocks of houses. But toward the east rolled the vast expanse of grassland and copses that Old Buxton couldn't lay a hand on. That much Evelyn had locked up for Corinne and Lloyd, fair and square, the lawyers had said. "I tell you, it's not just the greed. It's the dead end of it. What's it mean, Dorothy, where's it all go to, his cars, his country clubs, hob-nobbing with the big money politicos? He didn't do a thing for it all except get my mother pregnant so's he could marry the treasury. The man's an ass. I'm gonna kill him. Deserves to die." Corinne sat in her living room, staring at the wall, refusing to yield to Dorothy's pleas that she invite her father for Thanksgiving dinner. Dorothy was incredulous. "No, I got another plan, Dorothy."

Dorothy is driving Corinne's car out to the Miller place. "A shame Corinne's doing this to Lloyd. The boy is helpless." Richie nodded agreement with Dorothy; Lloyd didn't deserve this, but it was how Corinne wanted it. She wanted Buxton dead. This was as good as she could get.

Lloyd was ecstatic. Corinne's for Thanksgiving? Hot dog! "Just get him back by Friday night. Somebody sober needs to drive me around this weekend." Buxton was high as a kite already. Who knew what might happen if he were left alone?

"Your tie's all screwed up, Lloyd. Lemme fix it for you." Richie reached out, but Lloyd fell to his knees, grabbing Richie around the thighs. "Hey, buddy. What's goin' on? Dorothy. Help me here." Richie held Corinne's sobbing brother by the shoulders. That morning, Old Buxton had used a belt to convince Lloyd he'd better shut up about the plan to sell the boy's share of land so Buxton could pay off a gambling debt.

Dorothy and Richie gave the boy aspirin and a sip of scotch for the ride to Dorothy's church.

Houses along the streets of the Berkeley flats floated on wisps of November morning fog. In Dorothy's church, faint sunlight warmed the walls, a gold glow suffused the worship hall. Corinne and Richie stopped to introduce Lloyd – "Miss Corinne's brother" – and to greet the Martins, the Pages, the Widow Brown. They stepped aside to let Dorothy's parishioners crowd into their pews. With Lloyd, they found places at the back of the hall. Sunday hats lay like great bejeweled crowns on the women's heads; men flexed their wrists to free gleaming cuff links from the sleeves of the suit jackets. There would be coffee and cake after. But first, the Thanksgiving prayer. Dorothy grasped outstretched hands offered to her as she made her way down the center aisle to the pulpit.

"Lord, we come here this morning first to thank You, then to ask of You, and finally, Lord, to marvel at Your world. Hear us as we raise our voices in a psalm of thanks. Let us sing." The fog was lifting outside the church, the voices of the seated parishioners rose to the ceiling, then wafted beyond the hall. Dorothy read from the Gospel of Matthew. "Blessed are the poor in spirit, for theirs is the kingdom of heaven." The hum of response hovered in the air above the pews. Dorothy called on Deacon Matthews, who prayed for the world's woes to be washed away by the work of Dorothy's congregation. "Now let us take a moment to hear the better voice that is within each of us." Not a sound. Then a soft moan. Finally, a deep sob as Lloyd fell, once again, to his knees. Corinne smirked as her brother clasped his hands and murmured: "Sffah. Uhsad." Only Dorothy had understood his words. Saved. Lloyd the Innocent had been saved. Buxton the Bastard had been slain.

Lloyd's life began. Mr. Haines, Richie's father, needed a mechanic in his shop and Lloyd was eager to win the reward of driving his boss's red Mustang. Mr. Haines himself brought him home from a shopping spree with a new wardrobe, a new stereo system, an apartment just walking distance from Mr. Haines's garage. But Corinne wasn't done with Buxton.

Richie passed the bar, and started the long climb to the top of the mountain they had all chosen for him. The math professor urged him on, counseling tactics in addition to strategy. "Estate planning can be just about money, Richie, or it can be something greater. Now you want to let them come to the choice themselves, whether their kids'll blow the load, or whether they want to see themselves as first in a dynasty, creators of some sort of legacy, worth more than a wad of cash and longer-lasting than a fancy house." Richie was learning.

He had only to look at Old Buxton, reduced to drinking alone as the pipeline to his son's money drained dry and his tab at the country club ran off the spread sheet. Corinne imagined the man writhing in his chair, whiskey in hand, helplessly furious that his son was not the eunuch he had raised him to be, that instead the fellow was kneeling in a church run by a woman pastor and revving up motors in a garage owned by a man he imagined was an illiterate migrant from Oklahoma. Enough to kill a man. From time to time, Richie would drive Lloyd and the two women out to the farm, ring the bell to the crumbling farm house, have Old Buxton reach his trembling hand for the money gleaned from the sale of an acre or two of the land he could rightfully claim as Evelyn's husband. Wouldn't Richie like to see Lloyd a rich man? All's he needed, Buxton murmured as he shook with delirium, was to sell an acre here, an acre there.

"Oh, Mr. Buxton, sir, Lloyd doesn't like builders. No, sir, it's just gonna stand there, his land, and be green." The more Buxton hated this poetic lawyer from Berkeley, the more Richie aimed his words as a thousand cuts. "Lloyd's gonna make it preserved land, Mr. Buxton. No houses, no, sir". Then they'd drive over to Lloyd's and Corinne's woody and grassy land, an emerald eminence that ruled over the devastation of Old Buxton's housing developments.

But Dorothy worried about Corinne's murdering mind. "You do the right things for the wrong reasons, Corinne. You can't be so dad-blasted angry all the time."

"Oh, yes, I sure as hell can. The madder I get, the more your people are redeemed." Corinne snickered. Dorothy felt the familiar sting of Corinne's unkind stab at her beliefs, but held back. She had nattered on enough at Corinne's faith, her unshakeable certainty that the next mayor, the next governor, the next president was going to save them all. An old story. It would never work out that way, Dorothy believed.

And then, without warning, they discovered how it would work out. Corinne felt nauseated in the morning, was in the hospital by nightfall, and with little time left to her, gave her brother everything she owned on the condition that Richie fix the developers once and for all. Richie put the law into high speed. In a matter of days, the Miller ranch was immunized against the disfigurement of what passed for development, an expanse of what had been, now to become what always is. Lloyd did as his sister bade him, signed where Richie told him to sign so that the remnant of the family land would become a lasting public treasure. That meant a lot at the time.

No one in Corinne's crowd knew there was a song called "Long time comin'" until Dorothy sang it for the guests one afternoon, unaccompanied, unhurried, each word a history that for Dorothy was a living past. "Where did my pretty one go? Long time comin'." You could sing it over and over, it would never mean the same thing. Decades of meanings had flowed through her melody that day, and filled Corinne's bright yellow living room. Now the song was lingering in the hospital room. But daylight was fading. Dorothy asked her friend, "Corinne, does anyone know how good really gets done?" But her friend had gone on. Dorothy opened the window and let the question slip out into the evening.

~~~~~~~~

PLAYGROUND OF WRAITHS

KIT STORJOHANN

Despite my mental preparations—and the callousness I had thought my recent tragedies granted me—seeing the wreckage that used to be my uncle's farm, and my childhood sanctuary, tightens my throat. I knew that the land had been all sold off long ago. I'd been prepared to see chain-link fences guarding factory-like buildings where my uncle's legacy would have been transformed into a mechanized caricature of itself. A hint of fields and wild lands in the distance, or the babbling flow of the stream (now just a turgid worm hidden by reeds), would have been enough refuge for me. Instead, crows cackle their vague disapproval as I wade through a hip-high sea of grass to the rotted skeleton of the house I had known. I pluck a handful of dust-like soil from between briar-choked patches; it spills through my fingers with the texture of ash.

When I was young, this remote, rustic area had thriven under what seemed to be perpetually clear blue skies. Tidy farmhouses were comfortably nestled into their modest rural fiefdoms while sheep and cattle grazed all around in near-still tranquility. Fields of well-tended crops had stood in rigid formation, broken only by their now-fallow brethren, allowing foraging rabbits and wild greenery a season's respite before falling into crop lines once again. Today, however, a cracked, overgrown road has led me through a jungle of rust-colored, tangled, and matted grasses under a churning gray morass of sky. A sprinkling of dilapidated shells of homes, like the carcass of my uncle's farmhouse, are the only signs that people ever lived in this place.

I spent my summers growing up here. When I was very young, my parents would drive us from the suburbs every few weekends to visit my father's brother, who neither time nor progress could pry off the farm. Eventually my sister and I were invited to stay a whole summer, enjoying a piece of the life our cousins enjoyed all year round. She had wearied of the experience after two or three years, but I asked to be allowed to go back every summer. Those blue-skied weeks between school years were spent cheerfully tending a slice of the world considered—even in those days—a throwback to a dead era.

Growing up in this paradise, my cousins became my best friends. They listened patiently to my fears and secrets, and trusted me with theirs. My first kiss was shared with one of my cousins in a field, rolling and tumbling around when we were old enough to know better. A mélange of smells, twined with manure and rotting vegetation, transformed quickly from a pungent nuisance into a token of homecoming every time I arrived at the end of the school year. I'd learned the names and personalities of every one of the cows, even helping to birth several calves. A series of bloodhounds surrendered their traditional perch across the doorway at night in order to sleep at the foot of my bed — the last of the line, Smokey, being barely out of puppyhood in my last summer here. Nothing I saw on television during the rest of the year could compare to my uncle's stories on bath night as we each waited our turn for the tub. The domesticated uniformity of suburban landscapes held little promise for a nascent dreamer, but the fields and pastures dissolving into distant groves provided a comforting womb to gestate the yearnings I did not yet understand.

The woods, though, have sent forth creeping platoons of grass and scrub-brush to reclaim what was once my uncle's piece of the world. My cousins drifted off, one by one, into lives of their own, and my aunt had sold the farm almost immediately after he died. Now there is no sign that anyone owns it. The borders between properties have been erased by tangles of weeds. The old wooden rail fences have fallen and rotted to splinters, leaving only a scattering of warped posts climbing out of the grass like spindly fingers.

I wondered at the eventual fate my own house, hundreds of miles away in another sector of the suburban world I'd once imagined escaping. In the wake of all that had happened, the few friends I had left weren't surprised I didn't want to stay there any longer. Far too large for a solitary person and a growing roster of ghosts, it was eagerly snapped up by a young family shortly after coming onto the market. What met with less understanding from my social circle was the utter purgation of its contents—even the photographs and all the supposedly sacred keepsakes vanishing over the course of some yard sales and countless trips to the dump. Only a few suitcases of clothes survived to accompany me on my journey across the many places I had lived during my life—a sad wandering which I jokingly dubbed my 'tour of the battlefield'. My career was already a dead husk of routine, held together with less cohesion than the decaying farmhouse in front of me. Letting it collapse was a mere formality, much as it would be if the rotted joists of my uncle's house chose this moment to finally give way.

Feeling the inimitably unsettling sensation of someone's gaze, I look around, expecting the glare of some squatter or even a specter. If a dog were given as many decades as a human to watch its world crumble, it might look like the nearly-furless, twig-legged, rangy creature that stares at me from the creeper-choked road. Its teeth have been reduced to a few stubby fangs, around which the sagging jowls hang, but the eyes that are watching me are still perfectly black and puppyishly eager.

"Smokey," I whisper. The ancient dog regards me for a moment, then pads away, losing itself in the stalks of brown grass that crackle in the breeze.

~~~~~~~~

HEART ACHES

DAVID PORTEOUS

There are coincidences, amazing coincidences, and then this: too magical for words is what Darren Scott thought he told Julie at their chance meeting earlier today. It wasn't right, but he tended to be a suave star in memories. What he did recall accurately of the meeting in that Deli was her iciness for a first encounter in thirty-plus years. But now, seeing her twice in the one day, he had to keep his focus on Julie, as she headed off in the distance, unaware of him chasing her. This time he had recognized her hair-matching, silver-gray coat as he left the hospital and peered down the road to find where he parked before the numbing time at his father's bedside. An image of Julie in that coat had filled his mind since the Deli and their ensuing move to Starbucks; it was all he'd had to bolster his mood in the dismal hospital.

Just ahead, a train station had disgorged a horde that he had to zig-zag through, but he refused to lose her after their Starbucks tête-à-tête had left so much unsaid, unasked and, most importantly, unanswered. He endured protesting lungs by remembering their first kiss, though he had to ignore the image of her lowering her lips to his and saying: "Tall girls too much for you? This one will come...even go...down to you."

Like salmon going upstream, Darren pushed on, images of Julie in his mind as he struggled to keep her in view so she didn't slip out of his life again. He also pondered the unlikely events that had led him here today. He'd chosen to take local roads to kill time before hospital visiting hours, even though he hated traffic, but why stop to buy a cigar? His cardiologist had banned them now that a stent nested in an artery, and he rarely missed them, but today's inexplicable desire for one surfaced and he stopped his car then and there...

~~~~~~~~~

Choosing that seedy area's Deli after he saw teens doing drugs outside was a miracle. They had bags of 'fruit salads', stolen multi-colored meds with various long-lasting effects, often for a suddenly shortened life. Still disturbed by that as he went in, he was glad to see the only customer engaging one of two swarthy shopkeepers. She was tall and elegant, wearing a silvery-gray coat that looked too expensive for the district, so that coat, and then her profile held Darren's interest.

"Jules?" He could hear his incredulity. "Julie Pierce?"

"It hasn't been Pierce for...forever." She'd looked down saying that, as if nervous, but turned toward him and calmly added: "Hello, Darren. I wondered if you'd speak to me."

"You recognized me? Why didn't you say something?"

Her response was soft and hesitant. "Oh... You know."

"No. All I know is that some coincidences are amazing, but this is magic. Why not say hello after so long?"

"Well, we didn't part so magically, did we?" With that gentle rebuke, her hazel eyes twinkled a hint of mischief.

As crinkles radiated around eyes that once excited him, Darren was only vaguely aware that her pretty face showed few signs of her age. His mind was scrambling to reach back beyond decades, but he saw a wry smile twitch her lips and managed to mumble: "We didn't?"

"No, but let's not reminisce here. Buy what you came for, and then I'll let you buy me a coffee somewhere."

"Great! It'll just take a sec."

Seeing Monticristos amid cheap cigars, he raised a finger to the shopkeeper and pointed. He spun back in time to see Julie slip a pack of cigarettes in her bag, and felt relief from having a safe topic to restart a chat. "Both needing a smoke is fate! And shows that smoking can't be all bad...not for us." A memory flared, and he added: "Still menthols?"

"Lights. Token health gesture. It's my only vice now."

Paying for the cigar diverted him from a cute rejoinder to that, but he had to say: "You look stunning! So... Whatever you're doing for your health, Jules, it works."

He thought she'd ignored the compliment, but as

they walked to the door, Julie said quietly: "You haven't changed."

"Yeah, right. My hair's going white, and I didn't lug this weight around with me back then."

A glow he was feeling faded as she smirked while giving him a head to toe glance. "I didn't mean how you look."

After leading him to his Audi, Julie pointed to a shiny old Mercedes 450SE and told him to tail her to a Starbucks. He only then realized that she had known his car by seeing him get out of it, and again wondered why she didn't greet him. He hoped to recall how they'd split before the coffee shop, and tried picturing their affair back when he was singing in a band. Julie hadn't seemed jealous of the groupies, nor of his fiancée, Laura, so he'd chosen to believe that she was content in their secretive affair. If that fallacy itched in his mind back then, it hadn't done it enough to scratch to the surface.

A Barber Shop where they parked reminded Darren that a trim would end his wife's nagging, and he foresaw Julie's prickliness shortening their chat to give him time. Seeing a woman cutter buffet her customer with hefty breasts decided the matter. That had him grinning as he opened Starbuck's door for Julie, whose quizzical expression he had to ignore.

She sat and asked him to get her a cappuccino, a request sweetened by flashing eyes that made him feel young again, and ignore his cardiologist's mantras. He returned with her cappuccino and a double espresso.

"I see your passion for drinking mud hasn't changed."

Rather than risk revealing his heart attack, he said only: "But less now. No, I want this to be like old times, when we'd sit chatting in coffee shops forever. They were the days!"

"Nights," Julie said tersely. "After I'd hung out waiting for all the gear to be packed... If I'd been lucky enough to be allowed to go to your band's gig. Remember that?"

Darren's affable façade faded, but a tiny sparkle in her eyes kept him willing to stay, mostly to say: "Whatever I did back then to bury a burr in you, Jules, I'm really sorry. But... I've racked my brain and... See, my memories of us are great. Really great. Seems all yours aren't. So...what was it?"

She tried to laugh, but his intense gaze ended it. "Great, huh? Oh...it's too long ago to fuss about. Let's talk about now. What're you up to? Last I heard, you were in advertising."

"Got out. Full of 'poseurs', as we used to say. We were so pretentious! But I don't want to change the subject, Jules. Why won't you tell me what I did to piss you off?"

Julie stalled by pulling the cigarettes pack from her bag, glancing at a NO SMOKING sign and returning it. "I'd have done anything for you back then, Darren... Too often I did. It still hurts that you never knew how much I loved you."

"But...we were kids... Having fun, but not...you know."

"You were a kid! Having fun with every girl around. But I clung to any time you gave me, hoping you'd see I wanted you all to myself. My big hope...stupid as it was...was for you to love me like I loved you. So what did you do? Not change. Married Laura and, I heard, ruined her life by still having love affairs. No, not love. Flings! Heart-breaking flings!"

The response in Darren's mind seemed sure to drop him in the pit her tone had dug under his façade, but he let it out. "Thirty years ago! You talk like it was yesterday. I was no saint, but why so tough on me? Can't we just be glad to have met up again? Maybe I deserved that lecture once, but I... No, sorry. I'm trying to say that I don't get this hurt you've nursed. Not having me in your life didn't stop you getting on with it. You look great. Nice clothes...classic car...all good. Want to take a shot at explaining it? Please?"

She looked down at her hands, as if willing them to be steady while lifting the cup to her lips. He stayed silent, and used the pause to admire her retained beauty, seeing a ghost of honey-blonde waves in gray hair. He also saw a missing wedding ring's groove in her finger; that helped to turn his expression to compassion as Julie spoke, sounding more like she was explaining to herself, than to him.

"Sorry. Emotions are...shaky. I lost my husband...four months ago. Cancer. It's evil. For years I watched him fade, suffering as it spread...losing the will to fight. The end was a blessing, but it left me... You know. So I'm sorry... I just..."

He held her left hand, unconsciously feeling the groove as he said: "No need to say more. Or apologize. I'm sorrier than I can say, Jules. I saw two uncles...fade like that. No one should go through it...the dying, or who's left behind."

"No," she said firmly. "I must...explain. When life goes bad, you think of what might have been. I couldn't...without thinking of you...a lot. So seeing you get out of your car was a shock, but my memories were right there. All I could think was that if I'd done things differently I might have won you from Laura." She tried to smile. "It's funny. Over the years I've pictured us as a couple...having coffee together like this."

Darren's stifled chuckle cleared Julie's mind enough to register that his index finger was tracing the ridge on her ring finger. She slid her hand from under his to lift her cup with both, then gazed into his eyes, unwilling to say more.

He hoped that his expression looked reassuring. "Sorry. I guess what you said drew me to where your ring had been. I was surprised you don't wear it...but that's... Forget it."

"John wanted it with him. I didn't mind. It's ash now. No. Gold melts, right? Anyhow, it's gone. And it'd be silly to wear just an engagement ring at my age. But this isn't worth talking about. Tell me about your life. Nothing serious like I just... Make me laugh. You always could. That was one of the things I most... Oh, I don't know. Tell me anything."

"In my second marriage." His pause for her laugh was rewarded by a smirk. "Yeah. Big surprise. Ten years. Laura and I stay friends, but she's better off without me. Marriages get to be a pattern, don't they? And if the pattern has a flaw, like the guy's a skirt-chaser, it repeats. I did try to be a good husband. Really. But I was always ready to bed hop. Lousy thing to admit, but who better than you knows it's true?"

"Do you treat this wife any better? Tell me about her."

"Cheryl's a good kid... We're good for each other. Being different as chalk and cheese complements all each of us lacks. She's practical, too...can do anything she puts her mind to. Me? Well...still a youngster in my head, chasing dreams. But I've learned to shrug about what I can't do. This body keeps reminding me I'm not a kid any more."

Julie diverted from the topic of aging by asking, too gaily: "And what dream are you chasing now?"

"Writing...a novel. Still more like just a heap of stories."

"About?"

"Life, I suppose."

"Yours? What a colorful tale!" Her smile softened that.

"Not exactly mine. But I borrow bits from it."

"Do I rate a mention?"

Darren sipped his espresso to stall; one story had a tall band groupie whose soulful moans during sex led the singer to write sad love songs. After lowering his cup, he said flatly: "It's fair to say I blend aspects of people I know to make my characters. I guess that's what fiction is... It works for me."

If that disappointed Julie, it showed only in her changing the topic. "You called your new wife a kid. A young trophy? There's a surprise." She arched an eyebrow.

Darren chuckled, partly relieved to have the new subject. "Hell no! Almost my age. As to your other question... I gave up frolicking with strange ladies...and some were real strange! So age does have benefits, like putting an end to bed-hopping. Oh, sure, I still look. Just not up close."

"So laudable." Julie's lips formed a wry smile. "Cheryl is a lucky lady... Only woman ever to have you all to herself."

He chuckled dryly. "Yeah. Real lucky. What a prize."

A shadow of seriousness darkened Julie's eyes, but she cleared it with a bright smile. "And that hasn't changed... I'm glad. You're the most open man I ever knew. Say what you think...none of the games men play. It won't be news to you... given all your experience, but we women love honesty almost as much as we love men who make us laugh."

"Write that down. I'll show it to Cheryl next time she's giving me hell for it."

"Giving you hell for what?"

"Not engaging the brain gear before driving my mouth. Like, if we're at a friend's home and he asks how I like some new thing he bought... I tell him...the truth. It's sparked a few ear-bashings in the car ride home, I can tell you."

Julie's laugh held an echo of her mirth when with him at a park, naked, stoned on pot and Chablis, and giggling as a family hurried from the sight of them. He chuckled as he asked: "Know what I just thought of?" Her curiosity rose as he paused before saying: "A loaf of bread, a jug of wine, and thou beside me. Soon I'll be fat, drunk and in trouble for spooking good Christian picnickers. Remember that?"

Her laugh bubbled again as she said: "In the

park...that Sunday you gave up band practice to be with me! Oh, yes! I often think of that." She paused, clearly checking if what she said crossed some privately defined line, but then shrugged. "Well, as I told you. I've done a lot of thinking lately."

No other customer knew that a wall fell between the older couple there, but Darren and Julie felt it as they revived the past with: "Do you ever see...?" The reply was always 'no'; both had left their suburb soon after the affair and each new home took them farther from all they'd known. Neither let pain from old times mar a rekindling of the glowing bond they'd had, nor said more than needed if they had to refer to their marriages. They squeezed each other's hand to convey delight at anecdotes, and by the time Julie saw that an hour had evaporated, they were simply holding hands.

"Hell! I'm late! It's time for my appointment!"

Darren then saw a blur of movement. Julie's long hair swirled in unison with her coat's hem as she took her bag and strode to the door. He had to keep up; the most important fact about her had not been revealed.

"Jules! You can't go until I get your phone number!"

"No time! I'm late for... Your business card, quick!"

Before they got to her car, Julie had lit a cigarette while he was still searching for a card in his wallet. She opened her door, then spun back to get his card.

He held it tightly. "It's old, but the home number's right. You will ring?"

"Yes, Darren." Her eyes pleaded for him to forgive her haste, then glinted wryly. "And if Cheryl answers?"

"Ask for me. I'll say I ran into you today. Probably."

"You would." She leaned in to kiss his cheek, but he held her arm to prolong the contact. "Darren! I must –"

"Yeah, an appointment. Too important to stay?"

She sighed out smoke and regret. "Grief counseling. Help to get my head straight...a shrink one of John's friends knows. It's why I'm in this area, and why I can't be late. I'd look like I'm not interested. She does help...and I've talked about you, so after seeing you...I think I need to talk to her. I know I do."

Another swirl of the coat had Julie in the car and the engine of the 450SE rumbling. She looked up at Darren and smiled. "I am glad we...met up. And I will call."

As the door clicked shut, she spun the steering wheel and the Mercedes sped into the patchy traffic. He could only wave, and hope she saw that in her car's mirrors.

~~~~~~~~~

Now, with that vivid in his mind, he emerged from the crowd of commuters and saw Julie's Mercedes again, parked just ahead of where she was walking. As she was close enough to drive off before he got to her, Darren wanted to run, but closing the gap to her had turned breaths to gasps. He saw it as a heart attack's aftermath, so no cause for alarm, but felt it prudent to just suck in a breath and yell: "Jules! Wait!"

Her glance back before going to her car to then peer at the dispersing mob reminded him that her vision had always been weak. With flailing arms that would look strange in any other setting than people pointing to parked cars, he caught her eye. His relief was fleeting; an agitated Julie checked her watch.

She waited, fidgeting impatiently until he was almost to her, then called: "I've got to go, Darren! I said I'd phone!"

"Yeah, yeah. But –"

"No buts! I..." By then, he was close enough for her to see him gasping, and changed her tone. "Are you having a heart attack? Sit in the car! Get your breath. Are you okay? No, don't speak! Do I call for an ambulance? Oh, my God!"

With a wan smile of gratitude, Darren eased backwards in the door she held open and sat with his feet still out of the car. Amid gulped breaths, he said: "Don't call me God, Jules. But thanks. Actually... I did have a heart attack...few months back. But I'm fine. Or I will be. Really."

"Can I get you...? Like water? A shop...a Deli is just over the road." Her caring concern put a tremble in each word, and as her face lost its mask of impatience, her tears welled.

"I'll be fine, Jules. But can I just sit here a minute? Can you spare the time?"

"Of course! Then I'll drive you to your car. Where did you park? Why are you here?" Regret about peppering him with questions showed in quivering lips as she added: "I mean... That's if you feel up to driving. Should I take you home?"

"My place, or yours?"

"Darren!"

"Joke, Jules. I'll be good to go in a minute... But a

lift to my car would be sweet... If you can spare –"

"Forget it! Forget...everything. I'm so sorry I was bitchy. Nothing matters now, except to be sure you're all right. So wait here while I get some water for you. No arguments!"

Darren turned to watch her long-legged glide to the Deli, and smiled at this meeting also involving one as he settled in and closed his eyes. Above the traffic's roar he could hear his pulse's soggy thumping. His anxiety about that faded as the sound did, and by the time Julie was back and sat beside him he was feeling almost at ease.

She handed him a large bottle of Deer Park. "Here. Sip some water. Not too much. Take it easy."

Darren grinned. "What an advertising image problem! Our water's from a park full of deer, or a spring in Poland."

"Ah, good...back to your old self. Your color's better, too. You looked... Well, I was really worried about you."

"Must admit...so was I. I feel okay now, but can I sit a few minutes? I'm sorry if I'm holding you up."

"Forget it. There's no good reason for me to race off."

"But I thought from how you were as I got here that –"

"I...didn't know how to talk to you after being with... But the reality is..." She shook her head, as if to dislodge some disturbance, but a nibble of her lower lip exposed her failure.

"There's some great truth you can't tell me? Why?"

Julie frowned. "I...don't know." She got her cigarettes and was about to light one. "No! I can't fill you with second hand smoke if you had a heart attack. Sorry...sorry."

"Jesus, Jules! I didn't buy the cigar as a souvenir of that place I met you, so... Go on. Light up."

"Really?" Taking a chuckle as consent, she lowered her window. "Thanks. I need it. I tried to stop, but...they helped me cope with John's... Better to stop and just drink, but to my wine and cigs I added vodka. I'm back to just wine now."

"My cardiologist says that's okay. Banned every damn booze I could think of, but said a little red wine's good for us. He didn't define what 'a little' means... I didn't ask."

Julie's smile was the first since he arrived. "Still my old Darren... Hopeless! Won't let doctors tell you how to live."

"Think they're god! Your smile does me more good than docs do. And still being your Darren... Even labeled old."

Her smile died, replaced by an expression Darren sensed told of inner conflict. Unable to ask what it was, he sipped the water. She finally spoke, without looking at him, and he was more baffled by her rambling musing's bitter edge.

"Why would a shrink lecture me? I thought they just help you to see things right...but... See, I just tried to brush you off because that didn't happen. I know I started it...being late. It got Riva, the psychiatrist, cranky. But I said I ran into you and she asked how I felt about it. I let it all out. She always says to say what I'm thinking. But, hell! I did, and she really let loose on me. I was...still stunned by it when I saw you."

Rather than react, Darren used a sudden silence to watch Julie gnaw her lower lip and gaze blindly at traffic. Evidently sensing his scrutiny, she turned to him, but didn't speak. He offered a smile, hoping it looked sympathetic, but it faded as she focused on his face. Hers took on a look of surprise, as if she was only now seeing him clearly, and she diverted to what he assumed was safer terrain for her.

"You've had a haircut. It looks...nice."

"It's too short. I should've known better than to get it cut in that lousy area where we had coffee. Serves me right."

"Near Starbucks? Did miss big boobs cut it?" She then assessed the nuances of Darren's attempt at a blasé nod,

A short silence felt alarmingly long, so he tried to laugh it off with: "Yeah...be a big girl when she grows up, eh?"

"So the haircut's why you're still up in this area?" Her question clearly included reference to the buxom haircutter.

Darren said only: "That just filled time before going to the hospital, back the other side of the station."

Alarm flared through Julie's pensiveness. "A check-up? After a double espresso hit your blood pressure? That's so...! God, Darren! If I'd known, I wouldn't have let you drink it."

"I said don't call me God." He hoped his smile didn't show his delight in her caring about his health. "No, I visited Dad. Not that he knows... Had so many strokes he's always out of it. But I've got to go. You know how it is."

"I do... It's...hard. I'm so sorry, Darren." After a pause, she said: "And I know you two fought back then, so it's good of you to go now... But tough, I bet. Does your mother visit? Or isn't she still... She'd be very old by now."

"A feisty eighty-two. Hasn't seen Dad in twenty years. Still hates him. As their only kid, I'm stuck with that. Your shrink can tell you about symbiotic bonds...couples thriving on hostility. I know...raised in a non-stop war." Darren then thought to ask: "How are your folks? I really liked them."

"Both gone... Last year, when John's cancer was raging."

As Julie threw her cigarette out the window, Darren saw her tears and took her hand. He then raised his other hand to ease her head onto his shoulder. "Sorry. Didn't think before I spoke. At our age...likely they're...gone. But... Sorry, Jules."

"I'm...just shaky. They both passed quickly...not too bad. But odd. Dad was really healthy, but when she went...heart attack, he just...died. A month later."

"It's sort of nice." His tone held awe. "Not losing them, but...he couldn't live without her. Love like that is nice."

Julie raised her head to look into Darren's eyes. "As lovely as life gets...happy together. Wendy and I – remember my sister? – were lucky to grow up in that love. I've thought about that a lot over the years. Especially lately."

Reminded of her admitting to thinking about him, Darren realized that their day's conversation had come full circle. It seemed prudent to end it there, before anything too unnerving was said, but he couldn't break their locked gaze. It took all his willpower to say:

"Time's getting away. I should, too. Still want to play chauffeur, and take me to my car?"

"Yes." The bland reply was at odds with the intensity of her eyes as they peered into his. "If you think you're ready and want to go now."

"Go? Now? Honestly...that must be about the last thing I want to do... But, really... I think I should."

A frown flittered over her brow before she said softly: "Should I worry about you driving? Should I follow till you get home? You know...to be sure you're okay."

"No. Thanks. I don't think so."

Julie expelled a long sigh, which Darren interpreted as regret for having to end this unexpectedly warm reunion. He read her lapse into pensive silence the same...until she spoke.

"Then would you like to follow me home to my place?"

~~~~~~~~

Originally published in in the antholgy '*Strangers In My Mind*' by The New Atlantian Library / Absolutely Amazing eBook (2017)

RACING COCKROACHES

HELENE MUNSON

What insanity drove me to leave New York, only to end up in this decrepit city? That thought dominated Ann's mind as she walked down *Linien Strasse* in the center of the newly unified Berlin. A blisteringly cold January wind drove snow flurries into her freezing face.

In the Soviet days, the city had been treated politically like it was a suburb of Moscow. That was certainly true as far as the weather was concerned, she thought.

As the new millennium began she'd made some decisions for all the wrong, personal reasons, pretty much on a whim. She'd left her home of 20 years on Manhattan's Upper East Side, quit her job and resettled in Berlin, a city still struggling to rebuild its infrastructure after 45 years of communist sloth. Pockmarks from WWII grenades that splintered buildings had been patched over, but the city still had a long way to go as the new German capital it was supposed to be.

What had she been thinking? She'd moved to a house in East Berlin only to discover - too late - that it was located in a district where a lot of former Stasi officers lived. No wonder the neighbors seemed to watch her every move and treated her with suspicion. The Stasi had been well trained by the KGB. Whenever she unloaded her car she could feel their scrutiny, glaring from behind their polyester lace curtains to get a glimpse of her grocery bags and see whether she had bought her groceries at the discount supermarket or the delicatessen. Prior to the wall's fall, living too lavishly led to denouncement by the Stasi, but now none of that mattered. Those former informers had a hard time accepting that their skills were no longer needed, or valued.

On top of it all, Ann was out of a job. The moment she started talking, people noticed her slight American accent, making her even more guarded among people with lifelong indoctrination about Americans being the *Klassenfeind* - the enemies of the working class.

Hot coffee is what I need now, but this town doesn't have a single Starbucks...and a coffee-to-go at a bakery is served in the cups urologists give us to pee in! In Manhattan, everything had been available within a few blocks of Ann's Park Avenue apartment. She had worked at the *American Museum of Natural History*, the *AMNH*, on the West Side of Central Park, and loved the venerable atmosphere of the giant edifice that spanned an entire city block. Its equivalent in Berlin, the *Naturkunde Museum*, was just as venerable, but looked like the curators and cleaning staff had fled the day the Nazis came to power. It seemed that for sixty years the guards just opened the heavy, over-sized oak doors each morning and shut them at night. Nothing else had been done. Dust-covered exhibits lay in rows, the vitrines displaying hand-written explanations on pieces of paper. At the AMNH, by way of contrast, artifacts were part of multimedia displays, with sophisticated lighting and sound effects, not to mention printed, backlit texts.

There's no gift store here, either. One can't even buy a souvenir T-shirt. What a total no-no for any self-respecting American tourist attraction. She shuddered at the thought.

Ann had run the AMNH's gift store, and stocked much more than T-shirts. Her favorite merchandise was anything whose authenticity needed to be approved by the museum's curators. It allowed her to go to the top floor, closed to the public, where fascinating items that had been collected over the course of a hundred years, were held. She'd seen hapless creatures, bleached by age, swimming in glass jars of formaldehyde, and an impressive collection of preserved bats. In a large glass tank were live black beetles, which were put to work to eat the meat off animal cadavers, leaving only the bones. That was all hidden from the regular museum visitors who had no idea how those pristine animal skeletons on dis-play were obtained. Ann considered having her own key to this secret world a special perk of the job.

Whenever she visited the famous curator of entomology, David Grimaldi, she passed a glass case of giant Madagascar cockroaches that, like the carnivorous beetles, were alive. The entomology department's friendly assistant often let her take one out and pet it. The cockroach would emit its usual hissing sound, which always delighted her. Eventually the assistant allowed her to take home a breeding pair.

She kept them in a small terrarium and they did their thing: multiplied. Ann gave them names. The largest was Hulk Hogan; there was a stately Washington, a fast Jessie Owen and an agile Sammy Davis Jr., all named according to their personalities. When she packed up to leave New York, she could not bring herself to part with her pets. A small cardboard box with holes carried them transcontinentally to their new home in Berlin. She had smuggled them onto the plane. Unfortunately Sammy Davis Jr. got loose and lost. She had thought it wise not to alert the stewardesses.

Now, as Ann walked down a street in *Mitte,* the middle of old Berlin, she searched for a club she had read about in the newspaper. Many old Belle Époque buildings in the area had not been restored, and lacked modern amenities such as state-of-the-art kitchens, or even properly functioning bathrooms. Artists in search of low rents inhabited them. There were also lots of *Kneipen*; cigarette smoke-infested watering holes for local beer-drinking barflies, stranded there after Germany's reunification. The first hipsters were starting to move in and had discovered the club she had read about.

It was run by a Russian artist, Nikolai Makarov, who had lived next-door to Wolf Biermann, an iconic protest singer of the former communist Germany. Biermann had fled to the West a long time ago, but Makarov stayed. He was originally from Moscow and had moved to Berlin because he had fallen in love with a German girl. He was now running the Russian émigré Club *Tarakan*, which means 'cockroach' in Russian.

Ann had difficulty finding the house number; they never seemed to run in a logical sequence in Berlin. But finally she spotted an unassuming wooden door to a basement, down a few steps, and knocked. After a moment, a tall, bald and bulky guy with pasty skin opened it and motioned for her to enter.

She was in a room with floor-to-ceiling bookshelves amid several gilded, almost blind mirrors mounted on burgundy red walls. Most of the book backs were imprinted in Cyrillic. The furnishings were second hand, some antique, and in New York the place would have been labeled "shabby chic." But here in Berlin, Ann felt like she had entered a secret, literary salon in St. Petersburg on the eve of the Bolshevik revolution.

She sat on a sofa closest to the burning fireplace, grateful for the heat. The man who had opened the door came over, and with a heavy Eastern European accent announced: "Welcome! I am Pavel. You want drink?"

Ann ordered a beer and drank from the bottle, as no glass was offered. Looking around, she noticed several men playing pool on a table that filled most of the adjacent room, which was also painted burgundy. A man dressed all in black caught her attention. Long, scraggly hair hung down his back and an equally long beard reached down to his chest. She imagined *Rasputin*, but his attire was distinctly American: black shirt, black Levi jeans with a silver buckled belt and pointed-toe cowboy boots. She watched him for a while. Between hitting the white ball he took long drags from a cigarette and gulps of red wine from a large glass.

Growing tired of watching the players, Ann directed her attention to a stack of books on the table in front of her, all of which were imprinted with Latin lettering.

Ah, something I can actually read, she thought, and took a book of Russian plays from the pile, its title: *Early Plays* by the author Mikhail Bulgakov. A bookmark stuck out and she flipped it open to that page and started to read. In her mind she saw the characters talking to each other. A bunch of down and out Russian aristocrats who fled the revolution were mixing with the less savory segment of 1920's multi-cultural Constantinople society. They were arranging cockroach races to pass the time with something to bet on. Ann had reached a description of a fight starting because somebody was accused of doping the winning cockroach as Pavel returned, pointing at her almost empty bottle.

"You want more beer?" He saw the book in her hand, and asked "You like Mikhail Bulgakov?" Without waiting for her reply, he continued "But you know Bulgakov is thief. He steal idea of cockroach race from Aleksey Tolstoy. But Tolstoy copy from Arkady Averchenko."

Ann sensed that Pavel was getting ready to give her a lecture on plagiarism in obscure Russian literature, and she interrupted, smiling: "Maybe it would be more polite if we call it literary transmission?"

Without acknowledging her response, Pavel continued with a rhetorical question. "You understand that cockroach races are joke of Russian aristocrats on themselves? When emigrated to Constantinople, no more race horses, and no money, only cockroaches and alcohol." A thought flashed in Pavel's mind and, pleased with his own profound thinking, he added: "Kind of like us, just other way around. No more communism, with free schools and doctors, just capitalist money pay for cockroach races."

Not impressed by his wit, and to change the subject, Ann pointed at the man in black: "Is that Nikolai Makarov?"

"Yes. I work for Nikolai, prepare canvas for painting to send to America," he responded proudly.

"Can I talk to him?" she asked.

"Of course. Nikolai always friendly, especially to nice woman," he encouraged her with a wink.

The men had stopped playing pool and Nikolai Makarov was pouring himself another glass of wine. Ann approached him, saying: "I have read about you in the newspaper."

"Nice of you to come out and visit on such a stormy night," he said warmly. She liked him immediately. *He has kind eyes,* she thought. He asked her where she was from and when she said New York he was delighted.

"I spend some time in SoHo to sell my paintings at a Manhattan gallery. Here in Berlin nobody has money, but in New York people have lots of it," he explained.

For a few minutes they talked about the differences in life between Berlin and New York. Then, without any further introduction Ann blurted out: "I would like to challenge you to an American-Russian friendship race."

A broad smile lit-up his face as he asked: "Ah, you also breed racing cockroaches?"

Ann nodded, but had to explain: "Well, they haven't raced yet, but I am sure they are fast."

He took her arm and led her to a back room next to a small kitchen. A table in the middle of the room had a terrarium with cockroaches perched on sawdust in it, a different breed than hers. Nikolai saw Ann's look of surprise and explained: "These are African cockroaches, a close cousin to the more common Madagascar hissing cockroaches". He picked up one. "This is Pamir, there in the corner is Ivan the Terrible. The one sitting next to him is Olga, she's the fastest runner." Ann took Pamir from his hand and gently lifted him up so she could get a better look at him.

Softly rubbing his chitin body, she gushed: "He's really beautiful." Nikolai nodded like a proud father. The animal was clearly not the petting kind and tried to wiggle away, tickling the palm of her hand. She gently cupped it in two hands and gave him back to Nikolai, who put him in his pen.

From a nearby shelf he took two water glasses and a bottle of clear liquid with Russian writing on the label. He filled both glasses a third of the way, handed her one and proposed as a toast: "Let's drink to an American-Russian cockroach friend-ship race at the Palace of Tears." Seeing confusion in Ann's expression, he explained: "As you walked here from *U-Bahn Friedrichsstr*, you had to pass a building on your left looking like a big, dark hall. It was somewhat provisionally built in 1962, just after the Wall went up, for border inspections between the East and West. Families cried a lot when they had to say goodbye to their loved ones who left for the West, never to return; hence its colloquial name." After a pause, he added: "One day it might become a museum, but for now our cockroaches will make history there. It will be a big and newsworthy event!" Nikolai hesitated, gazing intently at her, then said: "Maybe you could help me with organizing it?"

"I would be delighted," she replied enthusiastically. "I'm out of a job right now anyway."

After a pensive moment, he said: "Well, if that is the case, maybe I can offer you a full-time job. I also run an art space called 'The Quiet Museum'. There is a lot to do. Pavel helps me, but I could use a manager who speaks English."

Ah, finally my language skills are an asset and not a handicap, Ann thought as she nodded gratefully.

Ann took another large sip of the clear, burning liquid which warmed her as she thought: *Maybe Berlin is not such a bad place after all...and could this be the start of a beautiful friendship?*

~~~~~~~~

UNFINISHED BRIEF

GERARD MEADE

He stands before the small, rapt audience with his arms outstretched; the pose of a martyr at his moment of ultimate sacrifice. He's meticulously dressed in a custom tailored suit and hand woven shirt, accented by an exorbitantly priced tie. That sharp look is betrayed by the thick black, tousled mane that crowns the ensemble and is the focus of his listeners until he raises his head, surveys the expectant stares, pauses, and delivers the punch line.

"I said, well...I said: 'Wow, you're actually pretty hot!'"

He nails it. His audience howls. It's funny but...it isn't. Knowing him well, his friends' laughter is the sort that slips out in response to unbelievable tragic news. The incredulous but sympathetic guffaws are nothing new to Josh, nor to the familiar group gathered at the end of the bar. The laughter ebbs, drinks are ordered, and Sam approaches, a concerned frown in place. A stray tear is brushed from his cheek and a cold bottle placed in his grip. *Ah Sam, dear, sweet, Sam.*

Sam knows him best and feels his pain, but they need to hear the rest. The gentle words are spoken on behalf of all, a nudge to go on. "And after that...?"

Josh takes a long, hard pull from the bottle and is finally able to resume. "Well, she didn't throw me out but...she did let my asinine remark hang for much longer than I cared to bear. At that point I think I would have preferred getting the boot. After that, it went pretty much as expected, I guess. I mean, I was flabbergasted at having blown what might be my only chance, but she acted as though nothing happened, cool and professional. Her questions were tough, really good, and I answered ok, but my confidence was crushed when I heard my stupid voice say what I never should have been thinking."

Josh downs the rest of his beer and Jack jumps to swiftly replace the empty. Not one in this tight cluster of equals, or near equals, could imagine themselves ever committing such an horrific *faux-pas,* but they collectively commiserate.

It's past nine on a Tuesday after another too-long day at the office. All in attendance are associates at the same huge firm and each works ridiculous hours. They comprise just a small segment of an enormous pool that performs the same tasks, hold the same aspirations, and remain junior in status. The company owns three floors in the ornate high-rise, and the employees are designated a location according to stature. Associates that have not yet been blessed occupy the lowest, mid-level lawyers and supervisors the middle, while partners and the senior elite reign from on high. Each day, hundreds of workers cram the elevators but mostly without interaction. An iconic figure from above is rarely seen amongst them, so to most they're mythological entities.

Everyone's in competition, and recognition is hard to come by. Josh and the lowest level residents around him are no different, but having worked together for a time, they've bonded and are surrogates for friends that became collateral damage of a young lawyer's quest. Simply put, it's easy to stop for a drink with someone you knew was working as late as you were—and would need one just as badly.

Among these peers that Josh considers his friends, he is deemed exceptional. He's been blessed in many more ways than most, and his refined appearance is rarely overlooked by members of either sex. He dresses above his pay grade, is brilliant, tenacious and seems more likely to succeed than the others. He is honest and humble, rare qualities in such a competitive environment, directs praise to all who deserve it and declines recognition if it's mistakenly accorded to him. Josh is Opie from Mayberry, with a young Brad Pitt look and a convincing demeanor that even the sternest of jurists or most skeptical of jurors would be unable to resist if he ever achieves his goal to apply his attributes in a courtroom. Unfortunately, he was also endowed with a less desirous trait, and while listening to the shocking tale, all in the group decide that lone imperfection will inevitably derail his dream.

In brainstorming sessions, Josh is truly incredible. His superlative mind and encyclopedic memory bring theories and alternatives that amaze even the agnostics in the firm. Often it's one such idea that wins out, but he doesn't even remember proposing it; one aspect of his affliction. Far more detrimental to his ascent as a barrister is his inability to consistently curb voicing what churns in his mind—an absolute boon for brainstorming; not so much for closing arguments. His misspeaks are unlike Rain Man's dry monotone or the abrupt staccato of Turret's; it's Josh's wonderment that makes it impossible for him to harness his reaction to potent stimuli. Most outbursts are innocuous—no harm, no foul—but others can be problematic. "That's brilliant!" or a favorite of his, "Hell yeah, baby!" are appreciated, but the rare 'accidents' have repercussions. As in: "Wow, you're actually pretty hot!"

Josh takes a stool at the turn and conversation resumes. The bartender places another brew before him with a wink, having listened in. They stay too late and drink too much but eventually begin to disperse. Josh appreciated the diversion, sharing his embarrassment helped to ease some of the pain, but it couldn't dispel the disappointment. Sam stops on her way out and tenderly caresses his cheek, her own sad smile in place, saying nothing, yet saying much. The guys bump fists, a newer associate asks just how hot she really was as Althea plants a wet one where Sam's touch still lingers. She giggles her parting remark: "You, my man, are the absolute *bomb!*"

Josh has another beer but wisely chooses a cab instead of the next and stews silently on the short cab ride to his studio. Without hesitation, he falls into bed and passes out instantly, still wearing a week's salary in clothing.

Four hours sleep after ten-plus beers never feels good. As Wednesday dawns, he's up on time but quickly abandons the thought of the routine morning run. He drags himself to the shower and attempts to wash away the suds-laden clouds of the previous night as the lowlights from that day's interview roll in HD. Josh frets that some overheard his remark—surely the assistant that had shown him to the office, blurting it out as he did before the door closed—and how fast news travels on the executive floor, but knows that his friends won't betray him. He dreads the long day ahead; it will be even worse in a steadfast fog with a pounding headache.

Surviving a roller coaster subway ride and the elevator's queasy rise, he arrives at the office on time, 7AM, and suffers the stares of those already at work, suggesting he's a slacker for coming in so late. He manages to get through the day, his fear of repercussions repressed by his work. Josh stays later than usual and skips the post-work cocktail, heading straight home instead. The next day's a bit easier, he looks and feels better and by Friday he's thinking it's possible that there'd be no blowback from his crude and inexplicable behavior. He's attacking a brief that needs to be set for review by first thing Monday. If finished today, Josh can take Saturday off and add two more days of separation from the Tuesday fiasco and it might just fall off the radar by then. He doesn't notice the messenger at his desk until the kid speaks up.

"Excuse me sir, I have a memo?"

Josh extends a hand, not looking away from his screen and finishes the paragraph. Accustomed to the rudeness of lawyers, the kid is almost to the elevator before the words carry to him: "Thank you!"

Print correspondence is unusual at his level, email and IM the norm. A fleeting hope that it's from Sam is dashed by the bold script on the envelope: '*Mr. Krieder*'. It's not company stationary, but smaller, and its color isn't one that's much appreciated in office communiques. Anxiously annoyed by the unwelcomed distraction, he considers putting it aside to finish what might save his Saturday, but ultimately breaks the seal.

Please stop by my office at four this afternoon, there are matters we neglected to discuss at our last meeting.

JA

JA? He's stumped, but it dawns dreadfully as he rereads the pink-hued memo. Jacqueline Avigneault is the partner he'd interviewed with and proclaimed 'hot'. His hands grow sweaty and his throat tightens; only one thing hadn't been discussed. Josh checks his watch and is dismayed to find it's already past three. He tries in vain to go back to the brief but winds up making several trips to the men's room instead. His thoughts are consumed, work is impossible, and he rummages for excuses explaining his behavior but that's an even more futile exercise. He makes a final stop in the restroom before boarding the elevator, it's there that he manages to compose what he hopes is a convincing apology.

The same assistant greets him and suggests he sit; Ms. Avigneault will be with him shortly. Josh tries to gauge her reaction to his presence, but finds her only professional and polite, just as her boss had been. He's pondering how many she'd told about his misadventure when a firm voice startles them both: "Mr. Krieder, come in."

The assistant springs up, the atypical personal summons surprising her. Ms. Avigneault holds out a raised palm.

"Thank you Alice, we'll be fine."

Josh follows the executive meekly and stops at her desk while she continues past and resumes her place behind. He stands tall with damp hands clasped before him, attempting a confidence he doesn't own. The partner allows an awkward moment to pass while studying the folder on her desk. She slowly removes her glasses and considers him with a serious, almost grim expression before allowing a polite smile.

"Have a seat Mr. Krieder, that's what the chair's for."

Josh undoes his jacket and obeys but sits forward on the chair's edge, alert, attentive, and shaking in his boots.

"I reviewed my notes from earlier this week and I believe we covered most topics. However, there are certain, ah, things we should address."

Josh simply nods and resists launching his apology. He waits for the reprimand he's sure to receive, and hopes it won't be followed by a description of his severance package.

"First off, I did want to congratulate you on the work you did in the Nash case. It's unlikely that anyone else would have dug up the obscure precedents you discovered. t led to a very favorable disposition in the matter, and it's just that kind of dedication that got you the interview. I'm also aware that Nash is not unique. Other similar contributions have not gone unnoticed, and it's important you know that your efforts are appreciated."

Surprised by the compliment, Josh waves it off, reluctant to articulate. He waits for the 'but'. He's not disappointed.

"Not all is positive I'm afraid. Next week the partners will meet to determine who is ready to accept an increased role with the firm, and while your work has been exemplary and most immediate supervisors agree on your assets, I have my concerns. You may recall, and I certainly do, that our interview didn't start off in traditional fashion. I've recuperated from the shock, but I feel we have to explore the matter further if I'm to make an intelligent recommendation on your behalf. I'm excluding the perplexing episode from your evaluation for the moment, *but*...I've not finalized the report. No doubt you recognize the need for this additional review."

Her look and the pause indicate it's time for a response. Josh inhales and prepares to deliver what might stretch the leeway into a pardon. Josh half-expects a trap, but responds with the reparation he crafted in the toilet, not the schoolboy excuses but the clean, carefully composed atonement.

"Ms. Avigneault, I'm sorry for my gross misconduct. I cannot offer any explanation for it, and believe me, I've tried desperately to construct something credible, but I was totally out of line. I meant no disrespect and I am absolutely aware of the inappropriate nature of such a crude remark, especially when being offered an exceptional opportunity to advance. I've hardly slept as a result of my carelessness. I still have no idea where that remark came from, and I sincerely regret the discomfort it caused you."

She considers him and his apology; he watches closely for her reaction. She lets him wait for what seems like minutes before lifting her glasses from the desk and replacing them. She shifts the file and folds her hands above it.

"There's more to discuss Mr. Krieder, and frankly I don't have the time to allot in my schedule today."

Josh reads indecision in her features. She scrunches her lips as she tries to decide. His eyes drift toward the lips, but his willpower's on top of it. She reaches a decision.

"Join me for dinner this evening. A car will pick you up at seven...I'm sure I needn't tell you to dress appropriately."

Josh is staggered by the unexpected demand and fights off thought/speak impulses. An awkward silence looms as his lack of response draws out, he stutters an unpoised reply.

"Well, yes of course but...I, I'll ah, make sure that I'm, appropriate."

Ms. Avigneault turns her attention elsewhere; he's been dismissed. Josh is imperiled by dangerous thoughts, looking back with his hand on the door lever. *Maybe I should call her Jackie?* Deciding no exit line is necessary, Josh passes the reception area in a daze, slips through the etched glass doors to the elevators and walks right past Sam as she steps out from one.

She's surprised to find him in the executive suite and is immediately concerned when she notices his trance-like state.

"Josh, hey Josh! Hello-oo?" No response. She doubles back and comes up from behind as he presses the call button.

"Hey, what's up bud, you ok?" Sam's on her way to an interview of her own and doesn't have time for distraction, but Tuesday's mishap is fresh in her mind. "Everything alright, Josh?" He turns and smiles in recognition, but offers no reply. "What happened, you don't look so good?" Josh wants to speak, always to Sam, but the tongue that performs of its own accord lays dormant. "Sorry, but I gotta go, I have a meeting. I really want to talk, and you look like you might really need to. I'll catch up with you once I'm done, ok?" A smile and a nod this time as Sam sprints away.

Josh boards the elevator perplexed, trying to justify the emotions and thoughts engulfing him. This whole dinner thing seems wrong, but he clings to the possibility of staying on an upward track, knowing the crux of the matter has yet to be fully addressed. The work day is now shot, as is tonight, and the weekend will be compromised by uncompleted work. Josh closes his station and leaves to prepare for a date with his boss. The complications of the arrangement multiply in his mind and jockey for pole position all the way home.

Even dressing for the occasion becomes troublesome and Josh finds he's struggling with each choice, not sure of the image he should project. He decides the stylish, conservative business ensemble is best and is in the lobby waiting at 6:50, fortified by two beers to settle his nerves.

The car pulls to the curb uptown, money territory, in front of a building that looks residential, not much different than the others they passed on approach. Sam's text arrives just as they drift toward the curb. *Josh, sorry I had 2 run before hope u r ok. Let me know. I'm at Stonewall's if u can stop for a drink, if not call me ok?* He's about to reply when a doorman opens his and the driver instructs him to ask for *Monsieur* Arniel. A brass plaque set in granite is the restaurant's sole designation, and it bears only a forename. Josh steps into a lobby unlike any restaurant he's ever encountered.

Before any embarrassing exclamations escape, a woman, dressed in *appropriate* business attire, greets him and asks for the details of his reservation. Josh passes along the name he's been given. She leads him to a bar area, introduces him to *Monsieur* Arniel, who's been expecting him and leads him through a regally appointed dining room filled with enticing aromas. *Mssr.* Arniel gestures to a private booth where Ms. Avigneault waits with a martini before her, seeming already aware of Josh's arrival. He slips into the banquette opposite his boss and the *sommelier* is immediately at his side.

"Good evening sir, what can I bring you from the bar?"

Josh expected to refrain, thought it best for many reasons, but Ms. Avigneault insists he join her in a cocktail. He asks for a Hendricks on the rocks. His drink before him, she begins with small talk, innocent

315

questions about his background, education, etc. Offering a silent toast, he sips the gin carefully and becomes almost comfortable with the harmless banter, but his stomach growls as bread is delivered and a waiter approaches. Ms. Avigneault shifts conversation to the meal.

"So, you've dined here before Mr. Krieder?"

"Me? Sorry...no, I've never had the pleasure."

"I am relatively sure you won't be disappointed. I have enjoyed many a meal here. Some were incredible, others... well, just memorable."

She laughs at her own joke and Josh tries to join in but his is weak and nervous. She reads his discomfort easily.

"Mr. Krieder, I recognize and understand your anxiety, but before we conduct business we are going to enjoy a fine dinner. This is my preferred method of attending to matters, let's say, best handled outside the office. I've discovered that they're resolved successfully when discussed over a leisurely meal, especially when the parties are unfamiliar. That will be the case for us this evening."

Josh studies the menu, considers her words, and takes a longer pull of gin. The food sounds phenomenal, the bread is incredible, and his appetite suddenly seems fine despite his anxiety. She asks if he has allergies or if any of the offerings don't appeal to him. Explaining that he pretty much enjoys everything seems to please her and she proceeds to order for them both—a...five...course...tasting...menu. Josh cringes, discreetly, as he envisions the extended meal. He sips more gin, almost spews it when, seemingly as an afterthought, she adds the suggested wine pairings which, she explains, will enhance the nuances of the chef's creations. Josh drains the last and sets the gin aside. Digesting the fact that the meal will go on much longer than anticipated, he wonders about the motive behind the fancy, elaborate meal. He's excited by the cuisine but concerned about the wine's effect; eager to be done yet curiously comfortable with the proceedings so far. His job may not be in jeopardy but the night is young and her cross examination has yet to begin.

Dining proceeds at a relaxed pace, limited conversations revolve mostly around the food. The wine does compliment the dishes, but Josh resists draining each glass. Eventually, Ms. Avigneault resurrects the purpose of the meeting during a break between the last savory course and dessert.

"Josh."

Wait...Josh?

"During the interview you mentioned a desire to become more practiced in courtroom litigation. I think that's where we need to begin. Unfortunately, I'll have to ask you difficult questions; it's only fair to the partnership and to you as well. It's important our discussion be completely honest. Are you with me there?"

The suddenness startles him, apparently his look reflects it. He reaches for his water, delaying, sips and replies.

"Yes. I'm sorry. A little sensory overload I suppose. Yes, I understand."

"Good. Josh, you've already shown that you're capable of excellent work. You've put in the hours, and shown a level of dedication that's exemplary. I...we, would be remiss in not acknowledging and rewarding such performance."

"Thank you, I appreciate the recognition."

"You should, and I suppose you expect to be rewarded for that effort. In a way, you have been. An opportunity was offered, and if you succeed in winning the position you'll be far closer to your goal, as I'm sure you're aware. At the completion of your review you'll be rewarded for the work you have done. What remains to be determined is the extent of our generosity, and I'll play an important role in the outcome. My opinion will be crucial. I documented your contributions, nominated you for the promotion, and of course, as we're both well aware, conducted your initial interview. Are you following Mr. Krieder?"

Uh-oh, Mr. Krieder? "I understand completely ma'am." *Damn why did I use that word?* "And I would like to once again offer my sincere..."

The desserts are served, four individual ones for each of them, architecturally arranged and accompanied by four small glasses of different wines. Josh waits for the pageant to conclude. "As I was saying Ms. Avigneault, I would..."

"Please Josh, hold your thoughts until we've finished; we wouldn't want the sorbet to melt."

Josh sighs but smiles. The closer they get to the end—of the meal and whatever she's leading up to—the further away it seemed to drift. It occurs that it's she, not the chef, that's orchestrating the meal; that thought he nearly doesn't corral, it comes dangerously close to slipping past his lips.

The desserts are as impressive as anything that had come before, and the wines different from any he's ever had. He has a buzz on, from the drinks for sure, but also from the overall experience; the food, the service, the *theater* of it all is unique and new to him. The final course is being cleared and Josh readies to resume the aborted apology. He's about to start when the *sommelier* returns, topping off their Port to ward off the evening's chill. Josh takes a deep breath and is about to begin anew when the waiter returns with a 'gift' from the chef and places a platter of *petit-fours.* Josh takes a hit of Port and waits. The waiter leaves and Josh scans the nearby vicinity for any other intruders. He shifts back to the table and spots a smile that's not quite hidden by Ms. Avigneault's napkin.

"I think it may be safe now so let me try this again. As I started to say, I want to sincerely apologize for my indiscreet remark at the start of the interview. I realize that nothing I say can erase that mistake but –"

"Well that is precisely where this discussion begins and the difficult questions arise. Mr. Krieder, I'm sure you have considered potential consequences of your...affliction, should it reveal itself during the course of a legal proceeding before the court, and that you're well aware of how damaging such an outburst could be. I'm sorry, but what I must ask is...well, have you considered seeking help?"

"Frankly, no, I haven't. I think...no actually, I convinced myself that it was something manageable and I've succeeded, for the most part, to contain it...up until recently I suppose."

A lengthy silence follows as Josh absorbs the blow, finds solace in the Port and the executive absently swirls her glass while carefully choosing her next words.

"Mr. Krieder...Josh, I think that was exactly my point. I have no knowledge of what it is you endure and cannot offer anything in the way of guidance but I'm sure there's someone who can. Perhaps you should consider seeking that person out if you envision practicing law in the courtroom someday. For now, for me, the issue is what I advise when I meet with the partners next week and I wonder, what do *you* think that recommendation should be?"

"Well, I...you know what I'd hoped, but after Tuesday and all...I really don't know what to say."

His euphoric buzz had fizzled, leaving only dulled senses. Josh despondently pops a *petite-four* and chases it with a splash of fortified wine. Ms. Avigneault isn't finished.

"Listen Josh, I mentioned rewarding you and I feel that you deserve it. At the moment however, I think it must come in a different form than you'd hoped. Not everyone is meant for the courtroom, and I'm sure you know the vast majority who practice law don't do it under the bright lights. Gifted as you are with your many talents, we can guide you toward a specialty that would be more...suitable. It will benefit us all. If, at some later date, your disposition were to...improve, we can redirect your professional path at that time."

Crestfallen but still gainfully employed, Josh nods that he understands and concedes that he's fortunate. Apparently his boss kept the incident to herself and is still willing to propose his promotion, but Josh feels like he finally made it to the big league only to learn that he will be riding the pine. He resolves to display enthusiasm, put disappointment on hold, and show his gratitude.

"Ms. Avigneault, I recognize the wisdom in your decision and I'm unable to proffer a rebuttal that might possibly alter it. I'm very grateful for whatever it is you have in mind and I assure you the work ethic you've graciously acknowledged will remain tireless. I'm indebted to you for this chance and very thankful for your unwarranted discretion."

She theatrically waves off his humility, Josh noticing that she's feeling the effects of her many glasses emptied.

"No need to thank me for something you have earned Mr. Krieder but the discretion part... Yes, you owe me on that one, and also my assistant for honoring the sanctity of my office."

The waiter is back, inquiring about coffee or tea; Josh prays she'll decline and finally release him. She asks and he refuses with a smile. His boss excuses herself and he grabs his phone to return Sam's text. His typing's interrupted by the delivery of the check. Josh stares at the elegant check holder on its silver tray, placed in the center of the table. He hadn't considered the evening's tab or if he should offer to pay. He sneaks a peek inside the fold and finds the total bill exceeds his monthly rent. His anxiety returns, as does Ms. Avigneault. He pockets his phone but not before noticing that three hours have passed since Sam's text.

Josh makes a feeble attempt at gallantry but his gesture is dismissed by Ms. Avigneault's assurance that the firm can afford it. The waiter returns with two gift bags of breakfast treats and they carry those toward the lobby while the boss offers a glimpse of his promotion's attributes. She surprises him as they approach the steps to the vestibule by entwining her arm with his and speaking in animated fashion.

"What's your appraisal Josh? Was it an incredible meal or merely memorable?" He hesitates before he replies.

"Ms. Avigneault, *that* was an absolutely incredible meal!"

"Very good, perhaps you will soon be a regular." Josh grows more comfortable in escorting his boss as they traverse the expansive lobby until she gives his bicep a remarkably strong squeeze. A rich baritone voice bounds off the surrounding marble and Josh glances where he thought the voice sounded but finds they are alone. His befuddled, slightly inebriated state prevents him from processing the words. He's stunned when it clicks. "And please...call me Jack."

His mind tilts and swirls as they approach the doorman, who does his thing and reveals her town car idling at the curb. Her familiar husky alto resurfaces as they come within range of the sentry. "Can we drop you somewhere Mr. Krieder? It would be our pleasure?"

"No, thank you," he falters, "Ms. Avigneault. That won't be necessary. I'm meeting a friend not too far from here and I think I'll walk. The fresh air might do me some good."

She turns back as the driver opens her door. "Very well. The meetings will take place throughout the coming week, and it's likely you won't hear until the following one. Be hopeful Mr. Krieder, and, of course, follow my lead." She chuckles coarsely. "And be discreet. I truly enjoyed our meeting this evening, thank you for joining me." Sliding into the seat she continues: "You know, Josh, as first words go, I gave yours a good deal of contemplation, and I must say that after my initial shock passed, I found that I appreciated them quite a bit. *Bon soir,* Mr. Krieder."

Josh stands at the curb, watching until the car turns the corner before firing off a text to Sam.

Hope u r still there. I just finished the dinner meeting, on my way and boy, do I have a tale for you!

He pockets the phone and the bizarre day's events wash over him, escalating his lingering buzz into a vague drunken haze. He'd made it; without any harmful outbursts, despite many golden opportunities, but in light of the evening's conclusion, would it really have mattered? He begins to chuckle, it blossoms to laughter. The doorman intervenes.

"Excuse me sir, perhaps I can get you a taxi?"

"*Mais oui monsieur, mais oui!*"

Sam reads his text at home in the kitchen. It confirms what she'd feared when she ran in to him on the exec floor, no doubt having just left Avigneault. His lost, shell-shocked image pained her...she recognized the symptoms. She sips her wine and the first tear trickles from the corner of her eye. She won't tell him about her promotion or how it came to be, won't mention what she'd wanted for them, or how it will never come to pass with all that's happened, or is about to.

Sorry, waited but gave up. Hope u'r ok, talk tomorrow

Josh is bothered by the short text. It doesn't sound like Sam but he's well beyond his capacity for drama and he sets the disquiet aside, giving the driver an alternate destination. It's time to call it a night, a long, strange one at that. He still has his job and his Saturday will be shot, but there's work that needs to be finished.

~~~~~~~~

THE LAST STOP

SUSAN ROSENSTREICH

Years ago, The Last Stop really was the last stop. Alvin was out of work, out of money. But not out of ideas. He corralled squatters living in the old ranch cabins in the hills behind Benicia. "We're gonna rig us up a fine café. Nice warm fire on these cold mornings. So whaddya say, guys?" They scrounged a grimy coffee urn and a two-burner gas stove from the farm hand at Mount Diablo. Alvin prestidigitated a menu of hamburgers or toasted ham and cheese, bought all the food and fixings on credit from Hank's Farm and Ranch Supply. It worked, paper plates, grounds in the coffee and all. Regulars from the ring of remaining farms, the occasional biker and truckers who took the wrong turn, they dropped in, left their small change, and chatted each other up. Years went by. One by one, the squatters peeled off, went on out to San Francisco or found refinery work over by Martinez. Next, they blasted a connector to Route 680, slicing up the cherry and peach orchards. What cows that remained ambled uphill, well away from the non-stop coda of cars, trucks and motorcycles, abandoning the café to people with vehicles. Now Alvin was the star, regaling the growing crowd with his stories of cherry groves that grew fruitier and the farmers who grew richer as cherries shriveled on spring branches and farmers sent their sons and daughters to law school. These days, the fertile delta offered only faint scrubland. But Alvin was pouring coffee way past midnight. "I need me some help."

Grace was a high school dropout. For about two hours. She could have stayed at the farm, at her Uncle Craig's, could have moved one place closer to the head of the table, closer to being boss of the farm, where Craig sat after Pop-Pop died. But Grace got up and walked out of class that day, bored stiff with the unit on presidential powers. She was pacing the town's main street, all three blocks of it back then, wondering what to do after she got to the town line when she saw the sign in the café window. "You need a bus girl, right? I need a job."

Alvin hadn't thought this out. Grace wasn't homely. But romance and the lovey dovey life, no sir. "Alvin," she had said, not one week on the job, "we need to get us some white table cloths and napkins, too." Alvin's café filled when he opened for breakfast and emptied when he closed up after dinner. What was he going to do with white table linens?

Then, one afternoon, Evelyn from the old Miller ranch comes careening into town, about to murder her husband sitting drunk in the house Evelyn's family had owned since statehood. She skids to a halt at the café. Next thing you know, The Last Stop is powering up the main street with a neon red and green sign.

Right now, years later, it's closing time at The Last Stop. Alvin can't stop yammering on about Evelyn's plan to rename the café. "I don't get it, Ev. Why you wanna change the name? We're still the last stop." Alvin hucks a trash bag over his shoulder. "The name does kinda tell the story, you know, of what was around here. 'Sides, say you were driving through town, you see the café, you wonder, 'Wow, maybe this really is the last chance for coffee' or maybe you ask yourself, 'now how come that's the name of this café?' Right?" Evelyn and Grace say nothing, put up the clean plates, set out flatware for the dawn breakfast rush. "You know, last, like in the last bit of what we used to have." He clunks his way down the outside steps to the garbage cans.

"I wonder is he right, Ev."

"Gracie, he makes not an ounce of sense. Would you just look at the street, what it is now? This is no Main Street U.S.A. This is some kinda silk route. Clothes from India in Marva's shop next door, flowers from Belgium down the street. I mean, Gracie, you and Alvin and I, we're ghosts. Those people driving through town? Phantom folk. People like them don't see people like us. We're from here. People don't know, don't care where here is. It's like a bad TV show, calling us The Last Stop. What about 'Alvin's Restaurant', plain and simple, no story, the whole truth, nothing but?"

The thing is, it isn't Alvin's restaurant any more than it's his café. On the wall above the dessert shelf, a photo shows Alvin in a sport jacket and his nice tie. Evelyn is wearing a pink all-season wool suit. Grace is between them, gazing unsmiling at the camera.

Evelyn's son took the photograph. They look like a family. Lately, Alvin has been dreaming that Evelyn wants him to sell the café. Alvin knows Evelyn wants no such thing, but he wants Evelyn to tell him she doesn't want it. He likes to hear Evelyn tell him what he already knows, such as "Seventy, Alvin, seventy." Alvin knows the speed limit is seventy, but he likes Evelyn to tell him as he drives down to the Oakland waterfront with her and Grace in the car, going after the salmon and squid for the week's menu. Alvin has always wanted to be married, have a family. It's a fantasy.

Years back, when she had stood at the counter in The Last Stop on that dusty afternoon, Evelyn had seen her reflection in the mirror on the back wall of the café. As she stood there recognizing herself, sunburnt and in need of a hot shower, Alvin snatched the job application from beneath her hands. "Forget it. I don't need no job application. Job's yours. When can you start?" What was his rush? Evelyn already had a husband. "Wow, Evelyn. That's some story."

But for Evelyn, it wasn't some story when she told Alvin about home life back then. It wasn't a story at all. "That's the problem, Gracie. Alvin thinks in stories, he's got the start and the finish all wrapped up in his mind. Well, I just don't see us, people from here, like that. You and I, it's real for us. If Alvin's so damn keen on stories, let him stick to his own ramshackle cabin story. He oughta think what made him call it The Last Stop, way back then, even. What it is right now. Now that's a story, not this fantasy stuff he spouts."

"I see what you're saying, Ev. Still, I'm pretty sure that squatting here, selling coffee and burgers to bums bouncing around the delta, that's just not real interesting to Alvin."

"How's it not as interesting as you at Uncle Craig's?"

Years ago, at the moment Evelyn is gazing at her reflect-ion in the mirror, Grace is at the sink rinsing coffee cups. Her apron is askew, a shoelace swims in a pool by the dishwasher. Evelyn, on the other hand, is wearing a blue and green checked dress that sways in rhythmic folds as she leans her forearms on the cash register, talking to Alvin. Evelyn drove Alvin and Grace by her old home a few weeks after she came to The Last Stop. "Just checking it out, see if the shithead burnt the place down yet now, thank heavens, he's shed my boy." Bougainvillea curled up the adobe walls. Evelyn had kept roses, but none had survived her abandonment. The women of the house always had roses, a garden of useless beauty kept safe from the grit of ranch life. Now, where paddocks and harvest yards had been, clumps of ochre and peach adobe homes sliced through the net of sidewalks and streets with names like Persimmon Path and Walnut Way. Beneath it lay Evelyn's world of roots, trails and waterways. Alvin and Grace peered into the haze. Groves of serene fruit trees, expanses of corn fields, floated into view, silhouettes of the rolling acreage that Evelyn had known in her childhood.

"Those ticky tack houses? Used to ride my horse right through the field that was there. Fields and groves, pasture back then, far as you could see."

That was then, this is now. Time moves. Though the photograph above the dessert shelf is in a glass frame now, Alvin and Evelyn and Grace still look like a family. Couple of years ago, they busted out the wall of the café, did the work themselves except for putting in the bay of windows over-looking the restored grasslands. Alvin does what he can to keep Route 66 behind a curtain of dust and haze. Grace and Evelyn, on the other hand, keep the windows clear of grime, so if you're having your coffee and pie, you can gaze at the ribbon of the highway twirling away over the hills into the valley beyond. The hated husband is dead. The court has declared that Evelyn's land is hers again. Her boy comes by the café for Sunday dinner, sometimes with Pastor Dorothy and Corinne, and that nice lawyer friend. Alvin gets on with the lawyer, 'Nam talk and all. They cluster around the café table, working on the deed to Evelyn's land. County park, open space forever, the rolling grassland restored, Evelyn's son gets the ranch house.

But the pressure is still on Alvin to change the name of The Last Stop. He pushes back. "I just don't get how you and Gracie don't think we have a legacy here, Ev. I mean, we have a responsibility. Here's this lawyer in his nice suit, the pastor from the church down in Berkeley, your daughter with good money, your son looking after himself just fine, Gracie and me with you in the café, all of us working out a way to bring back a piece of what you had, let folks know what used to be here. Don't you want folks hearing this?"

Evelyn opens her mouth to tell Alvin. "What used to be here? We're just ghosts. No one knows where

here is. Those folks who come in to rave over our coffee and our pie, they're phantom people. They pair up at random with the perfumes, flowers, scarves, spices we sell in this town."

But she holds her tongue. She knows what Alvin will say. "That's just what I'm talking about, Ev. You have this way with words, with how the world is. I can spin a tale, sure. But you don't spin. You lay it out in a real way. Here we all are, Ev, sittin' around the Sunday dinner table. Who are we, any-way? Aren't we worth a story? C'mon, Ev. We're listening."

~ ~ ~ ~ ~ ~ ~ ~

We thank our families, friends, readers and all who support and encourage North Fork Writers Group authors

Our Biographies ...

JOYCE DECORDOVA
Greenport, NY
GOING HOME - ©2017 / THE PAINTER - © 2018
SHADES - © 2017 / FREDDIE THE FLUFFER - © 2017

Joyce joined our North Fork Writers Group in 2012, and follows her three acclaimed stories in *7 Voices, Volume One* with four in this *Volume Two*. Our close-knit and supportive group provides Joyce constructive encouragement to develop her imaginative creations.

Joyce is a mother of five and grandmother of 17. She and artist Hector deCordova are familiar figures leading creative lives on eastern Long Island. While being a business woman, guidance counselor and social worker have been her careers, storytelling remains her passion. She hopes that this book's readers will enjoy the diversity of her offerings.

~~~~~~~~

GERARD MEADE
Ridge, NY
BAD BOUNCE - © 2015 / SOUND AVENUE - © 2016
GLORY - © 2014 / BAR ASSOCIATION - © 2015
UNFINISHED BRIEF - © 2018

Gerard is a retired chef, carpenter and musician-turned-writer who relocated from Astoria, Queens, to eastern Long Island in 1984. Although not actually a resident of the North Fork, fortune led him to our group this past year, and he was welcomed into the fold regardless of his non-resident status.

Gerard's stories in this *Volume Two* are his first published fiction. His brief memoir *Beatle Boots* was featured in Emily Spivak's *WORN IN NEW YORK*, published by Abrams Image in October 2017. He is currently editing his second novel, thankful for the support of his wife Lisette, and the generous, bright minds of the North Fork Writers Group.

~~~~~~~~~

HELENE MUNSON

New Suffolk, NY

THE ELUSIVE CONSUL - © 2017
THE PRINCESS & THE TURNIP EATER -© 2017
THAT SILK DRESS / RACING COCKROACHES -© 2018

"We must remember where we are from to know who we are, to understand where we are going" is Helene's guide in her mainly creative non-fiction focused on travel and ancestry research, recording journeys to explore cultural identities and remote areas. With a German mother and Chilean father, she grew up in Germany, Brazil and Liberia, holds Degrees from London and Oxford, and has lived in the US since 1982.

Helene joined North Fork Writers Group in 2016. Her writing has appeared in German and English publications, and an excerpt from her upcoming book, *Hitler's Forgotten Children,* is in '*American Ancestry*' 2018 Winter edition.

~~~~~~~~

DAVID PORTEOUS
Mattituck, NY

HEART ACHES - © 2001 / **BEING THE** *GOODBOY* - ©
2016

KNOW THYSELF - © 2015 / **LOST TRAVELERS -** © 2016

Australian-born Dave is a USA dual-citizen since 2008, retaining The Australian Writers Guild's Full Member status accorded to him in 1982. A member of North Fork Writers Group since 2012, he had four tales in *7 Voices, Volume One*, and 20 in his own *Strangers In My Mind* (Absolutely Amazing eBooks & The New Atlantian Library - 2017). His poetry has appeared in several anthologies over the years.

Dave's creativity thrives on our group's camaraderie. His four stories in this book, although each is different in style and genre, are as unmistakably Dave's as the dedication he applied to being our Editor of ***Seven Voices, Volume Two***.

~~~~~~~~

ANDREA RHUDE
Riverhead, NY
**GRANTED / THE LODGER
THE INHERITANCE** — ALL © 2017

A fantasy/horror/sci-fi writer at heart, Andrea has been writing weird, and apparently unsettling, stories for most of her life. Three years ago she scraped together enough courage to let the wider world read her work, and joined North Fork Writers Group. These are her first published stories.

Andrea is a Pratt graduate (1998, Illustration), and spent twenty years in the interior design field working as a muralist and color consultant. She has recently started an illustration business, which she pursues in parallel with developing her story-telling craft with our Writers Group's support. Andrea says of this creative load... Why do things the easy way?

~~~~~~~~~

SUSAN ROSENSTREICH
Cutchogue, NY
SLOW MOVING CLOUDS, 1957 / THE MATTER AT HAND
WHAT GOOD PEOPLE DO ABOUT US / THE LAST STOP
ALL © 2017

Susan joined North Fork Writers Group five years ago, but has written since age eight, keeping journals that recorded her life in four countries. Earning her Doctorate in French at CUNY Graduate Center ultimately led to her being Professor Emerita of Foreign Languages at Dowling College.

Susan follows her two highly praised stories in *7 Voices, Volume One* with four engaging tales in this book. All her stories are shaped by the different realities she has seen, laced with her worldly views. She and her husband Saul live in leafy serenity on Long Island's North Fork, but busily pursue their interests in social activism as well as the arts.

~~~~~~~~

WILLIAM RUE
Southold, NY
JUST DAYS - © 2010

Bill Rue moved to the North Fork of eastern Long Island's Peconic Bay in 2000, and joined North Fork Writers Group in 2016. A graduate of NYU's Dramatic Writing Program, he is the author of two novels, *Last Tango in Jacksonville* (2010), and *Sea of Troubles* (2017).

Bill's contribution to our book of '*Just Days*', a revised excerpt from *Last Tango In Jacksonville*, makes him a most welcome eighth *Voice* – and makes his engagingly insightful tale a bonus for readers.

~~~~~~~~

CHRISTOPHER 'KIT' STORJOHANN
Mattituck, NY
RECONCILIATION © 2013 / WINTER ROSES © 2016
AT THE CHAPEL IN THE WOODS © 2016
PLAYGROUND OF WRAITHS © 2017

Kit studied Creative Writing at Binghamton University and works as a photographer, film archivist and meditation teacher. A member of North Fork Writers Group since its founding, he explores odd corners of the human spirit by depicting characters in diverse settings, epochs, and genres.

Our group not only helps Kit to shape his work, but also provides the camaraderie that makes the potentially fraught endeavor pleasant and worthwhile. His writings have been published in *The Mindfulness Bell* and *Here Comes Everybody* [online version] in addition to his four tales in *7 Voices, Volume One,* and these four in **Seven Voices, Volume Two**.

~~~~~~~~~

Thank you for reading. Please review this book. Reviews help others find Absolutely Amazing eBooks and inspire us to keep providing these marvelous tales. If you would like to be put on our email list to receive updates on new releases, contests, and promotions, please go to AbsolutelyAmazingEbooks.com and sign up.

The New
Atlantian Library

NewAtlantianLibrary.com
or AbsolutelyAmazingEbooks.com
or AA-eBooks.com

Made in the USA
Middletown, DE
05 August 2018